HOW I BROKE
THE SKY

ALSO BY E.W. PARK

THE GREAT YEAR CYCLE (forthcoming)

Aelia
The Fires of Paris
How I Ended the Fourth World War

HOW I BROKE THE SKY

THE GREAT YEAR CYCLE: BOOK ONE

E.W. Park

FOX POINT BOOKS

Cover designed by Fox Point Books

Fox Point Books
www.foxpointbooks.com

Printed in the United States of America

Date of Production: May 2018
Fox Point Books

ISBN-13 978-0-9997715-0-1

For the Mericle-Wiebe family.

CHAPTER ONE

Lest We Forget

Ten minutes in, I lost sight of the rocket. This was supposed to happen. Of course it was, but I felt a nervous little jag in my stomach, as if a moth had snagged on my belly-lining.

"They have her audio in room 12."

I nodded, kept watching through the plastic window. Outside, the airstrip was puddled from last night and cluttered with tubing and wheely service-trams. The concrete had scorched in three perfect, burnt circles where the *Melet* had taken off. Elena was up there. I stared at the gray sky. If it were still clear I'd probably be able to watch for another minute or two. The *Melet* would still be a shiny, smoking speck in the sky; a meteor going the wrong way.

Giannis took my shoulder, I didn't turn. If the sky cleared, I might see her again. You will, I thought, in 26 hours. That's nothing: into orbit and back again. Just to show the committee that it can be done. And the Shan. We have to show them too.

"Nikos . . ."

I said, "Yeah."

She wasn't going to pop through the clouds, was she?

"Nikos . . ."

"Okay," I said, and I followed Giannis to room 12.

Past the potted ferns and metal consoles, room 12 was a windowless cube with six-foot speakers matted to every wall. The Director wasn't here—it was tradition that the Director never monitor the launch.

One of the technicians said, "Elena, diagnostic check-in . . ."

A pause that let sweat slip on my palms, then a staticky crackle. Silence again. Giannis gave me a 'calm down, it'll be fine' look. I ignored him, thought about the breathing exercises they'd forced me to practice for the past eight months: as if I were giving birth. Not watching my wife go up.

"Elena, just a quick check-in. We want to be sure the comm's working."

Pause, and I murmured, "Better be the comm . . ."

Giannis smiled, but I saw—maybe smelled—the animal tension on him. Another burst of static, and the techies were checking dials, flipping switches, adjusting the wind resistance, surface temps—I knew all of that, knew what every piece of machinery in the room had been designed to do. And right now none of it mattered. Elena was up there in a little shuttle, membranes of cloth and plastic and glass fighting to keep her from burning or suffocating or . . .

". . . can't . . ." Elena's voice over the speakers, ". . . not doing what . . ."

I grabbed the back of someone's chair, said softly, "Something's wrong."

"Elena, we want to be certain the comm's functioning. Confirm that you are receiving this."

"Something's wrong."

Crackle, static, hiss, then: ". . . Nikos, I'm . . . didn't mean to fight . . . this isn't what I thought . . ."

Giannis took my shoulder, I shrugged away.

"End it," I said. "Bring her back down."

Giannis whispered, "You know they can't. She has to . . ."

"Bullshit." I went for the head techie. "Over-ride. Do it, bring her back."

Someone said, "Her velocity . . ."

"Shut up. I know the way it works. Pull her back. Emergency override—do it."

The head techie said, "It's not . . ."

Static hiss, and then an animal shrieked over the speakers. We all jumped, and the hair on my arms stood, became goose bumps. Silence. Gone again.

Giannis slumped against a console, but no one else moved. One of the techies murmured, "What was . . . what was . . ?"

I stared at the speakers, felt my left eye twitch involuntarily, and my stomach coiled into a fleshy knot.

The head techie spoke quietly, "Elena . . . Elena, confirm that you're receiving this."

I couldn't move, and that young techie kept saying, "What was that? There's nothing—what was that?"

"Elena, please confirm that . . ."

"What do you think it was?" I said, and I tried to walk away. My legs weren't working.

Giannis said, "Let's not . . ."

I glared at him. "Stop."

He closed his mouth, and as I left the room, I heard the techies calling for a confirmation code. They were aborting, pulling the plug, bringing my Elena back. Don't think about what she said. She was trying to apologize for last night because she knew what was coming. Just like the last time. And all the others before it. Two years since the last New Amith space shuttle launch, and all the engineering brilliance in the world, the instant communication, none of it had changed a thing. And all I could think about was how I was glad she'd gotten it. Glad it hadn't been me.

What was that? The dying animal noise. Oh that? That was my wife, Elena. And no. No, I don't want to be there when they open up the cockpit.

* * *

When they opened the *Melet*—no.

I thought of something funny while I stood in St. Hostos, listening to the reverend. A street comedian—Vincent's Street—once spent an entire week on the corner of Farm's Square saying, "It is hot today, it is hot today . . ." And on and on. Was that what Elena had been thinking about? Why had it popped into my head in the middle of her rites?

3

Body charred like an overcooked goose, all black around the edges—hair gone—with pieces of red flesh and white bone sticking through. The only thing not burned was a stupid red-tipped pen she'd had in her pocket. Elena's lucky pen, with tiny nonsense writing on the side: *Made in the USA*.

As I fidgeted with the pen, I started laughing, and Reverend Alexander paused, pretended not to hear, while the rest of the congregation shuffled uncomfortably. St. Hostos was all stone with ancient effigies of long-dead senators and prophets in the floors and walls: royalty buried all around us. The *Melet* program paid for the service.

"A loving wife and constant perfectionist, I think it's easiest to remember Elena's laugh, her . . ."

I couldn't hear her laugh, and as I left the church for the crematorium, where the second rites would be finished, Giannis fell into step beside me.

"I thought it was a nice service."

I didn't answer, and we got in the corporate tram, alone with the priest, the Director, and a couple techies. Elena's body followed three trams back in a private car, shuttled by the black hydrogen balloon fixed to the top, same as ours, and draped with a red tapestry:

> Elena Healy, 1166-1140 L.M.
> "Lest We Forget the Sacrifice of Our Wives
> And the Price of Salvation"

The price of salvation, I thought. Alexander met my eye, gave me a terse, 'It is as it must be' look, then sidled closer on the speeding tram.

"We will all miss her," he said.

"I know."

"Some things are outside our reach." I frowned, but before I could respond, he continued, "The Goddess Tenda will watch over you as Cratus guides Elena to divine union." A pause. "New Amith was never meant to leave the ground. We are meant to stay in our paradise of plenty until the next age."

Should ignore Tenda (goddess of mourning) and go to Elle (travel) or Rosantre for luck. As guides, the gods of New Amith were only one rung above us. The old gods—the Bialu—and all the moldy prophets were higher. After all, they're the ones who had known everything that was going to happen, weren't they? That's why our calendar counted down, not up. Five-hundred years ago people had observed the feast days and sacrifices, but mainstream religion was about community now, not the divine. History was predetermined, meaning that salvation was a matter of faith—when you examined it at all, the whole thing became far too fatalistic.

The Director—a stiff old man—grunted at Alexander. "And what would happen if we all thought like that?" he said, waved a hand at me. "I don't mean to diminish the tragedy here, but what if people said we weren't meant to move this quickly—when they built the first trams—where would we be?"

"New Amith is chosen for other purposes," Alexander said. He opened a bottle of water.

"And the Shan?" the Director said. He indicated the water. "Yesterday's Nine Laws are about sacrifice."

Alexander took a drink and smiled. "You do not need to worry, this is part of my quota."

Giannis asked what he meant, and the Director explained that in the hours after Elena's flight, the Senate had passed a series of 'symbolic' resolutions. The third resolution limited the amount of water, food, and energy we were allowed each week.

I didn't understand, and I didn't care. Giannis noticed my tension and gestured to the Director. "We lost a great woman today . . ."

"Oh undoubtedly," the Director said, still watching Reverend Alexander. "But what if the Senate begins to think, begins to vote, as you do, as you would, reverend?"

"This might never have happened."

"And we'll find ourselves with another two-year ban on even *test* flights," the Director said. "And where has that gotten us? Every day the Shan send three or four or six new cosmonauts into space—how long before they launch their first warships?"

"You're being, I think," Alexander said, "unnecessarily dramatic."

"Realistic," the Director said, and he noticed me. "You must agree, Nikos, that without heroes like your wife nothing, no progress, can ever—will ever—be made. Every new challenge has its casualties and sacrifices."

I looked at him for a long moment, and Giannis smiled uncomfortably, put a hand on my chest.

"Nikos . . ."

"Elena is dead because of the people in this car," I said. "Don't ask me what I think."

The Director shrugged that away. "But I'm sure an educated man like you can see that . . ."

"I don't see anything," I said. "Okay? That's it."

The tram stopped: we were there.

* * *

The second rites came and went. Alexander sprinkled flowers on the casket, mixed salt with vinegar and a tuft of Elena's hair, said a prayer to Tenda, her brother Cratus, then Dela for forgiveness, and cranked the coffin, salt and all, into the furnace. She wasn't inside that box. The thing I'd seen in the *Melet* wasn't Elena, she couldn't have made that noise. The demon-cry we'd heard over the speakers, no.

I watched the coffin disappear into a wall of solid black marble. People told me how sorry they were, that their prayers were with me. A woman I didn't know even squeezed my arm and told me that she *knew* things would get better. I didn't look at any of them. The arched hall stank of disinfectant and old incense, the kind of stuff I smoked as a kid. A pale blue glow that was supposed to be comforting made me feel like I was swimming or still in the womb. No such luck.

Not Elena in the wall, she'd already been cooked. What good would it do to fry her again?

Giannis squeezed my shoulder. "Are you ready?"

"Sure."

I ignored the throng of grim techies and distant relatives.

"How are you?"

"What?"

"Are you all right, I mean how are you . . ."

"How do you think I am?"

Giannis swallowed, we left.

Outside, villas walled by green hedges stood on either side of the road. Trams waited for us, but I started walking instead. Unquestioning, Giannis followed. He wore the embroidered 'gitah', the mourning robe that had been a tradition of silver beads and black tassel for the past seven hundred years. I wore the same untucked suit I'd been wearing for the past 56 hours. Since I'd last slept. The clipper injections were still keeping me up. Whoopee.

"Where are we going?" he asked at last.

"I don't know, where do you want to go? Want a drink?"

"You've been on uppers for . . ."

"Calm down," I said, "I'm still older than you. And I need a glass of cold liquor."

"You need to sleep."

I walked faster. "You need to keep up. You giving up your routines? What's wrong—you're slowing down."

"Nikos, stop . . ."

"Come on—you don't want a run? I'll race you to the end of the hedge. That's 150 meters. Think you've still got it?"

"I'm not going to . . ."

"Go!"

I burst into a sprint, and suddenly tears streaked my cheeks: I pumped harder, used the adrenaline in my guts like some people use fire. I pounded the pavement, swung my arms, and heard myself growling. Shouldn't have . . . no—should not have—Goddamn it. Giannis was right behind me. I heard him panting, and I swerved, kicked gravel at him, he shouted, "Oh that's how we're playing!" And I charged for the finish: I beat him. Maybe he let me win. We both stank, streaked with sweat, and I doubled over, hands on my knees to breathe.

"You just . . ." he mumbled, "you don't know when to stop . . ."

"Nope."

"You're like dad . . . you know that? Every time I see you, I think you're turning into him a little . . ."

"Hey shut up, let's get drunk. I'm buying, come on."

He hesitated, his mental clock grinding: should I let my older brother tear apart his liver the night his wife was cremated?

"Come on." I nudged him hard, knocked him off-balance. "It's that or I pin you to the ground right here." Still hesitation. "I have to grieve somehow. Now let's go."

We went.

* * *

"When I say I never knew what to make of her, I don't mean I didn't like her . . ."

"Stop apologizing," I said, "you don't have to apologize for your feelings to me."

When we'd entered the bar, the bartender had read from a laminated card, explaining that a committee somewhere would electronically track our purchases to be certain we didn't exceed our monthly booze quota under the Nine Laws.

"And how many are we allowed?" I'd asked.

"Twenty-five drinks each month."

"That's my lucky number."

Was there a sudden supply shortage? Some reason the government had mandated nationwide rationing? The bartender didn't think so, and when I pressed him, he'd offered me the card; printed along the top, were the words: 'Our Sacrifice Shall Be A Symbol of Hope'. That didn't strike me as a legitimate reason not to get drunk every night. Worry about it tomorrow.

I called our waitress, ordered another round, and the percussion band in the next room continued to play. Crowds danced and laughed in the silver-halogen glow. We sat at a back corner, getting more and more slockered. Still Giannis was stiff, despite the alcohol. We hadn't had a brotherly moment like this since before I married, since the academy.

He said, "She was gorgeous, funny, she had a nice brain between her ears."

"Good ears too. And legs."

He smiled. "I wouldn't know."

"You never wondered?"

"Nikos . . ."

"I'm just kidding."

"You're drunk."

"I'm not."

"You are."

But I wasn't, and I said, "Never cheated on her, you know that?"

"Never?"

"Nope."

"Good for you."

But all those times I couldn't find her—I knew she was with other men. But what could I do? Elena was someone to come home to. What could I do? Cheat on her? No. Not because I hadn't wanted to, I thought. Because I couldn't, wasn't attractive enough or something—miserable human being, that's me. Just too much of a coward-prick to cheat, not because I'm a good person. That's the truth.

Giannis told me that I needed to sleep, shouldn't over-exert myself, and I said, "Screw you. Finish your drink."

He did. "All right, let's go. I'm paying for your ride home."

"I get to sprawl in the bed tonight, take up as much room as I want."

"Stop it."

It still wasn't real. I didn't believe Elena was dead, she would get home late, just like last week. No call, no explanation: there'd been a mistake. I struggled out of my chair, followed him to the door.

"I'm going to see you tomorrow," he said.

"No you're not, you have to work."

"I took the week off."

"Why?"

"Why do you think?"

Giannis had a post at the Lake Crossing Hospital: his first job since he finished his medical training at the Whle Monastery. Growing up, he'd tried to distinguish himself from me by observing the gods' days; Giannis had been the candle holder in our family, our little religious prodigy. Nevermind the secular practices, medicine was still intimately connected to the gods. Pain killers often came with incense. I got the sense it wasn't . . . he'd studied to become a doctor, but the job didn't match the brochure. Maybe it wasn't holy enough. And here he was, wasting all that training on me.

Outside, I frowned at the cloudy sky. Cool, like a spring night, even though it was summer.

"Should be raining," I said.

He called a horse on his comm. "Why?"

"Wash this smell off of me. I need a shower."

He grinned. "I wasn't going to say it . . ."

"Yeah."

A horse-drawn tram cantered to the curb, the plastic door bounced unevenly open. Electric lights popped on around the cushiony seats. Giannis gave the horse directions, the animal snorted and stomped that it understood and would I please get on the damn tram.

"Go back to work," I said.

"I will next week," he said. "What are you going to do?"

"I don't know. I guess I'll see where they are with the Vermice."

Giannis frowned. "The Director didn't . . ."

"What?"

"I thought he said that—you're going to go back to the lab?"

Before the Project, I'd been a genetic technician at the Maastade Academy. The Vermouse was a scrunchy groundhog that rooted through garbage and dug up crop fields. An adorable nuisance, I was convinced that the only reason they hadn't been hunted to extinction in the last century was their big brown eyes.

As Elena had trained for the *Melet*, I had periodically checked in on the loveable Vermouse to be certain the other techies didn't breed them into hamsters or rabid squirrels. Six years ago, a Senate committee had decided that vast plots of ruined land outside the Capital should be transformed from the trash dumps of the last half-century into tract housing. Enter the Vermouse. By stringing Vermouse genes with DNA from the Orchid Beetle and Caps Hare, we intended to create a new breed of Vermouse that would turn hazardous garbage into fresh topsoil. Last I'd checked—three weeks ago—the Vermouse was almost there.

"What else am I going to do?" I said. "We're almost finished anyway."

"I don't know," Giannis said, "I thought the Director said that the funding . . ."

My pocket shook. I ignored it.

"The Director said what? What about the funding?"

"I think they stopped it."

"When?"

"He was talking about the new budget, after the *Melet . . .*"

The Nine Laws again. Giannis watched as I fumbled with the button, produced the pebble-earpiece, and finally put it in. I was one of the few who didn't wear my comm constantly.

"Hello?"

"Nikos, hello." No introduction, I was supposed to recognize the voice: the Director.

"Hi."

"I wanted to check-in." I waited, and he said, "How are you?"

They'd probably moved my dossier from a standard black folder to a bright red one and put me on a 'suicide watch' list. Little did they know that I was too much of a coward for that. Nevermind that Elena wasn't really dead.

"Okay," I said.

"You're doing all right then?"

I said "Yeah, I'm fine. Has funding been pulled from the Maastade Academy?"

"You are talking about the new budget?"

"I don't know, am I?"

"Yes, priorities have been altered."

"After six years, they cut-off Maastade? Just like that? We were almost there—I told them three weeks ago."

I didn't care about the Vermouse, I cared about wasting six years of my life tinkering with rodents for the Senate, only to be shut down. I could have spent all those hours with Elena.

"The Nine Laws are about the greater symbolism of national sacrifice."

"Why? They didn't do this after any of the other launches. What's so urgent now?"

"Nikos, there's been a lot of discussion within the project, a lot of people—well you understand the need for a change, don't you? I had a conversation today with someone who was very persuasive. Do you know a woman named Aelia?"

11

"Nope. Why, who is she?" A Senator probably, someone who signed checks—or who told other people to sign them.

"Do you remember there was an article on the networks last week about a local dig?"

Of course I didn't. He wasn't going to answer my questions. "Yeah."

"You'll be sent as the project liaison for the dig."

This wasn't making sense. "I don't know what you want me to . . ."

"You'll contact the dig's supervisor, she's an albino. Her name is Anna." Albino: Shan. He gave me a contact number, then said, "Family history as ambassadors—that's how she got her pass."

"Who?"

"The supervisor."

We sat in silence for a moment. Restraint. Don't click off yet, wait to see what he's talking about.

Finally, the Director said, "Okay?"

"Yeah."

"All right then." And he clicked off.

The horse watched, tossed its mane, and Giannis asked, "That was the Project Director?"

"Yeah."

"What did he want?"

"I have no idea. Wants me to go dig up old pottery or something with someone from Shan."

Giannis started to say that it didn't make any sense, then stopped when he realized that it did. Keep me busy. Waste my time with a 'dig', now that Maastade is finished.

I had scribbled the 'dig supervisor's' contact number on my palm. "I have to call this lady."

"You know who she . . ."

"No."

"So call her."

I sighed, this was making me tired. I didn't have the patience for this. "You take the number, you can go."

"Nikos, if they want you on it, it might be--"

"Yeah."

I climbed in the tram. "Go back to work, Giannis, thanks for the drinks. Don't let me stop you from saving peoples' lives."

"You're not."

I thought about it. "That's funny."

"Go home."

I did.

CHAPTER TWO

Too Much to Think About

My Maastade keycard still worked, and I slipped in the back entrance without setting off an alarm. A converted Merr barracks, Maastade Academy was a slab of hulking concrete. The administrators had blasted windows and skylights to make the tunnels livable, but that only helped in the daylight. Unable to sleep, I'd taken a tram at four in the morning. The sun hadn't come up yet. I flipped a light switch, nothing happened.

The Director hadn't been kidding; the Senate had pulled all the funding. They'd probably even shut the water off. Following gray shadows, I wandered into the research wing and swiped my card at another door. No good. The older backdoor must have been rigged to a different generator. This one didn't respond at all. I paced, tried the card again, and began to curse. I pulled the handle: the door was unlocked. No power.

Inside, the lab was piled with monitors, papers, and empty cages. The skylight cast a white square in the center of the room, illuminating a mop and bucket. They were already cleaning up. I don't know what I'd expected to find. Our funds are cut, and a day later, the laboratory is transformed into a janitor's closet. I sat on a stool, rubbed my eyes, and thought about the launch. There had to be records, didn't there? In the flurry of death rituals and condolences, I'd never asked to see the mechanicals in Elena's file.

I heard a scratching.

"Hello?"

If attacked, I could always use the mop. A pause, and the scratching continued. It was coming from the opposite corner. On a pile of jumbled equipment, I found a cage lined with wood shavings. Inside, a Vermouse sucked an empty bottle, then froze.

"Hi there."

The Vermouse sniffed, then scratched the corner of its cage. They'd missed this one. Explaining the symbolism of national sacrifice probably wouldn't appease the Vermouse. Though it looked like an ordinary Vermouse, it wasn't. Its digestive system mimicked the plumbing inside an Orchid Beetle, balanced with the tough lining of the Caps Hare. It wasn't even a Vermouse anymore.

I opened the cage, and the Vermouse scrambled into my palm. Maybe it recognized my scent. Cupping the Vermouse with both hands, I left. Outside, the sky was smeared red and purple. Elena had a file somewhere.

At the edge of the parking lot, I let the Vermouse go.

* * *

"I want to see the records."

Giannis blinked, as if I'd just said that I'd grown a second penis.

"What—why?"

"I want to see them," I said, "come on, let's go."

Ten minutes after I'd returned from Maastade, Giannis had knocked.

"Wait, wait. Didn't you sleep last night? You don't look any better. You were supposed to sleep-in, call me when . . ."

"Yeah, my skull feels three sizes too small, so calm down." I motioned to the open front door beside him. "I slept. Come on, let's go. I called the base, the Director's there for another two hours."

"And we're going to see him . . ?"

"That's right."

"Why?"

"I told you: I want to see the records."

"What records, what are you talking about--"

"What do you think? The flight records. I want the cause of death."

15

"Nikos, we have the cause of death."

"No, we have a body," I said. "We don't have a cause of anything. She fried to a crisp."

"Let's get some breakfast instead."

I pushed past him. "Fine, I'll go alone."

"Nikos . . ."

"Don't patronize me, all right?"

"Did you see the inside of the *Melet*? Don't we know how she died? Fire, right?"

"No."

"We were both there when they . . ."

"Did it look fried to you?"

"Yes, it did." Giannis picked through the untouched pile of mail on my kitchen table.

"And where'd the flames come from? Fires don't just start. You know what else—I want to go over all of it again. I want all the records. What are you doing?"

Giannis held up an envelope. "Did you see this?"

"Come on."

"Wait. Do you mind if I open this?" He was already ripping the paper. "It's from an attorney's office at Fisherle."

"So?" He stared at the letter, and I gave in. "All right, Giannis, what is it?"

"Dett's dead."

"What?"

"Uncle Dett."

I grabbed the letter: Giannis was right. Dett had been our eccentric uncle-by-the-sea. He'd worked for Fisherle for decades, and their lawyers now politely informed us of his death—drowned in a ocean storm—and asked that as his only surviving relatives we come to Leim'en to inspect the estate and sign our names several dozen times."

"He died the day before Elena's flight," I said at last.

"It'll be good to get away," Giannis said. "I can't remember the last time we visited Leim'en."

I thought about it, then said, "He doesn't live in Leim'en, and I still want to see the records."

We argued for another minute, then he followed onto the stone steps outside my house. Bushes cut to look like orbs and stars were spaced around our lion shrine. A great beast with a huge mane and jeweled eyes hunched at the base of the steps, a trio of unlit candles between his paws: our household guardian. I hadn't struck the lights since coming back. Good job, I thought, hopping past him. Way to protect the lair. Nevermind the people who live here.

Giannis's tram waited in the street, a red hydro-balloon attached to the top. The nearby houses were similar to ours—to mine—one or two stories of steely brick, slated roof, solar panels, trimmed bushes or hedges and granite or wood or steel household gods on the lawn: their candles were all burning.

"You coming?" I called, waiting by the tram. Giannis was taking his time on the stairs.

"What did you mean?" he asked. "What records—what do you want to see besides Elena's records?"

"All of them: the other flights. I'm sure they took pictures, kept logs. I want to see it." He got in the tram, and I stepped in to stand beside him. "We know the story right?"

He nodded. We both knew the story: nine years ago, the first New Amith space shuttle is sent into orbit when the Senate realizes the Shan are days from beating us there. The launch is a success. Champagne and sex all around, except that the cosmonaut dies. The shuttle returns with a corpse. Gods, where did we go wrong? Let's fix it, and so—six months later—a second shuttle is launched with animals. No problem. Then a second cosmonaut. Mary Tasos, the famous astrologer. She dies.

The program disappears for almost a year, until an adventurous Senate finds the funding and sees dozens of Shan ambassadors landing every day on New Amith. Why can't we go there—but of course we can't use *their* ships. We need to build the ships ourselves. And, of course, the Shan— apologetically, oh so apologetically—can't risk the political consequences of a New Amith cosmonaut's death in one of their own rockets. So no, that's not an option. This time we get ambitious. Not only will we show them, we'll *really* show them. Two cosmonauts in the same ship. Two corpses, and the program dies for five more years. When it's jumpstarted again, three more people die, then the program sits in a closet somewhere for two years. And then Elena.

"We know the story," I said, "but that's all we know." Giannis looked at me for a long moment, and I frowned. "What?"

"Did you call the woman at the dig?"

"No."

"You should . . ."

"Don't change the subject. Do you know *exactly* what happened on those flights? No. Neither do I, and I know more about it than almost anyone. I had access to some of that in the training. But they never got specific, and we were too superstitious, too dumb to ask."

"They didn't tell you that it was mechanical . . ."

"Of course—that's obvious. I want proof of that. Elena's shuttle wasn't burned." He didn't answer, and I continued, "For her to die like that, the whole ship should have fried, shouldn't it? Not just *her*."

"They stopped looking for a genetic cause years . . ."

"I know, that's the point: I want to know why. I want pictures, records of the other deaths."

"They won't give them to you."

"Why not? I'm in the program, and my wife just died on one of their toys. They won't give it to me?"

He shrugged, tried to remain calm. "It's classified. Those documents— you'd have to be a senator or the program Director . . ."

"How do you know they're classified?"

He sighed. "Calm down. I don't *know*, but when things like that happen, the Senate appoints a committee that oversees information distribution, locks it up. Remember when there was an accident a few years back with . . ."

"I don't remember them saying anything about it being classified." Trying to convince myself. Truthfully, my skull was a swirling mess: I don't know what I remembered. I was too tired. She was my wife, even if the last six months—not the time for that. I owed her something. Because you're guilty. Because it wasn't working. Stop thinking like—because you're glad she's gone. Except she isn't.

Giannis studied me. He had that stern, professional stare, as if he were trying to read my thoughts. "What do we do when we get there?"

Always so practical, I thought. "What do you think? We knock."

* * *

"What do you call an armless man in a lake? Bob."

Yeah, that was my response too. But, that's me: must tread water, but how the hell am I supposed to—the security guard at the base stared at me. Might have been a kind of insane, 'Gods, was that a joke or a threat or . . .' look.

"Sorry," I said, "heard that one a few years ago. Did I miss the Director?"

"He was just leaving . . ."

Giannis gave me a look similar to clearing his throat. I waved him away, said to the guard, "We didn't finish reviewing some paperwork this morning, and you're telling me he just left."

"Yes, you just missed him. Do you want me to see if I can catch him?"

I thought, No, and said, "Yes, thanks."

The guard punched a few keys on his desk, something beeped, and he adjusted a circular comm.

"Calling Director Marcay: Director Marcay . . ."

This guard was all that stood between me and the base offices: a hall of beige tile and shuttle lithographs wandered away behind him. This desk was the only staffed security check-point: activity had been temporarily suspended since the 'accident'. Shut down by the Senate; 'Suspended Pending Review'.

After a few more tries, the guard shook his head, as if he were genuinely disappointed.

"He's not answering his comm. Would you like to leave a message?"

"You see?" I said, without turning. "See what you did, Giannis. You and your breakfast made us miss the Director. I forgot that they told me—you told me, didn't you?—that the Director might pack up if I stepped out . . ."

The guard nodded, already convinced he'd seen me that morning. "I'm sorry . . ."

I shook my head at Giannis. "The food was really that important? We just had to go eat . . ." If my hungry-tummy didn't growl, this might work.

Giannis said, "You didn't tell me he was leaving . . ."

"Because I forgot. Okay? I haven't slept, didn't eat—death does that, you know. Difficult to keep track, and now your breakfast, and I can't get the files the Director was going to give me. Five minutes earlier and I could have them." I pounded the guard's station. "Overdoing it—I can't do this, I can't keep . . ."

"That was you?"

I froze. "What?"

"I'm sorry," the guard said. "That was you—your wife who . . ."

"Yeah." I glared at Giannis. "And now I can't arrange the rites, because I don't have the insurance forms in the Director's office. We were going over it this morning, and . . ."

"You got a call a few minutes ago, from a . . ." He checked a log book. "Woman named Anna Antc'sh. She left her number." He recited it, but I already recognized this: the Director was determined to put me at that dig. No way around it now.

I adjusted my comm in one ear, told it to dial Anna Antc'sh's number, and the line rang.

"Hello?"

Giannis and the security guard watched, and I said, "Is this Anna Antc'sh?"

"Yes."

"Hi, this is Nikos Healy'll, I got a message that you . . ."

"Hi, yes." People argued in the background, and I heard a rusty mechanical beeping, like a fat robot woman backing up. "How can I help you?"

That caught me. "I—the Director told me to go to the dig as a . . . for the project."

"Okay."

I waited for more, heard her shuffling papers. "What does that mean, what do you want me to . . ."

"Come by tomorrow morning at 8:00. Okay?"

She clicked off. Yeah. I nodded to the security guard, as if I had everything under control. "You'll open it up for me?"

"What?"

"The Director's office." I started down the hall: I was a busy guy, after all. Phone calls to the security desk and everything. The guard punched the Director's codes, the door creaked open.

"Thank you," I said, and took a fraction of a second to scan the room: where was it? Cabinets, a steel desk with cleanliness demigods and smoking candles, posters, papers on leather chairs, a blackened window overlooking the main strip, where the *Melet* had sat for eight months in prep.

Where?

I went for the desk chair, and Giannis waited in the doorway with the guard. But where in the desk? Would Elena's file even be in here? What if it wasn't? No: it was. The Director was responsible, he wouldn't move it, wouldn't let anyone shuffle it around.

I sat at the desk. The security guard watched patiently, still convinced this was legal. Where? I pulled a few drawers, rummaging with the mess on a nearby chair and collecting sheets as if I knew what I was doing? Where? Papers on a circular table—no, and more under a potted fern. No.

And I found it: right on the desk, mixed in with a stack of stiff sheets marked, 'S. File'.

"Got it," I said, and we left. Just that simple. But, as I followed Giannis out. I clenched a fist on the papers, stumbled at the exit.

"Is that it?" Giannis asked, and we went for the tram. "You got everything?"

What was that python-tension inside my head? Adrenaline, but nowhere to run. Fists, but no one to fight—rage. Those incompetent bastards killed Elena—my Elena. She wasn't here because of the Director. Last night, I told myself she was out, or in the next room. She would be right back. And in the morning she still wasn't there. I wanted to find him, but felt mounting frustration, like a giant dog chained to a tree. And do what? Kill him? And then? Arrested, executed? You can't get away with it. So—so, you are about life, that's 'so'. You're a lot of things, Nikos, but you're not a nihilist. You care, even if you wish you didn't. She's dead, but your life isn't over. She is.

"Nikos?"

"Yeah." We paused by the tram. "What?"

"You look . . ."

"What? How do I look?"

"Did you look at the records, do they . . ."

I ripped the whole bunch of pages in half: right down the middle, then bunched my muscles, trembling, just waiting for him to say something. Say something wrong—come on. Provoke me.

"Okay," he said. "Do you need anything?"

I walked away without answering. A little part of me raised an eyebrow, tapped me on the shoulder. Umm . . . what did you just do, just like that and you're going to leave him there? He's trying to help, and you—don't care. Yeah, just like that. When I get home—tonight she wasn't going to be there, was she? Out again. I'm finished, I thought, and as I stalked away across the lot I put my comm earpiece in, dialed the base. The same security guard answered, and without putting up a fight he told me where the Director was: a lunch with four important senators and their wives; all schmoozing to save the doomed program.

I called a tram service, and they told me that one would arrive in ten minutes. Where was I going? One of two places: to kill the Director or take a nap.

The tram arrived, and inside a recording asked me to state an address or neighborhood. Which one? Home or the Senate?

"Destination?"

My comm rang: Giannis. I ignored it. His tram still sat across the lot and he watched me, leaning beside it.

"Destination?"

"The Senate," I said. "Take me to the Senate annex."

* * *

I stomped out. Need a weapon . . . weapon—why? Why not strangle the guy with my bare hands? Squeeze his dark throat until his cheeks swell and purple, his tongue flops out. Want to watch him choke and die. Took Elena away, they all took her away and it should have been me. Glad it—it shouldn't have been her.

On the way to the Senate, I'd been stopped at three checkpoints by unarmed soldiers. Wire fences were draped across the road, guarded by tracks of tire teeth that forced all traffic into one of two lines: entering or leaving. I'd never seen anything like it, and when I questioned them, the soldiers shrugged. The Nine Laws.

Pulse in my neck and ears, arms shaking, I stood at the base of the octagonal Senate building. 482 marble steps rose to the columned entrance, and bright statues of dead men and gods and a few of both, ringed the Senate house. Glass walkways sprouted like slick appendages from the marble octagon, linking it with annexes on both sides of the street, and I'd once heard that there were one-hundred layers of tunneling underground, dating from the middle of the Merr Dynasty, almost 2,000 years ago. And maybe even older.

The streets were ancient cobblestone, the buildings all government offices of glass and statuary and veined, multicolored marble. Blimps rocked in the breeze, tethered to the eight points of the Senate: one for each of the provincial capitals, each with its own patchwork flag. Why wasn't I moving? Weapon . . . No visible guards or soldiers. They had to be here, though I'd never seen them. Might not do any good to have a blade or a pyck. Back when I'd come for the base assignment, I'd seen them.

Up the stairs, and I reached the first landing, full of lounging bureaucrats, in their red-blue striped togas, all talking too loudly on comms. Three more landings and I reached one, then two, and now I stood at the summit: open bronze doors and 12-meter-high statues in white and black marble. I needed the annex. I stopped at the back of a line that led to a pair of soldiers. They were searching everyone. The Senate had always been open, but I didn't complain, and I didn't ask why. The Nine Laws, right?

I wandered through the Peletas entrance, with its frescos and latticework lamps. The tiles dated to the beginning of the Republic, 700 years ago.

23

More bureaucrats, but I was moving up the food chain: these preliminary halls were filled with darker togas—of course they were. I shoved my way through, took a left, around the parabolic corridors that wrapped the main chamber like concentric serpents. Around I went, until tile and fresco turned to purple carpet and signs directed me to the Butz'Da annex. Only problem was I might lose my unstoppable bloodlust if this went on any longer. There were over 500 kilometers of walkways and eight annexes in the Senate, each with another eight sub annexes, and ten times as many insectoid paths underground. Almost 5,000 kilometers of paperwork and togas under my feet. Finding the Director here might be akin to . . .

"Nikos!"

I stopped, and someone slammed into my back, dropping a spread of file-papers around my ankles. The Director smiled from the end of the hall. A soldier grabbed a nearby clerk and hustled him away.

"Nikos, I thought that was you," he said, trailed by a quad of dark-toga'd senators. Color determined by region: Nou green, Gat'ata silver, and so on. "How are you—you look better, healthier."

I watched them come closer. Yes, the people in the hall were making room for them, clearing a path: I wasn't the only one hallucinating here.

"Funding is always on the line, isn't it?" the Director said, and he named the four Senators, as if I were going to be tested later. "Walk with us for a moment—you're not busy, are you?" I started to answer, and he continued, "What brings you to the Capitol? You spoke with the dig supervisor?"

"Yeah."

"Interesting that she's an albino, isn't it?"

Not sure what to say, so one of the Senators said, "Should be sent home. That's what's interesting about this. We need border control."

He wasn't talking to me, and the Director was only half-listening. The Senator spoke the same way some people smoked: to pass the time.

"Interesting that some mongrel priestess can supervise anything without a drop of Amith blood in her veins. Just because her great-aunt . . ."

"Her mother," the Director said.

"Because her mother was a whore in white and blue."

By that he meant an ambassador from Shan.

"A well-paid whore," another Senator said, grinning. "She probably out-produced your Capital estates, didn't she?"

The first Senator grunted. "She may have out-produced the *cattle* on my Capitol estates. They should all be sent home."

"All right," the Director said to the first Senator. "Now back to our discussion. Will you explain the logic to Nikos here, Senator, just as you did to me. Perhaps the committee's referendums will make a kind of sense to a third party."

"Yes, and he's such an objective ear, I'm sure," the Senator said, ignoring me. "His wife was the one . . ."

"Everyone knows that the Shan have over 20—or even 30—ships in orbit, somewhere between Shan and New Amith, don't they? Why should we fall further behind?"

"It's not a matter of falling behind. You know the rationale, but unlike the members of the subcommittee, your job is bound to the program. Were you elected to my post, you would vote just as strongly against more funding. We will demonstrate our capacity for national sacrifice in the Nine Laws."

"You know," I said to the Director, "I came here to kill you."

The senators froze, and the Director smiled uncomfortably. "Really?"

"Yeah, but you didn't build the rocket, did you? You just made sure the money kept coming. You're just a placeholder like them."

"Why would you say that?" the Director asked, his smile gone. "That you came here to . . ."

". . . to kill you?"

"Yes."

"Obviously, I'm not going to anymore. There's no point."

One of the senators murmured into a comm, and a cluster of clerks appeared ahead, none armed. Even with the increase in Senate security, weapons—honest, burn-the-flesh-off-his-skull weapons—were tough to find. It would take a moment to unlock the cache in the next wing, to organize the guards.

"Did the others die like her?" I asked.

The Director frowned. "What others?"

"In the previous programs—every time they tried to send someone up, how did they die?"

"I don't know. We never . . ."

"Nikos!" Giannis pushed through the hall. "Come on." He yanked my arm.

I said, "Don't give him the funding, cut it off now."

One of the senators laughed, as if I'd just done a trick, like a performing cobra. "You see? Here is the voice of reason."

Giannis pressed me past the bureaucrats, they let us go. Have to get back to the exit before they call the guards.

"You followed me?"

Giannis hustled me down the front steps. A pair of soldiers in thick black armor rushed past, their lances hissing and sparking.

"Yes. I thought you might get a stupid idea . . ."

"Like what?"

He shoved me into a waiting tram and we started off. "Are you armed?"

I laughed. "What?"

"Are you?"

"No. How would I have gotten in?"

"I don't know." He slumped against the window and glared at the marble buildings and crush of tram traffic. "You're going to the dig tomorrow."

Not a question. I said, "What?"

"You're going."

"Why should I . . ."

"You're going, and then—maybe the next day—we're going to settle Dett's estate."

"So you're taking over now?"

He didn't look at me. "I'm worried about you."

"Don't."

"Just go, all right?"

Why not? Maastade was shut down. Alcohol and masturbation couldn't fill an entire day, could they? "They have a Shan running it."

"The dig?"

"Yeah."

Our tram slowed at a checkpoint. Giannis waited for more, then said, "So?" Good question. "Have you heard about the dig, what they're . . ."

"No, should I have?"

"I don't know. I heard about the Shan."

So had I. This is what I knew: One, New Amith has had five ages, from the first Amith Priesthood, which ended 4,000 years ago to this, the Fifth Age of the New Amith Republic. Two, Shan is a sister planet, which made contact with us centuries ago via radio signals and began sending ambassadors—like the dig supervisor's mother—three decades ago. The Shan is comprised of a motley network of territories, each governed by a warlord or local council, only recently united under nominal control of the Ckish.

Three, what New Amith has in unlimited fresh water, accessible food, and medicine, the Shan have in steel. The Shan grew as a pasty-faced conglomeration of tribes, slaughtering everything else on the planet. Those spears and guns held by the Senatorial guards were marked with the snake crest of the Ckish: imports. Of course, New Amith has had her share of atrocities. As Giannis once said, 'If we're entirely peaceful, why aren't we still living in the first age?'

However, crime and violence are virtually nonexistent, and the Senate provides for her citizens. The outer boroughs of every province are checkered with Tellen complexes: simple dwellings where those too lazy or distracted to work can live in relative comfort. Everything is provided: food, healthcare, even wine and entertainment. Officially, they are known as Senatorial complexes, but in the last century, since the poetic renaissance of Tellen, those free-standing buildings have been known as centers of art and learning. Not so on Shan.

Nevermind that a Shan ambassador would probably correct every last point I just made. The Shan have much to contribute, she would say, after all, I'm here, aren't I? Why would they send me to schmooze if military interests were paramount? Why would they send an archaeologist to 'supervise' a dig? The Shan want more than a gradual take-over of New Amith. Which is, of course, what all of this is about. The program, the tension in the Senators' eyes—fear of Shan warships, fear of a surprise attack and an end to a century of peaceful coexistence.

We passed the checkpoint and kept moving.

"I wasn't *symbolically* searched," I said.

"What?"

"They're searching everyone."

"So?"

"So here's another one." We were already approaching another roadblock. "What is this?"

"The Nine Laws are . . ."

"This isn't symbolic."

Someone had painted a segmented half-circle on a building adjacent to the roadblock.

As we rolled through the checkpoint, he said, "You're angry about the 25-drink limit."

"No."

"Then what?"

"I don't know."

When the tram stopped at my house, Giannis lit a roll, followed me up the lawn. Was getting late, and moths twirled around the candles someone—not me—had lit between the paws of my stone guardian on the lawn. I stepped over the lion-god's haunch, brushed a few insects away, and paused at the bottom of the steps. The charcoal-cinnamon smell of Giannis's roll brought a memory: laughing and singing with Elena in the bedroom of our first house. It had been Claure Day, and we could hear the parades and songs and fireworks in the street outside; one of the things I'd loved about that place when we first moved in was how close it was to the Market District, right in the center of New Amith, surrounded by people and excitement. One of the things Elena had hated a year and half later when we moved.

That charcoal-cinnamon smell had slipped under our cracked windows, soaking the sheets and drapes. And we'd lit up, bought a bottle of expensive—I'd thought it was expensive at the time—champagne. Gotten drunk and silly and made love six times, until I was finally sober enough to finish: she'd come every time.

"Did you stop by the house?" I asked.

"Yes," Giannis said. "How'd you know that?"

"That god didn't light himself, did he?"

I banged open the unlocked front door and pointed to a stack of carefully repaired paper. "What's that?"

"If you don't want them I'll . . ."

"You put them back together?"

He hesitated, smiled. "What else was I going to do with them?"

"Why?"

"Why not? You ran off, I had a free day, some time to kill . . ."

"Go home."

"Are you all right?"

"Yeah. Thank you. Go home—I'm okay."

When he was gone, I poured myself another drink and curled up in bed with the bandaged files. Late, but too early to sleep. The top page was marked 'S. File', with the words 'eval. of E. Healy'. My wife: 'E. Healy'. I started flipping and sipping. Cold vodka mix on my tongue, and I scanned the first few pages—there were hundreds of sheets—the way I'd reviewed before an exam at the academy. Columns of jargon and meaningless abbreviations; the project was technically a military operation. The army was notorious for insider-parlance. I slowed on the third page:

> Subject's death cannot be said to relate to a failure of a purely mechanical nature. Minimal damage to the *Melet*, significantly to the exterior, indicates that the fatality may have been due to a biological failure.

A biological failure, I thought. So she spontaneously combusted? Is that what this is supposed to mean? And hadn't I thought about it? Wasn't it strange that the ship hadn't been damaged, except where Elena's body had been: she'd fried and burned some of the circuitry.

> In comparison with the previous records, the temporary board of review has concluded unofficially that the most recent fatality may be said to be identical to those in the past.

I read it again, to be certain the liquor wasn't swirling or changing the words. A group of men somewhere had unofficially concluded that Elena died the same way the others had. No need to see the other files, I thought, they'd already done the work for me, and confirmed what I'd known: all the other space programs had burned in the same way. We could send rockets up, that wasn't the problem—we'd been able to do that for years. We just couldn't survive inside them, and that wasn't their fault, it was ours. Something in our bodies caught fire when we flew too far from the ground. Doesn't make any sense, so I kept reading.

Something in our cells, in our blood, something inside us broke when we tried to leave Amith. Heard that it couldn't be genetic, but maybe they'd missed something. Something in our blood. A footnote caught my eye:

See Appendix 382 – 490 for tseon lens recording.

I'd spent enough time with Elena and the *Melet* techies to know that a 'tseon lens' was a refined slice of glass used to build a telescope. Except that telescopes had been abandoned by the space program decades ago. No one could explain why, but the most powerful lenses blurred when they tried to look too far, as if New Amith were surrounded by a dust ball. And we weren't.

There were no external recorders on the *Melet*, and this file didn't include an Appendix. I stared at the footnote—probably a mistake—then continued.

Pages of technical garbage. I could decipher most of it, but there wasn't much point: it was a chart of the *Melet*'s heartbeat and pulse during Elena's last moments, and it was normal. The *Melet* had been fine: perfect stabilization, perfect oxygen and compression, it had been a perfect flight. The next few pages charted Elena's diagnostics. They weren't so good.

No, that's not right. As I compared and adjusted the readings, it looked more and more as if—as if nothing happened. Elena's chart was fine. Normal everything: pulse, perspiration, and it was all gone. No, not just like that:

Pulse: 61, 60, 63, 65, 63, 75, 81, 112, 0.

It rose, not too quickly, but Elena's pulse had snapped up at the last moment. I heard her, I thought, remembering her voice, and that terrible noise. It had happened so suddenly—too quickly and violently for the computers to follow. Something had happened.

She'd been terrified in a blink of light, and then it was over. What happened up there? Nothing on the next few pages, and then I shivered: a page of text, a transcript marked: *Pre-Flight Composition*. I'd forgotten all about this—before every military operation with a greater than 50 percent chance of death, a final statement was required. Not a will or even last words, more of a reflection, like the prologue of a book. Elena's began:

> This is a recording so I'll . . . I didn't want to leave one of these, but I have to, and no one will hear this until it's over. I love my husband, I love my life, but I love my gods more. [Laughter] That should be the end, right? I thought about other ways, but they're right—this is best. We've worked on this for so long. It will hurt—of course it will—but so would a bullet, right?
>
> I have to see them. They gave me a gift that's too great a burden to bear. Divine union in this . . . I have to love death as much as life.

Gods.

She knew what was coming all along.

I put the paper down, went to pee in the incinerator. When I'd finished, the urine was vaporized, I lit a candle in the kitchen and eyed the 'Beenizk Vodka' bottle. Half empty. Elena's last words went for a full page. It was a suicide note—had she really said those things? Elena wanted to kill herself, and she'd wanted to be closer to the gods when it happened. 'We've worked for so long on this,' she'd said. Who's 'we'? My comm rang. It was still in my left ear.

"Hello?"

"Nikos, it's Anna Antc'sh, I just wanted to make sure you're still coming tomorrow."

"Yeah."

"'Yeah', you'll be there?"

"That's right."

"Okay."

She gave me detailed instructions on how to get my security clearance from the archaeological board, along with directions to the site: it wasn't far. She explained that they'd found 'the ruins' under a field of wild strawberries in someone's enormous backyard. I didn't ask for details. I told her I'd be there, hung up, hid my comm on a bookshelf where I hoped I'd forget it in the morning, then went back to bed. I heaped the files onto the floor, blew out the lights. Go to sleep, I told myself. A part of me grinned and shook his head: no, we have too much to think about. Like what? What do you think? Fire.

CHAPTER THREE

The Black Doorway

My tram was late, and when I stepped into the harsh morning sunlight of a blocked-off villa, I wanted to go back home. Head throbbing, I pushed through a crowd of milling neighbors, past a street crammed with trams, and reached the gated villa-entrance. A pair of unarmed guards blocked the gravel path inside. They were both talking loudly into comms, ignoring me.

"The schedule was set last week, and it's not my fault if . . . no, I understand . . ."

"Have coverage when I get the call, not before. You can contact the compound at Vincex or you can wait."

Past the guards, the path circled to a stone and copper mansion surrounded by sparkly fountains and animal gods. Far beyond, across an unkept lawn, a cluster of tents poofed and fluttered in the wind. That must be the 'dig', out in the middle of some rich guy's backyard. I wondered how much they'd paid him to plow his strawberry field and whether or not he would own the entertainment rights to whatever they unearthed out there. All the trams and people in the street behind me—the controlled chaos—meant this was important.

"I need to . . ."

One of the guards glared at me, held up a hand, and kept talking, "Yes, I understand, but you need to be clear on exactly how our protocol functions. Just because you tell me . . . no. You need a letter from . . ."

The other guard was doing about the same. I might wait here for the rest of my life, it wasn't inconceivable. Maybe if I called Anna-the-Shan-supervisor—I didn't have my comm. Nice. Why the hell had I decided to hide it last night, what kind of brilliant plan had that been? Certainly it was obnoxious to be in constant communication with the world, but there were times, like now, when a comm would have been extremely useful.

"I need to get inside."

The first guard told whoever was on the comm to 'stop for a moment', then extended a hand. "Security clearance."

"I'm supposed to get it from the archaeological board."

Guard #2 shook his head and ended his comm conversation. "No passes issued after ten."

I reached into my pocket: Elena's red-tipped pen—I was still carrying it around—and my comm. The comm would tell me the time. "It has to be before ten."

"No, it's after ten, sir," guard #2 said.

Guard #1 continued to lecture whoever was at the other end of the comm, so I focused on #2.

"What time is it?"

He checked. "Almost 10:15."

"I just missed it."

"Yes sir. And passes are issued at the southern entrance. But, that wouldn't matter today."

"Why not?"

"No passes unless you're on the roster."

"So check the roster."

"It's after ten, sir."

"Is my name on the roster—can you look? It's Nikos . . ."

"No sir, it's after ten."

"Just check, and I'll . . ."

Guard #1 told his comm to 'wait', then said, "Rosters are at the southern entrance, sir."

"If I'm on the list, they'll know at the other gate?"

"It won't matter," #2 said. "It's 10:15, sir. No passes issued . . ."

I was already walking away. The southern entrance turned out to be on the exact opposite end of the estate, almost a full kilometer away, but I walked it: my tram was gone, and I couldn't go anywhere. How was I supposed to call another tram without my comm? Anna-the-Shan-supervisor had sent my ride. And somehow—after forcing myself to get up, shower, and settle in for a long read on the incinerator—I was late. They'd probably started without me. Exactly how all of this worked—the technicalities of burrowing under someone's strawberries and opening a prophetic tomb or ancient whorehouse—I had no idea.

Two more guards at the other entrance, but this side was an expanse of woods behind one road. Without the frenzy of trams and pushing neighbors, the villa's backyard was an over-run grove: weeds and whirly bushes protected by more stone fence and iron spike-tips. The guards adjusted a board of paper when they saw me.

"Your name?"

"Nikos Healy'll."

They checked, then waved me through. One, two, and I was inside—I wanted to hike across the lawn, past the canopy-tents, around the mansion and ask the cocksuckers at the front gate what time it was. People clustered around the tents, and I wandered through overgrown wine-country to meet them. Hmm. Not unlike the project, archaeological techies scurried around a junglework of machinery umbilicaled to two long trams, parked between me and the tents.

No sign of a Shan, and I was ignored as I reached the tents. Under the largest, a partitioned staircase of bright wood dropped into a hole like a well. Cords snaked and coiled out of the well, and people side-stepped around the mess of wires, crushed paper cups, and old wine-stalk supports. This had been a terraced yard for Nkeil red—I'd tasted it enough to know that we weren't missing much.

Older generations were supposed to be better, but most of the good wines—the fruity whites and deep reds—were imported from the coastal provinces or the mountain-country. The suburban villas of New Amith grew their own varieties and this territory was no different, and like all the others it tasted like cat piss. There had been a time—last night?—when I hadn't cared.

I stopped beside the hole. I'd imagined a door or a drum roll or something. Not the constant scurry of people in and out, like termites.

"You tell them to adjust the scope before we shoot in, I don't want to have to say this again . . ."

I turned—ah. She looked too thin, stretched almost, and—a ponytail of red hair. I'd heard about it, never seen it. Huh: red hair, like an exasperated glow-beetle surrounded by olive-skinned ants. Anna chucked papers at a circle of her techies and frazzled colleagues: an athlete on a track, in command.

"And I want the '9/14 without the last filter. The light'll hold, don't tell me it won't."

"AP-X?"

"No, a lower one. Try 1'E. Remus?"

An older guy answered, "Yes?"

"Have we cleared up the bug in receiving?"

No, not an athlete: a soldier. She's Shan, what did you expect?

"I'm telling you, I just spoke to them, and they think it's something with the line," Remus said. "We won't know until we replace it, screw in a full cage, but it doesn't feel like a drummed survey to me."

"Well it has to be," Anna said. "How long until we have the new line?"

"Not long."

"Check it, will you?"

"Sure."

Anna continued her stream of orders. ". . . take it out then? Okay?"

"I'll tell him . . ."

"Don't just tell him, make sure he understands."

"Okay."

I was completely ignored in the frenzy. "I want the news to wait—have you heard from central committee?"

The techie hesitated, watching me. Anna didn't notice and Remus said, "She bring you in to look at the cage line?"

"I hope not," I said.

Anna glared at me. "Who are you?"

"Nikos Healy'll. I'm from the . . ."

"Yes. Okay." Back to the orders and shouting—the chaos resumed. "Mitus, did you re-route the open AV?"

A techie called back, "I did, it's still no good."

"Route it again."

"We'll have to bring in another source."

"Then bring in another source. Barcuc's ass, am I the only one who wants to do this?"

"What do you want me to do?" I asked. See how helpful I can be?

Anna said, "What can you do?"

"You're having problems?"

She frowned, as if I'd just tried to throw a pie in her face and she couldn't decide how to react. "They sent you to make a report from the project, right?"

"Yeah."

"Okay. Here's the situation: nothing's working. We have power, but no feed. Juice, but no lights. We dig holes in the concrete and get nothing but black."

"I don't . . ."

"The room's black. It's all nothing."

"The room?"

"There's a room down—what did they say about this? That much?"

"Yeah."

"You don't have a background in this?"

I might. If I knew what we were talking about. "In what?"

"First Age Bialu Chambers. The ones on Shan pre-date the thaw of the Northern Ice Shelf."

"Oh."

"You don't know what I'm talking about?"

True, I didn't know specifically what she was talking about, but I'd been to the Academy, was better educated than her. I'd learned our history, studied scripture the way a good citizen should.

I asked, "There's a room down there that's the same as some found on Shan?"

She waved away her techies. I was trouble, need to coach the slow kid for a few minutes. "They're 10,000 years old."

"Like the ruins at Versa," I said. I'd seen them years ago, the crumbling bits of smooth metal and stone, overgrown and covered by modern buildings and roads.

"No, Versa only dates to your second age."

"And that's . . ."

". . . maybe 3,000 years old."

"Okay."

"These are much older," she said. "And they appear to be identical."

Oh gods, she was a Pnetian: red-eyed cult of Academy drop-outs who spent their time searching for the best high in the cheapest household cleaning products, and who had been famously taken to court by the Under-Admin Governor of the Academy for saying that New Amith and Shan were one and the same. The Pnetians gathered in remote communities, and when they did interact with us 'ordinaries', they tended to get tossed out of bars at 3:00 in the morning for screaming about the end of the world.

"The sites on both planets are identical," Anna said again. Here we go. She paused, called Remus, then said, "They should be."

"What do you mean? Can't you see?"

"No."

"Then how do you know . . ."

"The thermal charting and exterior markings are almost identical to a Hars'h Site on Shan." As Remus came back, she continued, "Traditionally the Shan sites are supposed to belong to the Rubay Era, the Gray Kings. That doesn't fit, of course, because the actual empires the Gray King legends are based on only date to about 2,000 years ago. These rooms are much older."

"8,000 years older."

"Yes."

"See—and you thought I wasn't listening."

Remus sat on a crate. "We still have last week's shots . . ."

"We can get those again," she said. "That doesn't do us any good."

"What can we do, Anna? It's not going to work."

She frowned. "I know."

We waited in silence for a long moment, then I said, "I just got here, but it seems like something's . . . not working?"

No smile, just a worn stare: she was thinking about something else when she answered, probably categorizing and listing and regrouping all the problems and potential solutions.

"I told you," Anna said. "We're blind. The room is black."

"I don't understand."

Remus nodded. "Neither do we."

"Did you open a door or something?"

"No, these things don't have doors, we have to cut holes in the stone," Anna said, her mind still elsewhere. "And the procedure is to peek inside— you know, check the air, make sure we're not going to release a plague or step into poison gas. We want to know exactly what's in the room before we dive in."

"And you can't see?"

"No, we can't. It's probably something to do with the machines, nothing else makes any sense."

"I thought you had an idea of what was inside . . ."

"I thought we did too," Anna said. "But there's a whole world of mistakes and complicated ways the computers can trick themselves into seeing things that aren't there. We had some basic images of the interior— from the outside—but those may be ghosts from a previous project or mirror bounces."

Ghosts and mirror bounces. Ah.

"Are you still going in?" I asked.

They answered simultaneously:

Remus: "No."

Anna: "Yes." She gave Remus a look, as if he'd just farted. "We are."

"Diving into a Black Room is . . ."

"It won't be black," she said, "we'll fix it." She shook her head, stopped him from responding. "We *will*. There's a reason for this: the machines are hiccupping, we just have to know why."

"How long has it been like this—have you been stuck?"

39

"Since we started, a month ago," Anna said. "But today we're making progress. Go make sure the stabilizing system isn't the problem. We'll be down there in an hour."

But we weren't.

An hour later, Anna was still shouting at her techies, while they cranked and rolled a 'robot-dog' down the hole. We followed it into a cut-out passage of mildew-dust and wooden wall-supports that dropped ten meters, then 15, and when we were maybe 20 meters underground—"22.6 meters," Anna said—the hall leveled out, and we 'walked' the three-foot robot to a sheer wall. Lanterns cast long, yellow shadows.

"Feed it," Anna said.

The dog-robot was cranked to the wall, where it pressed all four paws to the cold stone. Tubes along both sides of the floor hissed, pumping in oxygen, sucking out toxins.

A long pause, Anna gave me a tense 'please let this work' look. She was worried now: everything was working. They'd checked and triple checked the equipment. No hiccups, no reason the underground room was still a mystery. A comm beeped and crackled static. A flush of adrenaline: back at the project, Elena and beeping buzzes and comms and communication is . . .

Over Anna's comm: ". . . on the wall?"

She answered, "Yes."

"We're not getting anything."

"It's on there," Anna said. "They didn't ship the puppy in so it could break. Run a diagnostic."

"The diagnostic was confirmed before . . ."

"Check it again."

They did, then said, "No change. This isn't working, Anna. We've gotten calls from committee . . ."

Anna stared at the robot-dog, and her techies began to leave. "What do they want?" It was a rhetorical question; she already knew.

"They're asking for you . . ."

"Okay."

"They want to . . ."

"Okay."

"Are you coming up?"

She let the rest of the techies leave, we were alone with the robot-dog and an old stone wall. It might've been the middle of the night: the lanterns and dark walls made the passage feel . . . I don't know—*removed*. The rest of the world might have stopped, except for the wires and tubing that snaked in the corners.

"Yes," Anna said at last. "I'm coming up." But she didn't move. "Why isn't this working?"

Not sure how I was supposed to answer that. "I don't know."

"Me neither. There has to be a reason. You don't understand, there has to be a reason this thing isn't working."

"What does the committee . . ."

"They want to take-over. We're supposed to be inside already." The wall wasn't there anymore: a black doorway, but Anna was facing me, away from it. "Procedure: we can't go in if we can't see what's on the other side. You know how much work and luck let us find this place? If they take it away . . ." I grabbed her shoulders, forced her to turn. "What the hell are . . ."

"You said there wouldn't be a doorway," I murmured.

She was frozen, "Barcuc . . ."

The robot-dog lay immobile at the edge of the doorway—beyond was absolute darkness, like a dense fog. The lantern-light didn't break-in.

"I can't see in," I said. "That doesn't make any sense, I should be able to see."

Anna approached the cut-off, extended a hand, and her fingers disappeared into the—the room was visible in a sudden snap. A sharp jolt, and I shouted, grabbed the cold wall—someone had jabbed a sliver of glass through the right side of my skull, just above the ear. Pain—was gone, and I blinked, my spotted vision already clearing. Anna held her face with both hands, stunned. She looked as if a midget had kicked her in the back of the head: not sure whether to cry out or gape in surprise. I probably looked about the same.

"What was that?" I said, and my voice died as the room came into focus: the lantern light hit all four corners in a dim glow, just like it was supposed to. Writing on the walls, and worn mounds built into the floor and . . .

"That's a . . ."

"Yeah."

". . . skeleton against the far wall."

CHAPTER FOUR

Going Through the Motions

Anna pressed her comm. "Come down."

"The committee's . . ."

She switched off, and I followed her in. My stomach slowly curled, slick ice forming on the lining. The room looked like an ancient sewer-pot, just a stone bowl with faded, sediment-marked walls. The colors and rings circled the exterior, like a tree-trunk: this had been underwater or something, but that's not what . . .

"Nikos?"

Along the back wall, rows of curly text—old Menst—had been jammed to fill every centimeter of space. So that my eyes couldn't focus. Strange, over stimulating, and that human skeleton draped below. As a kid, I'd stomped on a black ant nest and watched the dirt fill with insects, like crawly-pebbles. After a moment, there were too many to take in— hundreds of thousands of ants squirming around their bashed home. That's what these words looked like: without the squirming or the antennae. Just too much tiny writing.

"Nikos, what's wrong?" Anna said. She sounded as if she wanted to be reassured. To be certain we were seeing the same thing—that she wasn't going mad.

"That skeleton . . ."

"Looks human, doesn't it?" She knelt over the remains. "It's old."

More writing filled the sides. What could anyone possibly say that would require so many words? More words in this room than I'd said in my life. Just on and on, but they hadn't been able to get the ceiling—tar-fungus blackened the upper corners of bare stone.

"I didn't expect this," I said.

Anna laughed nervously. "I did."

What was that—something's wrong. I heard it in her voice. "What do we do now?"

"I'll have to study it. It'll take awhile. You have something to report now—what are you going to say?"

Not much to it, I thought. Just this room. And the skeleton: Anna hadn't even noticed the room, the writing that made my eyes water—she saw the body. The room was a graffitied box of mold, just four walls with a slight depression in the center.

"You've seen this before?" I asked.

"What?"

"The room."

"Yes." She called her techies again, told them to hurry. "But not here."

"What do you mean? Not in . . ."

"Not on your planet, not on Amith."

I almost pointed out that it was called 'New Amith', after the Republic, but she probably knew that. Ambassador's daughter.

"You've found these things on Shan?"

"Yes."

I pointed to the bones. "But not the . . ?"

"No."

The nutball-Pnetians are right? No. "What does that prove?"

She gave me a 'if you can't figure it out, I'm not going to tell you' look, then said, "A lot of things."

"We both dug sewers under our . . ."

"We didn't build them. It was the same species, we were colonized by the same race."

She didn't have to say that; just making this dramatic. The Pnetians claimed that when the gods got involved—at the end of this Fifth Age—

they would unite our worlds. Nevermind that even more people wanted the gods to slaughter the Shan, when they finally—*poof*—appeared.

If both the Shan and New Amith were colonized at some point in the distant past by the same race—as Anna was suggesting—what would that mean?

"Think about the implications of a New Amith-Shan common past . . ."

"We'll suddenly be best friends?"

"Nikos . . ."

"No, I don't understand. Is that what you're saying, we'll stop the space race and the planet-side defenses, and you'll stop cranking out warships?"

"First of all, we're not cranking out warships," she said. "And yes, that's sort of a simplistic way of—that's what I'm getting at. A common history means a lot more than you . . ."

"I get it. What does all that say?"

"It'll take some time to translate." There it was again. Little twist behind her voice: something's wrong.

"You've seen the ones on Shan?"

"Yes."

"And these are basically the same, so . . ."

"Just because they look the same, doesn't mean they are."

"What do those say?"

She backed away from the skeleton, wiped off her hands and looked back at the hallway.

Why hadn't we been able to see inside?

She said, "Why are they taking so long?"

"Did you call . . ."

"You heard me."

"Did they answer?"

Anna frowned, pressed her comm. "Remus, get down here. Can you hear me?" She waited, stiffened. "It isn't connecting . . ."

"Something with the room."

"That doesn't make any sense."

"So." I went for the doorway. "It works in the hall."

Anna didn't move. Finally, she examined the carved walls, took a long moment as if she were afraid it would—poof—disappear. What's wrong? She knows something I don't. The moment we stepped inside—like an attack dog. She'd been trained to sniff out the bad—and something was *off*. But all I could smell was the mold.

"Okay," she said, as if convincing herself. "We need to preserve the skeleton."

"Yeah."

We returned to the hall. Wait—limbs tingled, as if I were drunk. And I wasn't. The lightness filled my toes and swam like frizzy soda up my ankles, through my calves and thighs . . .

Anna said, "Do you feel that?"

Through my dick and stomach, up my chest, out my arms, and when it surged through my neck into my face, I opened my mouth, "Anna . . ."

"What's . . ."

Voices, making music, and I felt heat change to substance. A calendar—our calendar. I didn't see it, I touched the colors of the overlapping, circular dial. Counting down, to the end of the Fifth Age, the end of the Republic of New Amith, as told by the Golden Age Prophets, as interpreted by the founder of the new Republic in the final days of the Merr. All just . . .

". . . bullshit."

I lay in the dirt corridor, Anna groggy on my left, staring blankly at me.

She said, "What . . ."

"Oh shit."

CHAPTER FIVE

Bad Timing

The door was gone: the stone wall and the robot-dog hadn't moved. But the skeleton had. It sprawled in the center of the floor. I tried to get up, but my arms and legs were dead weight, refusing to budge: eventually they did.

"It's out here," she said. "It shouldn't be out here . . ."

"Yeah."

Anna looked at me. "This has never happened before . . ."

"I should hope not."

"I'm asking you: this hasn't happened before?"

"I don't know." Of course I didn't, but for some reason, it wasn't strange that she'd ask.

Anna groped on the wall, smearing her palms with black dirt. "I don't understand, this doesn't make sense. We didn't move it."

"Maybe it got up and walked."

Footsteps hurrying behind me: a crowd of ravenous techies all screaming questions. They slowed when they saw the body, then continued, even louder:

". . . can it have come from?"

". . . requesting an update!"

". . . disappeared, how did that happen?"

Anna closed her eyes, as if she needed to soak up the shouts for strength. Eyes still shut, she said, "Quiet."

Silence. It was the damnedest thing.

"A moment ago, Nikos Healy'll and myself were inside the room," Anna said.

"... you can't ..."

"... where did the ..."

"However," she continued, and they shut up again, "as you can see, the wall has closed again. This body came out with us—no. I do not. Know how. But it happened. Now, it's obviously very old. Remus, assign a team and have it preserved upstairs. It's rotting as we speak—or have we all forgotten how to do our jobs now that we actually have something to do?"

The techies got to work, Anna ignored their questions, took a long look at the skeleton, then met my stare and nodded to the exit. She cleared us a path. Up the stairs, back into the tents and sunlight.

Someone said, "Anna, switch your comm to channel 3, the committee's on ..."

"In a minute."

"They've been trying to reach you since we ordered the puppy. You have to ..."

"In a minute," she said again, and we ducked into one of the service trams. The back was crowded with equipment crates and labeled tubing. She slammed the door behind us, flicked on a tiny white bulb.

"I'm not going crazy am I?"

I hesitated. "It depends what you mean by ..."

"Don't. I need you to tell me that you saw the same things I did down there. We were inside, right? And that skeleton didn't move. And when we left, I was seeing—no ... there were calendars and something to do with, I don't know. It felt like the end of the world. Then we're back in the hall with the skeleton: but we didn't move it." She paused. "Did we?"

"Well *I* didn't."

"Please ..."

"That's about right."

"Barcuc."

"Yeah." I slumped against the wall: I'd barely been awake four hours, and I was ready for a nap. "What're you going to tell them?"

"What do you mean?"

"About what happened . . ."

"The truth—what do you think?"

"What is the truth?" I asked.

"I have no idea, and that's what I'm going to say."

I grabbed her hand. She was shaking, slick with cold sweat. "You didn't expect that down there?"

She said, "No."

"There was a moment when there was something like warm milk or water filling me, when . . ."

"I know."

"You felt that too?"

"Yes."

I sighed, tried to bring back the release, the euphoria I'd felt. I couldn't, it had been too foreign, but—like something I'd forgotten. Like returning to the womb. We were all there.

"How long are we going to hide in here?" I asked at last.

"What do you mean?"

"I mean when are we going out?"

"We're not hiding."

"No?"

"No, we're—I wanted to make sure." She took a breath and opened the door and was surrounded by techies, all with questions and a handful of comms: she had 20 different people on hold.

I wanted this to go away, have to go away. Back to normal—empty house, remember? Normal's gone. As Anna was swallowed by the crowd of techies, I hurried to the main entrance, pushed past the guards and mixed with the street traffic. Find a tram, find alcohol, find—I shouted for a tram, got on. A part of me chuckled: just think, you have to write a report on this in the morning. Ha.

* * *

What was bothering me? She'd been distracted, and that stuck in me, like dust in my eye, irritating. On the ride home, Giannis called, said he wanted to meet for dinner, I asked why he hadn't gone back to his hospital to work, then told him I would be late. This was bothering me. I changed destinations, told the tram to drop me at the Yellow Lake Library. Four roadblocks later, I arrived.

A converted mansion, the Library was covered in ivy, like a leafy-carpet on the stone-bricks, around the old windows. Inside, it was what you'd expect: an old bathing pool in the entryway, donated gods in the corners and a sign that asked for a donation of ten denats. I swiped my ID card in a turnstile, told it to deduct ten, then wandered into a side room of humming computer terminals and jungle-ceiling. Vines had slipped through the cracks in the walls and run rampant: it smelled like an ozone-fern.

I popped a closed-circuit comm in my ear and sat at the nearest console—nobody else here. I didn't know the name of the villa or the dig. Nice. So how should I . . .

"Anna Antc'sh, I want information about her most recent projects."

A list on the screen: three sites on Shan, then the 'Wesler Estate'.

I said, "Wesler Estate." And it linked me to a cross-section of live network feeds and reports with titles like, "Possible Discovery at Yellow Lake Site" and "Shan Scientist Pushes Pnetian Claims". They didn't know yet. Anna was still there, screaming at her techies, trying to sort it out, before she made an announcement.

This wasn't what I wanted. I searched some more, but didn't— "Consular Suicide". The title turned out to be an exaggeration: the suicide hadn't been one of the two consuls, it had been a distant relative and old-blooded aristocrat named Famus Wesler'll. Lithographs of his stiff, bearded profile, and then with a plump wife and daughter. He'd been the one to—wife and kid both drowned and three days later, he kills himself. It didn't say how. That's why the villa was on the market.

That's why another bureaucrat and his wife bought it, discovered the ruins in their backyard, and gave Anna permission to dig. "After viewing Mr. Wesler'll's claims, the buyers searched the yard, and in a flash-flood discovered . . ." His claims? What claims? I went back, skimmed more records—until a Yellow Lake journal archive told me that the destruction to the Wesler Estate was not the work of vandals, but of Mr. Wesler'll before his death. Another link, another, and I found what I wanted.

Lithographs, pictures of the interior. Charred furniture, a scorched rug and smoke smears along the walls: he'd tried to burn it down. Now why would he—a picture of a burnt-out bedroom with slashes and writing on the wall.

To Hell. I Have Seen Hell. It Won't Go Away.

Okay . . .
There was more:

Open It To Bleed. My Vineyard. Do Not Go Down.

I took a breath. Calm down, he was a nut, he killed himself the next day. After he saw the room—no, after his wife and kid drowned. The article went on—a brief biography of the guy: famous family, wealthy, moved in high circles with Senators, Ambassadors and—why am I doing this?

I stared at the screen for a long moment, not reading. Don't want to go home. No need to see Giannis. I skimmed another page, nothing new. Just more pictures of the ruined villa interior and Wesler'll's nutty graffiti.

Grotton's Lif

The rest was burnt away.

Grotton? He was an old-world explorer, from the Gumay period. He'd founded modern Leim'en on the coast and promptly disappeared. That was the extent of what I'd learned about him at the Academy—why would this loon write the name of a 2,000-year-old explorer on his wall? No sense. Maybe I could visit the site and—no. They'd painted over all of it, torn down and rebuilt most of the walls.

But the bureaucrat and his wife had seen them—that graffiti was the reason they'd ripped up Wesler'll's backyard: they wanted to know what he thought he'd found, probably hoping for money. A door to Hell certainly sounded like something intended to keep peoples' grubby hands off buried treasure. Did that explain Anna's reaction? She'd been expecting more?

Blood-stained walls and a demon-statue, maybe. Not a boring square of writing and a skeleton.

No need to look at any more. I popped out the network comm and left on another tram. When I got home, called Anna.

"Hi, this is Nikos."

"Oh hi. Are you okay?"

And why that question? Yes. Of course I was.

"Yeah. You didn't tell me about the history."

"What?"

"The villa, the guy who owned it—why didn't you tell me?"

People shouted in the background, and she said, "You think I should have?"

"Yeah."

"Listen. They sent you to write a report for the project, right? If you think this relates to the space project, then go ahead and . . ."

"What happened down there?"

She yelled at someone else, then said, "I'm sorry, what?"

"I want to meet."

"Why?"

"Something happened down . . ."

"There's no need—we don't have to go over this again. The important thing now is the find. You can sit-in on the network briefings. I can get you clearance, okay?"

"About the skeleton?"

"Yes."

"It's a genetic-link between New Amith and Shan? It's what you . . ."

"Nikos, I can't tell you that now." She sighed. "Listen, I'll call you when I have the first conference agenda."

"When will . . ."

"Tomorrow. Okay? Thanks."

She clicked off. My tram continued home. What upset you down there? I wanted to ask. What do you know that I don't? Distracting myself. Look for questions that have answers: why did Elena—Giannis called.

I said, "Hi."

"Let's get something to eat."

"Yeah, all right."

* * *

Giannis was skeptical. "She didn't say anything?"

We sat on my front porch, drinks in-hand, watching nightflies buzz around the lion-god's candles. We'd just returned from the restaurant.

I said, "Maybe it was the skeleton, but I don't think so—something in that room was off."

"And now it's closed?"

"Yeah."

I'd told him about all of it, and he'd listened, as if I were a patient complaining about my ulcer: forced sympathy.

"Have you thought about why they gave you this?" he asked.

"What—why the Director sent me there?"

"Yes."

"No. To distract me, that's it."

"How about the records," he asked, then flipped his comm into the air and caught it the way he had as a kid; it had been a nervous habit.

"Thought dad broke you of that," I said.

"What?"

"That," I said and pointed to the comm he was bouncing in the air.

"No. You remember how he tried?"

"Of course," I said. "No calls, no tram time . . ."

"I used to store it up, practice my compulsive behavior at night, when I went to bed."

I watched him flick the comm. Of course, I already knew this. I'd seen him on more than one occasion lighting candles, blowing them out, and then striking them again; turning the doorknobs exactly nine times—he'd been able to hide it from our dad, but brothers knew. He couldn't bullshit me, but I just nodded. No sense letting him know.

He said, "You find anything?"

"In the records? No." It was true, but then I'd stopped when I hit her final log.

"You haven't finished her rites, you know."

"What—you forget that I had the ceremony, even draped the tapestry over her hearse?"

"You know what I mean," he said.

The third rites. Yeah, I knew, and he was right, but I said, "Just drink your beer."

"You have three days to mourn. It's been two. On the third day . . ."

"Knock it off." I wasn't in the mood for this. "You want to finish it, you do it."

"She was your wife. Both her parents are dead, same as ours, that means . . ."

"I know."

He hesitated, then shrugged and took a long drink. "I'm trying to help."

"You have nothing better to do than sit here and pester me? Explain to me why you're here again."

"I'm on vacation. And you don't have to be such a prick all the time."

"Sure I do."

After a brief silence, Giannis finished his beer, then stood to go. "I'll be here tomorrow morning." I frowned, and he said, "We're going to the coast, remember—change of scenery."

"Let's wait on that."

He stared to object, then said, "Okay. But we *will* go . . ."

"Yeah."

He left, and I locked the front door, stood in my bedroom doorway, staring at Elena's file. It hadn't moved from my bedside table. I'd tried to ignore—I started reading:

> Nikos doesn't understand. He's too sad and cynical, and I don't think he'll ever see. We're almost out of time anyway. They'll be here soon. He doesn't understand that there are more important things . . . we have to help it happen, don't we? Even Dett didn't understand that.

Dett? Was I losing it? I kept reading:

> It's a broken wheel, and we have to fix it—the Republic won't be saved through faith alone. We know that, even if

Dett does not. I don't know—it feels pointless to talk about this now. After all, the world is going to end in less than a week.

At the bottom, a line was written in a different color ink, separate from the rest:

We never had a child. Nikos and I will both forget her death.

That was the end. I felt like I'd been kicked in the gut. What the hell was this. She was insane. 'We never had a child'—of course we never had a child, why would she write that? And then 'We know that, even if Dett does not.' 'We' again. My Elena said this? No. I set the pages aside but couldn't stop staring at them. Yes, she wanted our relationship to fail, but she wasn't—she didn't say those things. Gods, why was I shaking? She already had someone else. Long ago, the certainty had grown in my mind, like a building; first the concrete and steel bones, then the mud flesh and wooden walls. Elena was cheating on me, but where's the proof? Forget the crazy suicide transcript. But I couldn't.

She'd been anal, always careful and neat; it wouldn't be like her to make a mistake, to leave a clue, but no one was perfect. There were always chips in the paint. I went to her dresser: I'd never touched her things.

Top drawer: lined with slippers, perfume scent of her three favorite scarves. Purple, purple, red. Her colors.

Next drawer: folded blouses on the right, jewelry boxes and old lithographs on the left. I was looking for proof of an affair, I told myself, not evidence that she'd gone mad. Everything was stacked and labeled meticulously so that I knew exactly when the black and crimson lithograph of our house had been developed. (Quintillis 9, 1144)

Same all the way down: the drawers were arranged exactly as they should be. Nothing out of place, and she'd been so Goddamn organized, so precise. The closet was no different. On the left: my outfits, wrinkled and draped on wooden poles, and there were hers on the right: organized by color, assembled so that a trained chimp could dress sharply in less than a minute.

I rummaged for a few minutes, then propped against the wall. No secret letters or mysterious stains. And now my forearms and fingers stank of her: flowers and oil smell of her summer perfume. I made the mistake of rubbing my face, and the odors shot anxiety through my nervous system, as if I were a trained bear. Mindless impulses told me I smelled Elena, that she was just in the next room, or taking a bath. Rationally, she wasn't. She was ash.

I took a few deep breaths; that only made it worse.

The candle by my bed went out. My comm buzzed, and I squeezed it out of my ear, put it on the table.

The kitchen floor creaked.

Elena . . .

I opened my mouth, shut it, and stood. House completely silent and filled with gray darkness: my eyes fought to adjust. Wait. Houses creak at night: materials adjust to changes in temperature, contracting as they cool, when it gets chilly. Shouldn't be chilly out, should it? I heard someone breathing.

Gone—holding her breath in the kitchen. Still that Goddamn perfume, so my gut twirled and said, 'Elena, it's Elena!' Except it couldn't be. Breathing, or was it me?

I crept to the doorway—kitchen on my left, so I pivoted through the doorway, feet sliding silently on the carpet. Empty darkness. No one—the front door was open. Giannis. Had to be, he had a key.

"Giannis?" I waited. "You there?"

Maybe he came and left. Forgot something or wanted a free beer or—I stepped in a cold puddle. Floor slick with water, and I dropped to one knee—not just one pool. Someone tracked water in from the door. All the way across the kitchen and back—I turned—to the living room, but no . . . the tracks went into my bedroom. I'd just been there. While you were looking in the closet. Someone came in, blew out the candle.

I shivered, rose, and balled my hands into trembling fists. Too late to hide: I'd already called out Giannis's name. One step, two, and another would put me back in the doorway—I slid inside. Wet stench of dead fish. When I was ten, we'd gone to Cape Entan and—forms piled on the floor and walls. Cold slush around my ankles, and I caught the doorway with one hand. People—no, *bodies*. Swollen and discolored, crawling with white rice, and something scuttled out of a woman's mouth. I heard low singing from the next room, some kind of instruments in the background. Someone turned on music somehow. Too dark to really see the bodies—two of them. Two: a woman and a—gods—child, and someone moved behind me.

I spun and slipped in the slime, splashed backwards, into one of the squishy bodies. Skin cold and rubbery, and a wheel clicked and turned on my living room wall. No one there. The music was getting louder, very proud, but something was off about it. Another language, but somehow I understood: *". . . Your warriors' valor, your pioneers' virtue, Alighieri's vision, today shines in every heart!"*

I watched the concentric circles spin on the wall in opposite directions, insects nibbling at my ankle. If I turned my head, I would see something new *behind* the world, like a puzzle-image made of nonsense shapes.

"Youth, youth, spring of beauty!" the song continued, louder. I heard footsteps on pavement, marching. Turn your head, a part of me said, look and see. *"In the hardship of life, your song rings and goes!"*

"Nikos!"

A woman rushed into the living room.

"Elena . . ." No, it was Anna. "What's happening?"

She was terrified, looking back. "Nikos!" she shouted again. She didn't see me. "Please!"

"Anna!"

The song: *"And for Benito Mussolini! And for our beautiful Fatherland!"*

The ground shook, the ceiling fell, and I jolted awake. Elena's file spread across my lap. The candle flickered and continued to burn on my right. I counted the sequential rings in the remaining wax: three hours had passed. I hadn't gotten up, hadn't looked through the—no, my hands didn't smell. No perfume. My comm still in one ear. My heartbeat gradually slowed, and I organized Elena's file, deliberately put it aside. Just a nonsense dream.

I searched the dresser and found a note at the back, behind a false wall. She hadn't really hid it—she'd known I'd never look through her things.

Elena:
We didn't fully understand what they plan to do. I
discovered last night. Bombs, Elena—this isn't going to be
ushered in with prayer or meditation, but with slaughter.
That isn't what the Gods want, I can't believe that. If
nothing else, think of Nikos. Don't go on the flight. I need
your help now. We have a few days, that's all—we can stop
them. Both of you must help me. The Gods will return
either way, you have to believe that. Millions of innocent
people. Please. You don't have to be one of them.
—Dett

She wasn't just crazy anymore. Something else . . .

My comm rang.

"Hello?"

"Barcuc, there you are . . ."

Anna.

"What's wrong?" I asked.

"I just woke up. Had a dream that you were dead—I wanted to make
sure . . ."

"I'm here."

"You're all right? Did I wake you?"

I told myself this was a coincidence, and the candle danced. No wind in
the bedroom.

"Am I awake right now?" I asked.

"What? Don't try to scare me. I called you because I need you to tell me
that everything's all right."

She had the same panic in her voice I'd heard after the Black Room.

"Everything's fine," I said.

"They're recalling us—me, I mean."

"What?"

"I got a call," she said. "I have 24 hours to report . . ."

To report: everyone on Shan—man, woman, child, cripple—was trained
and kept in the Ckish's roll sheet for a potential military draft. A real war

hadn't happened in three generations, but the last time one of the minor tribes had revolted, every Shan had been recalled from New Amith.

Bad timing. Nevermind that in the week it would take Anna's shuttle to hop back to Shan the uprising would almost certainly have been squished.

"There's a war?" I said.

"I don't know."

She sounded distracted, as if she were watching a monitor as she spoke. Maybe she was.

"You're an archaeologist, not a . . ."

"Yes, I am." Tension in her voice. "I'm Shan."

"Yeah."

"I must sound crazy right now. It's all the stress, I know. I've been working—I'm still at the site—and I get a call . . ."

Why was she telling me this? "I'm sorry."

"Just—I don't know. That dream was very real."

"What are you going to do?"

"What do you mean?"

"Well," I said, "you have 24 hours. What happens if you don't go?"

"I have to go," she said. "I almost wish I hadn't found it now. What's the point? I know it's just because it's late, and I'm on edge, but I already feel drained. I wish it hadn't rained so much."

I started to say that it was all right, get some rest, then stopped. "What do you mean?"

"I wish we hadn't found this in the first place."

"You found it because of the rain . . ?"

"It flooded two months ago. Remember the week when it didn't stop raining out in the vineyards? That's when the property went up for sale."

She knew about it too: Wesler'll and the bureaucrat. "Why then?"

"I don't know, but when they were touring the grounds, an aide and his wife found the washed-out tunnel. The flood cleared it. What's the matter?"

My research at Yellow Lake. No sense in putting it off, you have to tell her. So I did. The dream of drowned bodies and Anna running. The wheeled calendar on my living room wall; I left out Elena. When I'd finished, she was quiet for a long time.

"Nikos . . ?"

"Yeah."

"Were you going to tell me?"

"What—I just did."

Another pause. "We have to . . . Barcuc, you're telling the truth?"

"Yeah."

"If you're playing with me, I swear to the gods . . ."

"I'm not."

". . . what do we do?"

"Come over."

A pause, then she said, "You're sure that's a good idea?"

"No, but what else are you going to do? Pack?"

"Okay. I'll be there in a minute."

She clicked off.

CHAPTER SIX

The Beginning of Another

No question, it was going to be a long night. I waited for a long time, just staring at the wall, feeling like I should get up—make some coffee or something. Eventually, I went to pee, and as the incinerator vaporized the urine, I splashed some water on my cheeks. Awake, at least. I thought about Elena and re-read Dett's note.

What's in the cabinet: spray perfumes, comb, two of Elena's favorite earrings—the hand carved, wooden diamonds—and a plastic rectangle full of her razor blades. I stared at them for a long moment, not thinking about anything—except, two days before the flight . . . what did she say?

Oh, what? You'd love to see that, wouldn't you? A way out, so you can mope and move on. And everyone will feel so sorry for you.

Shut up.

Like me to draw a hot bath—you know why they do that? It loosens the blood vessels, stops the wounds from clotting. I wouldn't give you that, you prick. You want out, you do it.

She threatened me with them, more than once, then turned the situation inside-out: her depression was my fault. And then my inadequacies kept us from—no need to go over it again. I wanted alcohol but was already too dehydrated. Drank two full glasses of bottled water, thought about the decorations, the frog-statues over the oven: a jade protector dijin. Thought about the crazy note—never had a child . . . forget her death or something. How could you forget the death of someone who didn't exist? A few minutes later, Anna knocked, and I offered her water as she came in.

"Thank you."

We sat in the living room: she had a bleary-eyed, 'why-haven't-I-slept' look. As if she couldn't decide whether to be a professional insomniac or fall asleep.

"I don't know what I'm doing here," she said at last.

"What was your dream?"

"What?"

"Your dream—I told you mine. What was yours?"

"You were dead."

I forced a smile; this should have been ridiculous. In the sunlight it would be—but not now. Not unusual for basic reality-rules to alter at midnight, or whatever time it was. My smile faded. Those bodies might still be in my bedroom, I might really be dead: how long until day-break?

I asked how she'd seen me die, not because I wanted to—because it was too quiet.

"I came here, walked in and found you in the shower." She shrugged it away, took another drink. "You're okay?"

"Yeah. Don't I look . . . probably not, right?"

"You researched the villa?" I told her I had, and she continued, "We didn't know what to expect. Thermals showed a match to sites on Shan—it was the same."

"Except for the skeleton."

"Yes."

"I want to know . . . something was—something bothered you down there, didn't it?"

She hesitated. "What makes you think . . ."

"I was there. What was it?"

"I don't know."

"Come on, we both . . ."

"It was too normal." I started to ask what the real reason was—but she was serious. Anna said, "It was *exactly* what I expected."

"Except for the body."

"Yes—that was more." She paused. "It feels good to talk about this. You won't write about this if I . . ."

"No. I was assigned to this to waste my time."

"I know. Your wife was the one in the last rocket. I follow the news. It shouldn't have been that normal."

"Isn't that good?" I asked. "It's what you guys wanted . . ? A Bialu, an old skeleton?"

"Yes."

"And Pnetians—you think the old gods, Bialu—may have been our ancestors, settling on both planets. How'd they do that? They had spaceships or something, right?"

"Presumably."

"Then they were at least as advanced, probably more, than we are. We know almost nothing about them, except a dozen different legends, which may or may not even . . ."

"We know about them," she said. "They're the old world gods of your scriptures and the origin of Shan warrior deities . . ."

"They weren't gods," I said, "we've got one of their skeletons."

She sat up again. "So? What does that prove?"

"You're serious?"

"Why couldn't gods die? Of course they do. They live, just like we do, and sometimes they move around physically—just because they're above us, controlling the physics and elements of the worlds, doesn't mean they're invulnerable."

I'd heard this argument before, and had given up having an opinion, years ago. Basic triumvirate of existence: Ae (Creation), Bjell (Conflict), and Cia (Destruction). Both Creation and Destruction inevitably lead to Conflict, which must lead to the opposite, in a lopsided, eternal triangle. Thanks to Conflict, the universe and everyone living in it had formed, including the Bialu; old gods who had guided humanity to agriculture, birth control, and so on in the first age. Then, for reasons I'd never understood, the Bialu created a pair of gods—Meyy and Hebet—to watch over Amith.

Naturally, Meyy and Hebet hadn't wasted any time, spawning more than fifty god-children who had produced hundreds of inbred lesser gods and so on for another generation. All of whom—along with any consuls, senators or businessmen deified by Senatorial decree—still tended us today. Waiting for the end of the Fifth Age, when that arrangement was scheduled to change somehow.

In the first age of Amith, a society of wisemen and prophets had been in direct communication with the Bialu. Their priesthood led to the second age of prophet-kings, who directed all society toward a perfect realization of the gods' plans on Amith. This was after the Bialu left.

I'd attended the Academy, after all.

The specifics had faded from my memory, but in that second age, most scriptures were recorded, under the guidance of 2,500 years of emperors with unnecessarily frilly names like Gi'mae's'will, Ruler Of All That Is Good In This Land Of Abundance, As Has Been Bestowed By His Most Holy Lords Of The Air And So On And So Forth.

Gi'mae, Lord Of Men And Beasts, Director Of Copulation and all his heirs and their heirs had also claimed to be in contact with gods. They created vast, often contradictory cosmologies—all corrected in our *modern* Fifth Age, of course—to explain the universe and ensure the perpetuity of their reigns. I'd grown sarcastic and disillusioned during my later years at the Academy and had begun to interpret every reference to a Bialu or a lesser deity as a political tool. Nevermind that a good chunk of the population still burned candles and sacrificed at their neighborhood temples.

The universal cosmologies established by the Golden Age Prophets split and changed when the Worldwide Prophetic Empire broke into the Gumay Kingdoms. The third age saw scores of competing nations claiming direct relationships with the gods—often to the point of absurdity. Universal scriptures were challenged and rewritten and burned, as needed by whomever happened to rule his chunk of the world. Which meant that— nevermind the thousands of years of changes still to come with the Merr Dynasties and the Republic of New Amith—the Golden Age scriptures had undoubtedly been altered since they were supposedly handed down from the gods.

Enter the Bialu skeleton we'd found and an intelligent, hyper-religious Shan archaeologist like Anna. The situation was too complicated, too contradictory for me. Which was another reason I'd long-since become completely ambivalent. Were there gods? Maybe, probably not, but if they kept the rules of physics and cellular evolution going, what difference did that make to me? Again, I was not an atheist. I just didn't care—except I had to now. No choice.

"There's no reason the gods couldn't also be physically alive—and if they were, die," Anna was saying. "You think the skeleton proves the Bialu weren't gods?"

"I don't know that it proves anything, except that we don't know who the Bialu were, who we are, or if the skeleton is even a Bialu at all."

"It is."

"How can you be so . . ."

"It's a common ancestor," she said. "The first tests already show that. It explains why we have similar creation and foundation mythologies, it explains the identical ruins on both planets. The skeleton explains more . . ."

"Except our dreams," I murmured.

She paled, as if she'd just remembered why she was here. "What do you think's happening?"

1. We're nuts.
2. The Bialu *were* gods, that was a door to Hell.
3. Damned if I know—what about Elena?
4. None of the above.

I said, "The skeleton's real."

"I know, we just . . ."

I grinned. "Doesn't mean it was a god." And before she could object, "Maybe it was, maybe not. Either way, that room was something we weren't supposed to find—I think it was meant for them. It's been sitting there for a few thousand years—it's like putting a dog in a flight simulator. The Naake's designed to teach Elena how to handle the stress of take-off, not meant for a Labrador to just wander in."

She frowned. "Designed for Elena?"

"What?"

"That was your wife, wasn't it? You said a flight simulator is designed to teach Elena to go into orbit."

"No, I didn't, I said cosmonauts—they're built to train cosmonauts."

"I know that, but you said . . ."

"No, I didn't."

"Okay." She held my hand. "It's late."

"Yeah, and I'm still not tired."

"I'm exhausted," she said.

"What are we going to do about this?"

"What do you mean?"

Just a bad dream, I thought, but I said, "The room and the dreams: what if they don't stop?"

"I don't know." She paused, wiped her eyes to keep them open. "It's just a room. What makes you think it's anything else?"

"It opened, it closed. Rooms don't just do that. Did you hear a song?"

"A song? I don't know," she said. "I did hear something behind everything, people talking in another language, but I understood it. It was almost as if they were behind the walls or something. Except I knew they weren't. That sounds insane, doesn't it?"

It did, except that was my song too. "Does the name Alighieri or Benito Mussolini mean anything? Do you recognize those?"

She didn't, and I asked, "Why the calendar?"

"What?"

"Both times—in the room, and in my dream, I saw a circular calendar. You know, the old-fashioned, wheel kind?"

She nodded. "I saw that too."

"The calendar's important."

Anna grinned. "You sound tired."

But I wasn't. "It was our calendar, you saw that?"

"Yes. Shan calendars aren't circular, and they go up, not down." She pressed a hand to my chest, to feel my heartbeat: it was going too fast. "Are you all right?"

I ignored the question, fought off the blood-rush her touch brought. A great black dread formed in my mind. Right behind the room. I began to see a black doorway when I closed my eyes: I'd already gotten used to it, noticed it now—and it was still there when I blinked. Lay back, close your eyes. The doorway was there.

"Are you all right?" she asked again.

I was back in my living room. Too quiet, dark outside; just flickering candles on either side of us. "Yeah."

"You want to go to sleep?"

Gods, she was right, I was tired. My arms and legs were too heavy to move. That irrational dread—I felt like a horse two hours before a cyclone-cloud. Can smell the mistake in the air, the electrical, gods-what-is-that-heading-for-me scent. I'd heard about it—never been in a wind-storm myself—but I'd heard stories of animals breaking loose, trampling one another to death on the eve of a weather-catastrophe. Consumed by fear: too much, but I wasn't there yet.

With Anna, I could almost pretend the dream hadn't happened. Just take the doorway for granted: of course it's waiting in my skull, sitting behind my eyelids. Something bad. Disaster.

"It's okay," she said.

No it isn't, I thought, and I nodded, tried to push out the—what? Irrational adrenaline.

I asked, "Do you know about the calendar?"

"What do you mean?"

"The New Amith calendar—it's counting down to the Sixth Age, right? The end of the Republic of New Amith."

"Yes."

"What's it based on?"

"A few sources, but I think it's taken from Hostos's books, part of the end chapters in the Scripture of Ten Sons."

"The one about the civil wars . . ."

"Yes."

I remembered Hostos. He was one of the last prophet kings, writing during the fall of the Golden Age Empire. The civil wars that had started as a family quarrel between the Emperor's ten sons had slowly grown and burnt the Second Age to the ground. Two generations later, the Gumay Kingdoms—fluctuating anywhere from ten to over 1,000 independent nations for the next 600 years—had begun. There was a brief period in there, when everything had almost been united under the Summer Queen before she disappeared, if I remembered correctly, but mostly it had just been fighting. Lots and lots of fighting.

Hostos had been one of the ten heirs to the Prophetic Empire, convinced the world belonged to him: I remember sympathizing with his situation. Throughout his narratives, Hostos had been the victim of unending intrigues, one of which had decapitated him less than a year after he finished his works. Bits of him had supposedly been buried—minus his vanished head—below the deepest catacombs of Hostos Temple. The same Temple where Elena's rites had been conducted. The current building was temple number five, if I remembered correctly. His original tomb was long lost.

"He lived nearby," I said.

"Who?" Anna said. "Hostos?"

"Yeah. He was buried a few kilometers from here."

"His calendar—you can't think that has anything to do with this?" When she saw my expression, Anna continued, "Nobody knows where he lived. We only know where he was supposedly buried. Most of the records from that time were lost a hundred years later."

I went for the bedroom: Elena had a copy of the Scriptures. The gods only knew where my Academy books were. I think I'd sold them to pay for a party. Yes, there it was, on her side of the bed, buried in a box, under a mound of wrinkled clothing.

"Here." I returned to the living room, tossed the book between us.

Anna flipped to the end. "It's late."

I sat beside her, and she found the annotated beginning of the Books of Saint Hostos. Midway through the introduction was a paragraph titled 'Calendar Origins' over a stiff drawing of a simple, circular calendar. Anna paged past it, to the center of Hostos's narrative, stopping at a section someone had titled 'The Six Ages'. Anna handed it to me, and I read:

> I see the end of our Godly Age, full of reason and universal
> well-being and the beginning of a darker time. The gods
> gave us the power to write our own destiny, lost now. Torn
> and plundered by Salee'bl and the whore he calls mother,
> ruined by weak-spined advisors, too afraid for their own

lives and estates to stop the slaughter. At Mon'touth, they hung eight thousand children and nailed mothers to their birth trees after forcing unspeakable acts upon them.

This next age, our third in this world, will last until the world has recovered its strength. In Amith, a Tartar will give birth to the Summer Queen to unite the world. The third age will last more than thirty generations of men, as told in the writings of Sury.

A note here told me that 'Sury' was a physician contemporary with Hostos, who was referenced in several other books. Too bad for Sury, though, none of his own works had survived.

When the third age ends, an imperfect time of hereditary strength will dominate much of this world—nothing in the face of my father's dominion or the poor lands usurped by a mob of illegitimate worms. If I could crush them under the banner of my family's name and heel, I would. But their strength grows, and while I am still most powerful— what is power in a world of traitors? What use is it?

Hostos spent another four paragraphs meditating on the nature of strength, nations, and finally concluded that the first family—father, mother, children—was the basis for all rule of law. I'd heard it before. Many times. Hostos wasn't the first, and I doubted he even thought he was; chances were, he hoped his readers might think he'd come up with it. They probably had.

I flipped a few pages, then stopped. The purpose of monarchy, the falsehoods of Batrian divinization, the state of anarchy in a plurality of monarchies and . . .

I said, "Huh."

Anna shifted on the couch—her eyes were half-closed. She'd been drifting off. "What?"

"Do you remember this?"

"What?" I showed her the page, and she said, "My eyes are a little blurry, which part are you . . ."

"'On a plurality of monarchies . . .'"

"Yes, I know, he talks about how it doesn't make sense to have more than . . ."

"'On a plurality of worlds'."

"Hmm?" She concentrated on the book. "Oh, I remember that. It's all about . . ."

"No," I said. "Look how he starts it. He's just been ranting about man's failure and all that, then he comes back and says, *'So that after I returned from the well, I understood what I had seen'.*"

"And what does it say there?" Anna indicated a side note and read, "*'The well, here, is Hostos's personal doubt. He has been on a search for meaning in the chaos around him, and has returned from a mental 'sckek', meaning 'well' or 'cave''.*"

Before she could continue, I went back to the text.

> I understood what I had seen. A perversion of the gods' world, split like a woodblock into an infinite array of chips, some landing close to one another, others flying very distant. This will tempt us now and in the future. Our world is only one of many, and we claim—like arrogant princes—to be the only true realm.

He was drifting again, getting wound up about his personal problems— enjoying the scrape of his pen, rather than telling me what I wanted to hear.

Hostos continued:

> The falsifiers of gold and time no doubt exist in the otherlands, but their suits may be striped like a Bae. They could be . . .

"Wait," Anna said.

I paused, "You . . ."

"Go back to the falsifier part. What was that . . ?"

> The falsifiers of gold and time no doubt exist in the
> otherlands . . .

"Let me see that." She checked the side notes. "Here. In the original, untranslated text, the word is 'teut'."

"Ah."

"Do you know old Menst?"

"Yeah, but it's been awhile since I . . ."

"'Teut' means a lot of different things: time, lifespan . . ."

"'Calendar', right? That's what you were going to say?"

She gave me back the book. "Yes."

"Do you want me to . . ."

"Yes."

I started reading again:

> . . . may well be striped like a Bae. They could be even more
> numerous, unending like a plague of vermin.

I paused, said, "He goes on for awhile about how horrible human nature is . . ."

"Does he mention a well again?"

"You mean a *metaphorical* hole?"

"Does he?"

I checked. "I don't think so."

"Then it's probably . . ."

"Here." I showed her the book, read along with it:

> A hole so deep and changing that it mimicked the folds of
> my brain-tissue when I slept. In that place, I understood
> the course of the Ages: the six ages, the last of which would
> be the end of everything and the beginning of another.

That didn't make sense, so I read it again: no, the words hadn't changed, and I wished I remembered languages, had a copy of the original text. They kept it in a vault at the Purple Archives in the third annex of the Capitol.

"Why would he write that?" I asked.

Anna shook her head, and she slumped back on the couch, eyes closed. "I'm too tired, it's too late for this. Gods, if I'd known you planned to peck through the scriptures, I wouldn't have come over."

I ignored her groans. "You want me to scribble you a summary? Look at this—can that be right? *'End of everything and the beginning of another'*?"

"Nikos . . ."

I read further:

> I traced the ages in that place—the bright candle-glow
> passed through my body, as if it had been made liquid.

Anna stiffened, and I thought, I understand—I almost understand, almost get this. Hostos continued:

> And when it had finished, I counted the candle-marks on
> the wall and numbered the visions I had seen in
> otherworld, and it totaled to roughly 245 generations of our
> short-lived.

A long side note told me that until the standardization of the Merr Dynasty, the time span of generations and generational cycles had been extremely subjective. The specifics: Hostos was writing in the Second Age, about 6,500 years after the beginning of history. He had predicted a Third Age—the Gumay Kingdoms—just two generations after his text: 30 years. And—what do you know?—30 years later, the Empire of the Golden Age Prophet-Kings split. Almost 30 years on the dot.

Hostos had been terrifyingly accurate. Or, as the side note told me, perhaps not so terrifying after all. How impressive was it if, for instance, councils in the Merr Dynasty—Fourth Age—had systematically altered Hostos's texts to match history?

Or, I thought, if those same councils had gone further and left Hostos alone, but had forged numerous other documents, had changed history, to match his words—wasn't that worse? The Merr had used Hostos as a Saint of the People, a 'look-how-much-better-things-are-now' text. Hostos was the perfect Merr Patriot. His scripture was bound to an argument in favor of an all-powerful nation, ruled by wise and beneficent monarchs. A return to the Golden Age Prophets, when we could 'write our own destiny' as Hostos said. Perfect excuse to slaughter opposition and censor dissent, as the Merr had, and then to claim direct descendence from Bar'schal, one of the most famous Prophet-Kings, who was himself, of course, in personal communion with the gods. Hostos was the obvious scriptural basis for a Second Age Defense of the Merr—there were others—but none like Hostos. Unless he was a fake.

Anna: "Had enough?"

I looked up. "Hmm?"

"Ready to sleep? Should I . . ."

"245 generations is . . ."

"3,670 years," Anna said. She knew it by heart. "Fifteen years each."

Hostos: 6,470 years after history began. Difficult not to think of it rightside-up—as counting down to the Sixth Age and the end of the Republic. We were in the year 1140 L.M., or around 9,000 years after the beginning of the First Age. The math worked out: 6,470 + 3,670 = 10,140. We were 1,140 years from the Sixth Age.

I went back to the text, read the last line again:

> . . . and it totaled to roughly 245 generations of our short-lived.

That's when the *'end of everything and beginning of another'* was scheduled. The chapter continued with Hostos's vague—and accurate—predictions for the previous five ages, all based on generations of 15 years.

Anna's breathing had changed: deeper, more regular. She was sleeping. My forehead ached—tired. But, I flipped to the next page. If I put this off it would feel silly in the morning, and I might never look back. Something to do in the morning . . . Giannis. He planned a trip to the coast, hadn't spent any real time there in a long time, since before the Academy.

Hostos:

> And I have shown why the Ages must continue, all of them stretched but the last.

The chapter continued for another page before a new break—'On Patronage'—returned the scripture to political bitching. There weren't any notes about that sentence: just Hostos explaining, in archaic translation, that the ages were all 'stretched'—except for the last one. So the Sixth Age won't be 'stretched', I thought. Good to know.

And it was too late, because I couldn't look away from those words: that sentence was separate from the surrounding paragraphs; someone—Hostos or his translator—had wanted to emphasize it. To make a point, or maybe the rest of the paragraph had been lost, or it was a formatting mistake, or it was too late for me to read the scriptures.

I paged backwards: no single-sentence paragraphs anywhere. Forward: nope. I tossed the book aside and put a hand to my head. Just one sentence separate from the rest. Blink: that room was still there. More chapters: On Justice, On Pre-Science, On Slavery . . .

"We have to go back to the archives."

Anna woke up. "What? Which archives?"

"Yellow Lake."

"I have to report tomorrow . . ."

"Now," I said. "We have to go now."

Why? If I didn't fall asleep, I wouldn't dream of dead people and wheels on the walls.

"You already looked at the records."

"The Weslers had money—they had servants too, didn't they?"

"I don't know."

"What happened to them after Wesler'll died? There has to be a record."

"We know what happened," Anna said. "They drowned."

I gave her a 'really?' look, and she said, "Okay, they didn't *just* drown."

"They knew about the Black Room. We have to find their servants."

"It's the middle of the night."

"And you have to report in the morning. We have to do this now—the gods only know how long you'll be gone. Please."

She started to object, then stretched. "If it's open . . ."

* * *

It wasn't. We took a tram to the Yellow Lake archives: predictably locked and dark, but—before Anna could argue—I found an open window and scrambled inside. Lights came on, but no alarm. I let her in.

"I can't believe you did that," she said.

"What are they going to do, deport you?"

"Nikos . . ."

"We won't be long."

I lit up one of the terminals, started searching for anything related to the names 'Alighieri' or 'Benito Mussolini'. Nothing, so I went for more Wesler records. Where would they keep a servant log—not on the networks. There would be private documents, buried in receipts and catalogs of gray pay slips. Did Yellow Lake even have a Nail Market? Probably not, so I searched—no, the closest Nail was in the Brevda District, further in-town: Brevda, unlike Yellow Lake, was an ancient smattering of farms and coal mines that had groaned when the Capitol grew around her. Yellow Lake was rich villas near a lake that wasn't yellow.

Anna looked on over my shoulder. "You think they were hired in Brevda?"

"Probably."

Logs: the Brevda Nail had a record of transactions. I went back—when did Wesler turn off?—then checked the Nail log. Ah, and there it was. I tapped the screen, and Anna made a surprised, impressed sound, as if I were a trained dog and had just rolled over.

> One(23) male servant(6), one(50) female servant, Wesler Household, 21687, (M) servant at 93 to M. Secr'l, 31922, (F) servant to Lagone Community, 32962.

You didn't have to own workers to decipher that scratch: the Weslers had two servants—a 23-year-old kid and a 50-year-old woman—who left after the Wesler deaths. The kid contracted out to someone else, and the woman returned to the 'Lagone Community'. Maybe her family?

I looked up Secr'l's identification number, found a comm ID and called.

"Nikos, it's the middle of the . . ."

". . . yes?" Someone—a groggy M. Secr'l?—answered.

"Yes, I'm calling about the Wesler servant—the one you hired . . ."

"I'm not discussing that anymore," he said. "The court documents, the rites—you're going to have to contact Fles if you want more."

Rites? "His original sponsor . . ."

"It's all with old Brevda—you'll have to go to them, okay? You're going to hear the same thing from Fles: the debt's settled, *more* than generously. And *nine times* they said a drawstring wasn't pulled. Okay?"

A drawstring. "Then the rites have already . . ."

"Yes, of course. He was broken—it was a gamble when I hired him, but that's what happens sometimes." A pause as he woke up. "Who is this? You're not . . ."

I clicked off, dialed a scrambler, then stared at the console monitor again.

Anna said, "What?"

"The first servant's dead, and whatever killed him had a drawstring."

A noose.

"That's suicide," she said.

"Yeah."

And M. Secr'l had known something was wrong, but he hired the kid anyway.

Which left the woman. She returned to the 'Lagone Community'. I looked up Lagone, found another comm number and called. This time Anna didn't try to stop me.

"Hello?"

"Yes hi, I'm calling about a servant who returned on the . . . 17th of Junis from the Wesler Estate, I think . . ."

"Who's calling?"

Quick: who are you? "My name's Nikos Healy'll, I'm calling from the Archaeological board . . ."

"Hold on."

Anna said, "That's an original alias."

"We don't have any reason to . . ."

She clicked back on. "Mr. Healy'll? Okay, what are you calling in reference to?"

"The woman from the . . ."

"Yes, Mr. Healy'll. What is this about?" i.e. why the hell do I care? And why call in the middle of the night?

"As you may have heard . . ." I gave her a ten second version of the two-hour Anna-conference earlier that evening, then explained that for important and confidential reasons, I needed to speak with the woman.

When I finished, she said, "You want to know if she went in the room?"

"Yeah."

"She went into the room." Not a question that time, and I realized I was holding my breath.

"She went in," I repeated.

"Yes."

"Where can I . . ."

"You can't." She's dead, I thought. Another one. "She doesn't . . . she has difficulty with new people."

Which means—what? "I'd like to try."

"You're not a member of the Wesler family?"

"Not directly, no."

"You're a sibling—someone related to Mrs. Wesler'll?" A rustling before I could answer, then she said, "When did you want to see her?"

"As soon as . . ."

"Can you come now?"

Now? "Yeah."

"Okay . . ." And she gave directions: north, north, west, north. Through the Ghte Forest, into the lowlands . . . "Mr. Healy'll, are you with me?"

"Yeah."

"Where are you now—the estate?"

Close enough. "Yeah."

"It shouldn't take you more than six hours by tram."

"Okay, thank you."

"Just so you understand—don't expect anything."

"I understand." I gave her my comm number, asked for her name.

"Oh don't worry, you won't see me."

"No? Why not?"

"By sunrise the Prophet will be awake."

The comm went dead. I stared at the console for a moment, then said, "I think we have to go tonight."

"Where—to see the Wesler servant?"

"Yeah." I got up. "We can get a long-distance tram at the Brevda terminal."

"How far is it?"

"Less than a kilometer, it shouldn't . . ."

"Not the terminal. How far is the . . ." She checked the screen. "*Lagone Community?*"

"Six hours."

"It's almost 1:00 now. I have to report at noon."

"You said you had 24 hours . . ."

". . . until my flight *leaves*. I have to be there five hours in advance."

I went to the door. "We should have just enough time."

"If we go, then come straight back, I'll still be late." She shook her head. "I can't go."

I was running on adrenaline: six hours in a tram would fix that. "How long will you be gone?"

"I don't know."

"A month?"

"Nikos . . ."

"Who's going to take over the site when you're gone?"

"They haven't decided yet. Your Senate will appoint someone."

"The servant went in the room."

"What?"

"The woman on the comm—she knew before I even asked. This servant knows, she can tell us what happened."

"We know what happened."

"Stop it. We don't."

Anna shook her head: she wanted to tag along. "Go without me."

"No, you know more about it than I do. You'll ask questions I won't. Come on." I opened the door.

"Can we make it five hours each way?"

I smiled and thought, No. "Absolutely."

She followed me outside. "If I don't report . . ."

"You'll be back in time."

We took the tram to the nearest Brevda terminal. Chilly, wet air, and the cobbled streets were full of terraced stone apartments and dark gas lamps. The only lights: a pair of dim flames at the tram terminal. I hired a tram at one of the automated kiosks in the terminal waiting room, then went back outside to wait with Anna. A six-wheeled tram with an extra-large hydro-balloon rolled up, took my fingerprint on a blue door pad, then started north.

"I've never been to one of these before," she said.

"Yeah, me neither."

The Prophet will be awake.

She squeezed my arm. "Are you okay?"

"Sure, why?"

By sunrise.

"Okay," she said. "Wake me when we're there."

Anna curled awkwardly against the opposite window and fell asleep. Never been there—where?

To a Pnetian commune.

CHAPTER SEVEN

The Lagone Community

After an hour of checkpoints, we switched from the Ryock—a loop of 8 concrete lanes that coiled around the Eastern suburbs like a fist—to the ancient T'en'n, the Bread Road. Still dark, not much traffic, and the patches of renovated farmland, kilometer-wide villas, and provincial hamlets turned to prairie. The flurry of signs, lampposts and parked trams darkened, as if we were going out to sea, away from shore. I'd never been on a real ship.

Thousands of years ago, the black flatness out my tram window had been part of the Ghte Forest. I'd read stories about the man-eating cats and venomous birds that had harassed the villages and hunted even in the Merr courtyards. Of course, the Merr had needed metal, which meant they needed fire, which meant wood—and why metal? For weapons: so they'd leveled hundreds of kilometers of Ghte to make guns to slaughter anything that survived the de-forestation. Naturally, they'd found other uses for the guns as well.

But it hadn't entirely worked. Hills popped up in the plain. My eyes couldn't focus in the dark—I'd been up to the Ghte more than once, so this was nothing new—but I still imagined that I could see the regular lines and too-straight-to-be-a-hill angles. The prairie was scattered with mildewed blocks of stone and half-buried arches: some well-documented, some obscure. Most were Merr, but not all of them. Some were older, and some much older.

The grassland bumped and grew bunches of trees, as if someone had dropped a handful of acorns every 30 meters. The handfuls clumped together, turning grassland to thorn bushes, and we entered Ghte Forest. I'd never been impressed by forests. Yeah, nice old trees, and Ghte was known as one of the oldest, least explored—despite how close everyone lived: the only way to explore Ghte was to cut it down. Not practical anymore. Cheaper to fly timber from the Vaan territories in the south than to hire the minor city of workers to chop up lion territory.

Might be exciting if a man-lion attacked or a cobra-bird grabbed the roof-balloon, but I wasn't counting on it. So I drifted in and out of consciousness, until—hours later—we descended. The Forest peeled away, became grass, then crusted to dirt.

Anna was still asleep.

I rubbed my face, stared at the bleary salt-basin. Gnarls of pumpkin-cacti looked like ink-spots on white crust.

The clock on the tram read 6:04. Five hours in this tram. My legs ached, I was getting hungry, and I had to piss. Best not to think about it. Never been past Ghte: I hadn't known it turned this barren, this quickly. Tree, tree, bush, tree, dirt. And more dirt. I'd heard about the salt-flat, but had never seen the lowlands. Little to no rainfall, scraps of plants, a few vultures, the occasional beetle and a network of Pnetian communes. Outside, the air faded dark blue, then gray, and I squinted in the early-morning glare of desert-sunlight.

After 50 kilometers, Ghte was a blob of green at the lip of the lowland crater behind us. I cranked down my window, smelled dry, sweet air—as if someone had sprayed berry perfume—and craned around to look: the road was half-buried in dust and pebbles and it led to a pile of tin barrels. The sun came up, and the barrels became a trio of 30-meter-high generators that towered over a nest of single-story buildings—all connected.

Anna stretched. "Are we there?"

The entire complex was surrounded by a moat, razor-wire fencing, and guard towers.

"It looks like a prison," Anna said.

"Yeah."

This wasn't what we'd expected.

Our tram stopped at the moat. A peeling speaker-box on my right crackled, said, "—ello. How can we help you today?"

It was a man's voice.

"Hi. My name's Nikos Healy'll, from the archaeological board—they told you I was coming, right?"

"No. How can we help you today, Mr. Healy'll?"

"I need to see a 50-year-old female servant who returned here on the 17th of Junis."

"What does this concern?"

"She's been connected to a recent archaeological discovery in the capital, at her previous employer's residence. I understand she may be able to help us understand some of the things we've found."

"Thank you for your interest, Mr. Healy'll." No pause—he didn't need time to think about what I'd said. "But unfortunately, the individual you're referring to has been given class C status, meaning she cannot receive visitors. If you would like to leave a reference number, we can be sure to contact you or your superior should her status change."

Anna murmured, "She's quarantined . . ?"

"Is there anything else we can help you with today, Mr. Healy'll?"

"Yeah, I'd like to learn more about you."

Anna gave me a look, and I shrugged: *we have to get inside.*

"Certainly, please state your reference ID number."

Shit. I fumbled in my pockets. "I'm from the Wesler Estate."

"We understand. Please state your reference ID number so that we can speed our authorization process along."

I found the scrap I'd used for notes at the archives. Ah: Wesler Household, 21687. I gave him the number. Again, no hesitation, and he said, "Thank you, Mr. Healy'll. We'll be with you shortly."

They couldn't have random nuts wandering in, now could they?

When the intercom clicked, Anna said, "You want to be converted?"

"We can talk our way . . ."

"I don't feel comfortable with this."

"They don't have cults on Shan?"

"Not like this, not . . . *automated.*"

The bridge dropped, linking us to the perimeter gate.

Inside the gate, the tram stopped—behind us, the bridge raised again, and a man in a light yellow toga came to meet us. The nearby buildings were all windowless blocks, like barracks.

"Please step out of the tram, Mr. Healy'll." I did, and he came to shake my hand. "How are you this morning? Would you like anything to eat or drink?" He noticed Anna. "Hello."

She jumped out, intimidated by the ugly buildings. "I'm from the site at the Wesler estate."

The man gave me a disappointed look. "I'm going to have to ask you to leave."

"Wait, we're just here to talk."

"We came to see the Wesler servant," Anna said. "We'll pay whatever you ask, but we need to speak with her."

He hesitated, and I noticed the closed-circuit comm in his left ear: he was wired directly to someone inside. From what I knew, the Pnetians were organized in a complex, organic hierarchy, and each commune had its own Prophet. I wondered what this one sounded like.

"I heard that there has been an incident on Shan," he said. "You have all been recalled."

"That's true," Anna said. "And you know I don't have time to debate this. We have to see the Wesler servant. Now what do you want?"

The man motioned to the nearest building. "Come with me."

We followed him into a conservative hall of doors with a staircase at the far end. He stepped into the first door on the left: a small, marble conference table with manicured ferns and soft music playing in the background. Two mugs of coffee and plates of peppered ham had been arranged at one end. While I sat, burned my tongue on the coffee and began to eat, Anna waited.

"My name is Seg'v," the man said, and he arranged a pile of folders.

Anna asked, "What do you want?"

Seg'v watched me finished my ham and smiled. "I can have more brought in if you'd . . ."

"What do you want?" Anna's voice rose. "We rode for six hours because someone told us we would be allowed to see the Wesler servant."

"Someone was misinformed." Seg'v stiffened. "I ask that you remain calm or I will end this conversation."

I finished my coffee, and before Anna could answer, I said, "Okay, Seg'v. I don't have much money, but what will it take?"

"The Lagone Community is quite comfortable."

"Then what? We wouldn't be sitting here if there wasn't something."

"I can see that you're both tired," he said. "And I understand that your wife recently passed away, Mr. Healy'll."

I tapped my ear. "You ran a background check?"

"Of course. We verify all of our visitors. There is the possibility that the most recent accident will lead to a cancellation of the Space Program indefinitely."

The 'accident' he was talking about was Elena. "Why should you . . ."

"We want it to fail."

I felt sick, it could have been the ham. Anna grabbed my hand and said, "You want the space program to end?"

"Yes."

I hadn't expected this. Anna said, "I thought you were only concerned with spiritual . . ."

"The two are connected," Seg'v said. "We're not as removed as you might think. We believe in the same pantheon, recognize the same gods. This isn't a reform movement."

No, I thought, it's a cult.

He continued, "We've simply returned to the values of the First and Second Ages. Our current deities are transient—valuable, but temporary. The old gods *will* return. Works are the structure of that salvation."

"*Salvation,*" she said. "Why do you care about the Space Program?"

Seg'v said, "You asked if we could make a deal for contact with the Wesler servant, and I've answered your question. After you speak with her, you—Mr. Healy'll—will do whatever you can in the future to end the project."

"Why?"

"I'm sorry, I don't have the answer to that."

"Let us talk to your Prophet or ask him . . ."

"Mr. Healy'll, I'm told everything I need to be told. It won't do any good to press this."

"He wants my word—is that it?"

"Yes."

"Fine. Now let's go."

Seg'v led us back into the hall, and I noticed the vent-speakers spaced between each door near the ceiling. Simple walls but I imagined a honeycomb of cooling fans and multicolored wires in-between. We went down stairs, through a hall of transparent plastic wall-wrap, and into the basement of an adjacent building.

As we walked, Anna pressed close, her hand brushing my fingertips. We didn't speak: what was there to say? Why in the name of Hebet's left nut did a Pnetian 'Prophet' care about the space project? And even if they did, how did they expect to ensure that I kept my word? Of course I wanted the project to die. We wandered through a hall of dirt root system walls. Moist air, like a swamp, and he stopped at the last door on the right, blocking it.

"She's in here," he said, but didn't move.

"Why are you keeping her locked up?"

"She's free to go at any time."

"Are you going to let us in?" I asked.

"You will make sure the space project is abandoned?"

"I told you I would." I nodded to the door. "You *are* afraid of her—she's a 50-year-old woman and you're scared."

He stepped aside. "Why do you say that?"

I smiled: why was I nervous? "You're sweating."

I opened the door.

CHAPTER EIGHT

Make It Work

She didn't look 50. With full black hair, huge eyes, and a large body of muscle and breasts, the Wesler-servant looked 30—better than me, probably younger. In this cell of paper walls and potted plants, she looked more well-rested than I did. Seg'v noticed the way Anna was examining the walls: the servant had scribbled detailed columns of text and diagrams. Nonsense words and geometry—with one dominant scrawl:

> We Should Be Called Rome

I said, "You let her write on the walls?"
"We wanted to see what she would say."
"Yeah."
They'd given her a bucket of pens and drab paints—colors with names like charcoal, smoke, and deep-sea black.
Anna said, "What's her name?"
"The Weslers called her Kysa, but . . ."
Without turning from her wall-work, the servant said, "Kysa's fine."
Anna frowned. "Kysa? That's her name?"
I said, "Anna, what's . . ."
"I've heard the name before."

Seg'v went back into the hall, shut the door, and I approached Kysa. Anna squeezed my hand, but Kysa didn't turn, writing a stream of blocky red letters below a cone-diagram.

"Kysa?"

"Yes."

I waited behind her. "They said you weren't responsive, we didn't know . . ."

"I'm not responsive," she said, finished her work and stood. Fingertips inked purple and black, she frowned when she saw us. "Who are you?"

"We're from the archaeological board. I'm Nikos Healy'll, this is Anna Antc'sh."

Kysa didn't shake my hand, she nodded to Anna. "We'll be working together."

Anna turned to me. "She was assigned to the dig by the Senate committee." I didn't understand, and Anna said, "She's a Senatorial advisor. She's returning to the Estate permanently." To Kysa, "Aren't you?"

Kysa nodded.

Anna said, "And you were there when . . ."

"When it opened? Yes."

What did you see, how did they die? "What does that mean?" I pointed to her main banner.

"It means we should be called Rome. I've seen it and heard the people there singing. That's what it's called."

"That's what what's called?"

"The Capital city."

"Who calls it . . ."

She pointed to a long stream of text below the 'Rome' statement—I went to read:

> In date and place and
> space between
> I've seen them love and
> fight and dream.

The Weslers taught her iambic quatrameter. It continued like that, without specifics. "What's this mean?"

"They didn't show you?" she asked, and when I stared back blankly, Kysa shrugged. "I don't know why they didn't show you."

"Who?" I glanced at the door. "What'd they . . ."

Kysa asked, "What do you want?"

Anna said, "What did you see? The room opened for you?"

"You've been there, haven't you?" Kysa said. "What'd you see?"

Anna said, "An empty room."

"No." Kysa smiled. "Don't lie to me. What did you really see?"

As I watched, Anna's cheeks lost their color. "I didn't see anything."

"You did. You both did, but you don't understand it."

And you do? I said, "We both had nightmares."

"I know." Kysa laughed sharply. "Trust me, I know. What did you see?"

"A calendar, drowned people."

"Drowning is the most humane death. People don't hurt when they drown. They struggle a little bit, but they don't hurt."

Yeah, okay . . . "The Weslers did."

"No."

I waited: more happened in that mansion. "Why'd they drown?"

"Why not?"

Anna said, "Did you do it?"

Kysa shook her head. "You don't understand?"

Anna said, "No."

"Do you believe that your brain exists?"

"Yes."

Not sure how much more of this I could take. Why would the Senate assign a lunatic-former-servant to oversee the dig?

"Why do you believe in your brain?" Kysa said. "Have you seen it?"

"Of course not."

"But, you believe it . . ."

I cut her off, "Yeah, all right, I get it. Tell us what happened."

"That's the difference between us," Kysa said, "I don't."

This was bothering Anna. She went to the wall to examine Kysa's illegible writing and diagrams more closely. She'd drawn a row of circles with lines radiating out from the center.

I said, "No?"

"No."

I smiled, tapped the side of my head. "My brain's there."

"Do you know what year it is?"

"It's not 1140 L.M.?"

"It is," she said, "it's also 8088 in the C.L. Era and 1942 A.D."

"Oh yeah?"

I didn't ask her to explain, but she did anyway. "They showed me that. Our life is the smudge." She stuck a finger in a cap of gray paint. "But there are others." She poked dark red with her thumb, then blue-black with her middle finger.

"You're not going to wipe that on me . . ."

"All together." She dotted the wall gray, then pushed red on top, then black, stirred the smear and it turned brown.

"So the world's brown?"

"Yes."

"All the people overlap and mix?"

"Not *people*," Kysa said. "Time and space do not exist—you knew that before you came here. We've been created to feel them, but that doesn't make them . . ."

"They're real for us," I said. "Yes they are."

"You both know what the room is," she said quietly. "More than I do. But your bodies are rejecting it—going into shock. It showed me other versions of New Amith, and one is so close you can almost touch it. I'm sure you'll see it too."

"It *showed you*?"

"Yes. That other world is all around us. You can almost hear them singing and marching right now, can't you?"

The song again. "I didn't see anything," I said. "What I saw happened in a dream—it wasn't real. The room was just a box of mold and old Menst." I glanced at Anna. She was still concentrating on the wall; back to being an archaeologist.

"You don't believe it yet," Kysa said, "but you will."

Anna tapped a section of the wall. "What's this mean? 'The fire is buried with Grotton'?"

Kysa shook her head. "I didn't write that."

"You did," Anna said, "It's right here."

"No, I didn't." Kysa sat in the opposite corner facing the wall. "My mind is breaking, I write nonsense. I'm going insane."

I went to look with Anna. "You're sure that's what it says?"

"Look at it."

The door opened. Smiling, Seg'v stepped inside. "Mr. Healy'll."

I said, "Wait . . ."

Anna tore a strip of paper from the wall, I gave her Elena's red-tipped pen, and Anna started to frantically copy the gibberish.

"Please, Mr. Healy'll. That's enough."

Kysa said, "I didn't write that, I didn't write that . . ."

"Come with me," Seg'v said.

"Just . . ."

"Now, Mr. Healy'll."

We followed Seg'v out, he shut the door, and we left. As our tram rolled over the bridge, back into the salt basin, Anna gave me back the pen and glared at what she'd copied.

"This bothers me," she said.

"What?"

"That wasn't just poetry—that line I read in there. It was mixed with specific directions." She read, *"The Capitol spire is in the Center, The Ye'ts Route circles the winter tilt*—that's just the pattern," she said, when she saw my expression. "It probably means that the Ye'ts curls in a semi-circle, following the sun's path. It's a road, isn't it? In the Baat Mountains?"

Anna's red-tipped pen writing was the same color ink as that line Elena had written about forgetting a dead child we never had. Huh. But damned if I knew about the Baat Mountains. "Sure."

"It's a specific *thing*, a description. And then: *The Fire is Buried with Grotton*." She rubbed her swollen eyes. Six hours of pretzel-sleep wasn't enough. "And there are several more, one that doesn't make sense. I may have read it wrong: *Fisherle brought it in, we will bring it down.* It's more of a verse . . . . What?"

I swallowed. "How's it spelled?"

"What?"

"'Fisherle': how did she spell it?"

Anna spelled it for me. "Nikos . . ?"

"It's a shipping company." Giannis was going to enjoy this. "In Leim'en."

"How do you know?"

"My uncle used to work for them."

"He doesn't anymore?"

"No."

"Why not?"

"He's dead."

"I'm sorry, was he . . ."

"It's okay." Outside, the sunlight made the lowlands look even more pathetic. No choice now. I told Anna about Elena's suicide note and Dett's letter. When I finished, she was quiet for a long time.

Then she said, "I wish I could help you."

"What do you mean—you're not going back to Shan, are you . . ?"

She frowned. "Of course—I have to."

"You're not interested in this? Why would she write the name of a Leim'en shipping company on the wall? And why would Elena and Dett . . ."

"What do you think?"

"I don't know, but we have to go to Leim'en."

"We do, do we?"

I ignored her tone. "Yes. You think so too."

"I can't. When I get back I'll . . ."

"You don't even know what's happening on Shan. *'When I get back'*— when's that?"

"I don't have a choice."

"Do you think Kysa was just crazy?"

Anna said, "I don't know. Do you?"

"No. And neither was Elena. The Nine Laws aren't random. Something's about to happen that we can't see yet."

"Like what?"

"I don't know."

"What's your plan—to just show up at the shipping company's headquarters?"

"We have to settle Dett's house . . ."

"What?"

"Dett was my uncle. He died at sea a few days ago, so there were no rites. We have to take care of his house."

"It didn't go to your parents?"

"It probably would have, but they're dead too."

"I didn't . . ."

Before she could apologize again, I said, "I'm unstable. You wanted to return, but I wouldn't let you."

"You're joking."

"No. You were forced to come with me to Leim'en. What can they do?"

"It wouldn't be me . . ."

"Exactly." I waved away another objection. "I don't care—they can lock me up, it doesn't matter. I want to know what this is."

"They might not . . ."

"They'll believe it." My eyes hurt. I'd been awake too long, didn't want to dream. "I would."

"You're kidnapping me?"

I smiled. "Looks that way."

"This is a bad idea. They'll catch you."

"Yeah."

We didn't speak for a moment, then she said, "It makes sense, doesn't it—what she said?"

"Who, Kysa?"

"Yes. She said our minds went into shock in the room, and we're trying to cope with it—that's why we had dreams."

"We were traumatized?"

"Yes."

I didn't want to think about this. "What did we see? It was just an old room." She didn't answer, and I said, "You don't think so?"

"I don't know, but we had simultaneous nightmares after going down there."

"You'll come with me to Leim'en?" My comm rang, and I answered, "Hello?"

"There you are."

Giannis.

"Hi."

"I'm at your house, where are you?" He didn't wait for an answer. "We're going to the coast today to settle Dett's estate. I already called the Fisherle people."

I hesitated. "Okay."

Giannis waited—he'd no doubt prepared point-by-point rebuttals to my expected objections. "Okay—you'll come?"

"Yeah. I'm in a tram now, we'll pick you up in a few hours."

"Where are you?"

"I'll tell you when we get there."

"Who's we?"

"The woman from the dig is with me."

"She's Shan, isn't she?"

"Yeah . . ."

"Haven't they all been recalled?"

I took a patient breath. "Giannis, I'll see you in a few hours." I clicked off.

Anna was watching me. "Who was that?"

"My younger brother."

"He's coming along?"

"Apparently."

She shook her head. "That's not a good idea. The more people involved . . ."

"He's my brother, it'll be all right."

She stared at me as if I were an abstract painting: from a different angle I might make sense.

Anna tapped her Lagone-scribbles. "I *do* want to know why she wrote this."

That servant—Kysa—is coping with it too, I thought. She saw the Black Room. "Gods, I'm tired."

Anna sat beside me, pressed my head to her shoulder. "Here."

"You're being kidnapped, you know." She *was* more comfortable than the window, but not much.

"Go to sleep."

My brain chuckled: no, I don't think we'll be doing *that*. But I could pretend.

CHAPTER NINE

A Modern-day Oceanman

The fishy-salt smell and sea-air frizz in my hair brought memories of our annual trips to the coast, to visit uncle Dett. Dett had been dad's brother, some kind of middleman in the trade of lobster-traps via Fisherle shipping. The linked cages they plopped along the reef tended to rust or break loose, meaning more business for Dett, who—as far as I could tell—had done nothing more than order new shipments for local trappers and create piles of unnecessary paperwork.

All of that bought him a yellow-roofed house overlooking Marke's Harbor and the Eastern Ocean. I spotted it on a sharp outcropping of rock and overgrown cacti on the cliff below—our tram bounced along a mountain-side road that curled and dipped from the highlands and inner valley of the Capitol out to the villages that sprouted like moss around the lip of ocean. Dett had chosen that airy view for obvious reasons: access to his boat, the view of isolated palms and overgrown rock paths leading to the harbor and its bea-comb of multi-colored shops, houses, brothels, and wharfs, all dominated by a thicket of masts and limp flags, and by the ocean. And because it was close to Leim'en. The same city Grotton-the-explorer had founded 2,000 years ago. The same explorer that nutball aristocrat and Kysa had written about on their respective walls.

Anna turned in her seat to look out over the edge of the road. "Wow . . ."

I'd seen it many times, and the ocean never seemed to change.

95

"Huffer whales," Giannis said, and he pointed to the horizon, past a quad of anchored steamships, too large and heavy to pull into the provincial docks. "See them?"

We squinted, and Anna leaned her forehead against the glass as the tram continued its automatic course. She frowned. "Where?"

Giannis leaned close to her, rolled down the window—stronger salt-smell on the wind—and pointed out. "Look there."

Now I saw them: a family of underwater shadows near a rocky outcropping that would block our view in a moment.

"I don't see them," Anna said.

"Follow the line of that rock . . ." Giannis said.

"You see the barge on the right?" I asked. "The steamer?"

"Yes."

"Look above that."

A pause, and one of the whales broke water—like a gray-flesh submersible. Anna caught her breath, and as the first whale dropped again, two more surfaced, then a third geysered a plume of water into the air. Gods, it went high: above the masts of the nearby fishing ships. Thirty meters of water fired straight up. In another moment we rounded a bend and the whales were gone.

"Did you see Dett's house?" Giannis asked.

"Yeah."

Anna opened her mouth, but didn't say anything—Giannis grinned and told her about uncle Dett-the-lobster-middleman.

We needed to eat before meeting the Fisherle lawyers at Dett's house. I hadn't told Giannis much; he still thought this trip was all about the estate. It had been too long since I'd seen the ocean, I'd forgotten how it used to affect me. Staring at the water had always made me question my life and promise things would change when I returned to the city. Then I got lazy again.

Giannis picked a new restaurant on the boardwalk—'Butterfish'—and we sat outside, overlooking shallow waves and littered riggings. The rocks and sand under the walk were filled with warrior crabs, cracked seashells, and colored glass.

Giannis had a mango drink, while Anna and I stuck with water. No sense pushing the stomach too early. During the breakfast conversation, Giannis politely grilled Anna. He was fascinated, like the first New Amith Senators to greet the Shan when their Ambassadors began arriving 30 years ago. As if she were a forgotten relative—and maybe she was.

Anna's tribe was called the Na'ska. Her family had a long tradition as part of the Na'ska warrior caste, and since the unification of the major Shan tribes under the Ckish—a warrior-priest from another tribe—the Na'ska had intensified their militarism. Relative peace on Shan—until now?—with the Ckish Dynasty, should have meant an end to the era of Na'ska warriors, shouldn't it? I thought so, but it didn't: the Na'ska had extended the franchise, enlisting 80 percent of their people as soldiers. For the old aristocracy of Na'ska warriors, conscription was complete, requiring men and women over the age of 15 to be trained. After learning to kill, Anna had been granted a special status, because of her mother's position as ambassador. So, rather than handle pycks, Anna was allowed to dig up ancient garbage. However, now that the Ckish had recalled all the Shan, Anna was required to drop her moldy beads and join the cause.

"But you're still here," Giannis said.

Anna finished her fish. "Yes."

I hadn't wanted to jump right into this. "She has an extension," I lied. "Anna's important here: she has until the end of the week."

"That's great." When she didn't respond, he said, "There's a place to swim just a few kilometers down the road. Remember, Nikos? Lots of fish."

"I remember the sea-snakes."

"Oh please," Giannis said, "that was one time . . ."

"And you broke my leg."

"No, I didn't."

"He did," I said, and to Anna, "Giannis pushed me off a rock—twenty meters above the water, and after I jumped, my leg cracked underwater. A sea snake grabbed my ankle and yanked me under."

" Unbelievable," Giannis said. "That's not what happened."

I didn't remember what happened, but he was leaning close to Anna, maneuvering his arm around the back of her chair—she didn't seem to notice or mind.

I asked Anna, "Have you ever seen a sea-snake?"

"I don't think so."

Giannis said, "They have them all along the coast, but they're usually not that large so close to land. And they never attack people—except in self-defense."

"Like when someone's pushed on top of them."

Giannis gave Anna a conspiratorial look. "Don't listen to him. He's always the victim, whatever happens."

I looked away, to the ships and ocean. "I wonder if everything's still in Dett's house. His furniture and things."

"Why? Are you looking for a new couch?"

"Sure."

I let them talk about the whales we'd seen, while I tried to remember Dett's home. I remembered as a kid being impressed by glass jars of preserved deep-sea fish. Dett bought them off a passing privateer or something. He'd had a strange collection of books from his time at the Academy—the gods only knew what he'd studied. I remembered books about provincial bordellos, a lot of indecipherable maps, and a whole bookshelf full of early Republican comedians. He might have specialized in 700-year-old jokes.

A pregnant woman entered the restaurant alone, and a couple stopped eating to offer their table. One hand on her belly, the woman slid into an empty seat, thanked them. A waiter cleared the table before arranging a stone fish. He lit incense on the fish's back, said something to the woman, and brought her a menu.

Anna was fascinated. "What is that?"

"She's pregnant," Giannis said.

I smiled. She was as big as a tram: *really—she's pregnant?*

"I know," Anna said. "Why did they do that?"

"It's for good luck," Giannis said. "Part of the worship of Nosan. She's the goddess of the moon and spring. Festivals and weddings used to be dedicated to her. The fish commemorates the feasting. So she's been the goddess of birth since the late Merr Dynasty."

"You *did* learn something at the monastery besides how to write a prescription," I said.

Giannis shrugged. "You knew that too."

"I didn't know the history."

"These gods are important." He looked uncomfortable. "Even if some are only a few hundred years old, they're all we have right now."

Funny thing to say. I changed the subject back to the whales. Finally, while Giannis paid, Anna cornered me on the sidewalk outside.

"I should go back," she said. "I wasn't thinking, this is too dangerous."

"It'll be fine."

"It won't. People notice, did you see them watching me?"

"They weren't watching you."

"They were."

"Came all the way here," I said, "we should . . ."

Giannis: "Ready to go?" He exited the restaurant, motioned to the waiting tram. To Anna, "Is everything okay?"

She got in first. "I'm fine."

"Let's go then. What? Nikos . . ."

"Yeah."

"Are you . . ."

"Yeah." But I wasn't.

* * *

Thought it was bigger, but Dett's house hadn't changed much. Unless places disintegrated and shrank when people died. Like the parable of the forgotten daughter, who just pops out of existence, vanishes one day. No, Dett's house still squatted on a bumpy mountain of granite and wild orange-trees, the kind of place a priest might design after trading the gods for the Sea: reverent and cluttered with shells.

They crinkled and clinked underfoot as we left the tram and hiked up Dett's vertical front-drive. Spiky posts in the drive created a barrier to keep out trams, ornamented with just enough inscriptions and faces of dead merchant-captains that Dett could claim were aesthetic. And, of course, the shells. Crab shells, conchs and seashells, glittery, purple, tiny ear-shaped—he'd probably hired a transport to dump a bedload down the mountainside.

"It hasn't changed," Giannis said.

We went to the front door, flanked by dead plants and a cracked bird protector-god. The stained glass in the front windows was intact: scenes of ships and whales and tiny, treeless islands.

"Okay," Giannis said. "What do you want to do?"

I tried the doorknob: it opened. My stomach tensed, I let the door open wide. Entry hall of dark oak, more dead plants, and adjoining rooms. Kitchen ahead, library on the left, and there was a cluttered artifact-study to the right. I wondered where he'd slept.

A pair of lawyers ambushed us in the kitchen, and we spent an hour signing forms at the table. I asked about Dett's body and was told that Fisherle had already disposed of it. Nobody wants to let a drowning victim ripen. I tried not to think about it. When we finished, the lawyers left us in our new, jointly-owned house-by-the-sea.

Giannis showed Anna a counter full of family lithographs in the kitchen. Mom, dad, Dett, and a baby. Me. They all looked so young: dad's close-cut hair, trimmed beard and small, brown eyes. Mom's plump cheeks and sarcastic smile. I remembered this picture: I'd seen it before. Most of what I knew about my mother had come from pictures like that. Stories dad had told. Little snatches of childhood memory: old feelings that probably weren't genuine anyway, more influenced by stories and anecdotes from my father, the parent I'd known. Giannis had once said I *should* remember more. I was a year and a half older than he was when she died. Should have more memories.

Mom: liver failure when I was two. Dad: heart attack while we were away at the Academy. Alcohol and meat.

I'd known Dett better than my own mother, and Dett was a crazy uncle who pawned lobster traps and lost at cards. And who had apparently thought of himself as a modern-day Oceanman. Pieces of ship-junk were mounted in every room, the more bizarre finds displayed as centerpieces. A pile of old coins, a glass case of preserved slime with suckers and at least one eye, a painted shard of a woman's face—front piece—and books. Lots of old books.

I sat on a cushiony couch in Dett's study and stared at the disorganized trash he'd left. Had this man really sent Elena a note? Had he known that she intended to die? I didn't see a difference between the model ship Dett had left on a mound of garbage in the corner and the blackened strip of iron that hung over his desk.

Anna and Giannis bumped around in the kitchen, testing the heat and water, talking too loudly about the lithographs. Strange. There had to be some order to this—I had a hard time believing that 'crazy uncle Dett' wouldn't have organized his moldy treasures somehow. Why was this bothering me? Just confronting the remnants of someone's life, of course it caught—but no. More to it. There was a connection here.

I started around the study's perimeter. No labels or descriptions with Dett's paintings and dead fish, just a 'Here It Is' mentality. No explanation needed. Except . . . I was missing something. Anna and Giannis stepped into the doorway.

"Are you ready?" Giannis asked. "See anything you like?"

I went to the prominent iron bar mounted over Dett's desk. It was twisted, slightly warped, as if someone had poked half into the oven, and on the unburnt section—tiny writing? Yeah, there were definite, faint characters. Maybe something in Dett's desk would—no. One look at the clutter made me turn back to the iron bar.

"Come here," I said. "See if you can read this."

Giannis didn't move. "What?"

Anna came closer, and I said, "Why would he stick an iron bar—this is trash—over his desk. It's the most prominent thing in the room."

Anna stared at the iron-writing for a long time, then said, "Do you know what this is? Does it say anywhere when this dates from?"

"No . . ."

"It's a K'aur'is dialect."

Giannis approached. "A what?"

"What is this?" Anna touched the bar, glared at the rest of the room, as if she hadn't noticed it before. "I don't understand . . ."

Here it is again: anxiety under the surface, and I don't know why. I closed my eyes, the Black Room—and I was still in Dett's house.

"Okay," I said. "What's that . . ."

"K'aur'is—it's not, it's a Shan dialect," she said. "One of the Minebelt tribes used it, all of these artifacts are in museums now on Shan." She looked from me to Giannis, as if this were an elaborate joke. "You knew about this? What is this—how'd you get this?"

Giannis laughed. "I can honestly say that I have no idea what . . ."

"Nikos?"

"What?"

"How'd this get here? Do you know how much trouble this could get you into?"

"Why, it's just a . . ."

"It's a Shan artifact. They're not supposed to leave our planet—obviously someone brought it here. Do you have any idea . . ."

"No. We came together, calm down. Gods, what's . . ."

"Barcuc, you're both—this house belongs to you now. This was smuggled from our planet to yours."

Giannis said, "How do you know . . ."

She shrugged. "You could both go to prison for the rest of your lives. This breaks about 20 laws on Shan and another 50 over here."

"So what is it?" I asked.

"Nikos . . ."

"If I'm going down for the rest of my life over this thing . . ." And not for that *other* thing. "I'd like to know what it is."

She shook her head, scanning the room for contraband. Finally, she focused on the iron bar again.

"I don't know—I can't read any of this, but it doesn't matter what it actually . . ."

"It does," I said. "What—is it a weapon, is it a flowerpot?"

"Probably a crossbeam."

"Oh yeah?"

"Yes," she said.

Giannis said, "It's from a house?"

"It's from something that had crossbeams," Anna said. "They built a lot of things—houses, ships, even primitive mechanized armor. Any structure with a skeleton has crossbeams."

I thought about that, started to ask about the Mineland tribe that had written on this pole, then said, "Wait—when?"

"What?"

"When was this built?"

"I don't know," she said, "awhile ago."

"So we have to get rid of it," Giannis said.

I ignored him, asked, "How long is 'awhile'? Five, ten years?"

"No, no, no. This probably dates to the Blue Revolutions. It's around 8,500 years old."

"And they were able to build houses out of . . ."

"Iron? Yes. Just like you. In your Prophetic Golden Age, a lot of things were just as—were more advanced than they are today. We have the same patterns on Shan: technology goes up and down."

And someone smuggled it here, I thought. Why would they—so a screwball like Dett could buy it.

"How much would something like this cost?" I asked.

Anna: "What?"

"You have an idea of . . ."

"No."

"How would he afford this?" I said. "Dett sold lobster traps, how could he afford to buy a Shan relic?"

"He afforded this house," Giannis said.

Doesn't make sense. I didn't want to look anymore, didn't want to see the other scraps Dett had hoarded with his lobster-Fisherle loot. No need, but Anna was already roaming the walls, scrutinizing each item. She tapped a shiny white hook.

"This is Shan," she said. "It's a fossilized Gatt'a'y tooth. A sea-tiger—they've been extinct for thousands of years—that's how old this it."

Giannis asked me what we should do, and I said that Dett had probably paid half his profits for a decade to collect this stuff—no reason we couldn't make some of his money back.

Anna indicated a shred of green cloth. "Layer Mesh—this might be the oldest piece here."

Giannis said, "It's from Shan?"

"Yes." She gave me a serious look. "You can't sell these."

"We're already in trouble, right . . ."

"No," she said. "You can't sell these."

"If we did . . ."

"You can't."

"How much would they bring in?"

Anna didn't answer, and Giannis said, "Come on. He's not serious." To me, "Stop messing with her."

"Yeah," I said. He was half-right; I'd been half-joking. I didn't need money: the program and the Senate would pay me to sit on my ass for at least the next 20 years.

"Are these—the rest of these—from Shan?" I asked.

Anna took a long look at the wall. "I don't know."

That's the connection: the ones on the wall are Shan, the ones on the floor, the mess on the desk—all the rest is homegrown.

"What?" Giannis was watching me. "What's wrong?"

"Nothing."

Except that Dett was a Pnetian.

"Fine," he said, "are we ready to go?"

"You have to declare these," Anna said.

"I will," I said.

"Let's get in the water," Giannis said, but Anna was already shaking her head.

The Pnetians believed that Shan and New Amith were intimately connected—what had Seg'v said at the Lagone Community? Salvation through works. The gods were returning, but they needed help. And Dett had mentioned bombs. Only days left. What if our calendar is wrong? I thought. What if the Pnetians *believe* it's wrong?

We walked out to the tram.

"I have to go back," Anna said.

The Shan artifacts had either pissed her off or drummed up some latent nationalism.

"Are you sure?" I said.

"I should . . ."

"Come to Leim'en. It's less than an hour away. We'll look up the Fisherle address. It might take an hour for another ride to get here anyway. You can wait in the tram."

"Oh, thank you."

"If you don't want to . . ."

"Fine. Just to Leim'en."

"Calm down, those shark teeth aren't going anywhere."

As we got back in the tram, she told Giannis, "Your brother doesn't have any common sense."

Did she understand? I didn't want to talk about it in front of Giannis. Why? Anna and I were discovering this together. Jealousy, I realized. I'm afraid Giannis and Anna—so what? I met Anna's stare, and she touched my hand. Yes, I thought. She understands. And that's why she's afraid.

CHAPTER TEN

Leim'en

C ouldn't see it until we were right on top of it: the Coast. Leim'en hunkered around a gaping semi-circular harbor, crammed between volcanic cliffs and muddy water. In the deep, of course, the sea still glowed a bright blue, but here, near the beige-tin press of towers and shipyards, it had clouded. Generations of fleets docking in the artificial bay left tracks of grime, spills, and their own decomposing bones. I'd once heard that over 3,000 ships had sunken in Leim'en harbor.

And the Myein Barrier—a plastic, half-submerged reef they'd built several thousand meters out—kept the water from circulating. Just as it locked out hurricane-waves, it turned the harbor into a saltwater lake, linked to the ocean at either end. We had to go up and around from Dett's house—most of the coastline was too rocky.

We watched our track continue around the lip of a vertical cliff that dropped to a mass of 20 story Leim'en housing complexes. And more roadblocks.

"What's the Fisherle address?" Giannis asked.

"I have it."

"What is it?"

"I gave it to the tram." He was getting antsy, and it made me nervous. "603 Hal-f'or'd Street. I gave it to the tram when we left."

He nodded, and our tram slowed at a cluster of stopped vehicles ahead. Beyond, the road finally descended—at a 75-degree angle—into the outskirts of the city.

Anna went to the front windows to get a clearer view of the congestion. "There are so many people. It's so *packed*, not like your capital."

Old and cramped the way the lost city of Amith was supposed to have been back in the day, Leim'en had been the dominant eastern port of the Capital continent until shipping began to slow in the past decade. Leim'en still dominated these trade routes with her army of convoy ships and barges, all swarming around the docks and harbor—but shipping changed.

We couldn't fly too high, but we could still fly. And there just wasn't room around Leim'en for an airstrip to hold the gas-sucking puddle-jumpers that hopped from one side of the world to the other without stopping to catch their breath. Talk of torching Sumu's Island—that half-mile strip of warehouses at the southern edge of the harbor—hadn't brought action. Leim'en didn't have the money anymore, and as her shipping monopolies slowly dwindled, so did her ability to change.

Already too late to buy up the island, level it, and then fish for bird-contracts. So Leim'en puttered on with a pond full of dirty steamers coughing up rust-colored clouds, in water sludged with time—the city was getting old.

Yeah, Leim'en was the opposite of New Amith Capital.

Giannis said, "Can you believe this traffic?"

I said, "Yes."

The Capital sprawled for kilometers, tumbling from villa to Tellen housing complex to village center. When the New Republic began 700 years ago, someone—probably a committee of someones—had chosen the ruined hulk of the Merr Palace as the new capitol building, and a city grew around it. It wasn't coincidence that it was a short tram ride from Leim'en in the East and the Durges River in the west. That's why the Merr put it where they did—and the Republicans saw no reason to relocate. New Amith capital had crept out unevenly, engulfing ancient towns and bits of cities, as it still did. The thin strip of the Leim'en'a mountain range separated the Capital from the Coast.

Finally through the checkpoint, our tram bounced down the cliff-road into blocks of vertical housing. Sidewalks packed with people: fruit and fish vendors, musicians, and uniformed police. Never saw police in the Capital, but this wasn't the Capital.

Giannis said, "Do you know where the address is located?"

"How would I know where that is?"

"I don't know."

"Only one of us needs to know where we're going," I said, meaning the tram.

Some of the narrow roads were blocked off to trams, and we thumped in a pothole through an intersection that ended at a street-market. Getting closer to the ocean, and the air was getting worse. Behind us, the rise of sharp peaks had faded yellow with smog, as if our rear window were dirty. Not the window.

Steam-powered street cleaners huffed along the ancient asphalt, fouling the air as they sprayed and swept the ground. No one collected the garbage here, they just rotated in shifts, sweeping it downhill, until it piled on wharfs and shoreline rocks, and was finally dumped in the harbor. Cyclical rainstorms and the mountain brooks kept the city from dying of cholera, though the last major outbreak had been—what?—20 years ago? Still in my lifetime. What had caused that?

"A garbage strike," Giannis said.

"That's right . . ."

"They went three days without spraying."

Three days and 20,000 people had gotten sick. Could have been worse in a city of four and a half million.

The main roads of tourists, performers and police changed into blocks of crumbling warehouses and abandoned foundries. Empty lots, no people, and no trams. What little crime there is happens in places like this, I thought, watching a flock of pigeons through a collapsed wall in what had once been a red-brick factory.

"Do you know where we are?" Giannis asked.

"I haven't visited Leim'en anymore than you have."

"I don't know where we are."

Without turning from the window, Anna said, "Neither do I."

Giannis was getting worried, but somehow this didn't bother me. I wasn't excited either. We were looking for the address from the Fisherle legal forms. Dett and Fisherle were connected to Kysa and Elena, but I didn't really expect answers. A little more activity, and at least the buildings on the next block were intact, still smoke and ash pumping out of the ten story chimneys overhead. At least they were making something.

The tram stopped.

I checked the address, then squinted at the surrounding factories. All nondescript slabs of utilitarian cement and brick with pipes smoking on their rooftops.

"Is this . . ."

"I don't know," I said and got out of the tram.

Giannis didn't move. "You don't think this is it, do you?"

"Yeah, I don't know."

Anna hopped out and coughed. "Barcuc, this is terrible. How can they breathe this?"

Giannis said, "It's a shipping company, shouldn't it be at the . . ."

The ground shook. When it ended, I realized that I had fallen into an instinctive half-crouch at the open tram door, one arm around Anna.

Giannis: "What the hell was that?"

Anna was pressed against me, breathing hard, one hand clamped on my left knee. "I'm sorry," she said.

I helped her up and started for the nearest building. No one rushed out screaming, no evacuation siren in the streets, so it was just a minor quake.

"It didn't feel minor," Giannis said.

"Are you going to wait in there?"

He got out of the tram. "Maybe the tram couldn't find the address."

"So why would it bring us here?"

Naturally, there were no street signs, so I went to the nearest door—locked. Smoke rose from this factory, which meant there had to be someone inside.

"It's not that one," Giannis said, and he indicated a rusted square nailed randomly about three meters up: 605.

So it was next door.

"At least we know it didn't drop us in the middle of nowhere," I said.

Giannis gave me a look and followed behind Anna to the next building. "You realize this is probably going to be nothing."

"Yeah."

"Good, I just . . ."

"Okay."

The next building was 601.

Just a concrete alley between them. It snaked back to what looked like another stretch of derelict warehouses and factories. Down the drainage-pipe, sewer-grate alley, with Giannis complaining and there it was . . .

Halfway down the alley, I stomped across a rusted cellar door marked 603.

"Fisherle is underground?" Giannis said.

Anna tried to coax me back. "Don't . . ."

I banged on the metal flaps, waited, then banged again.

"Nikos . . ."

"It's not locked."

I picked up the door with both hands—teeth snapped at my fingers, I lost the door, fell over backwards, and the metal smacked down again hard, clomping a snarling black . . .

"What the hell?"

"Are you all right?" Anna was checking my fingertips. "Barcuc, that was . . ."

"A dog," Giannis said. "I think it was a dog." He backed away.

No sound through the metal.

"Why can't we hear it?" I said, arms and chest tingling with adrenaline. I was breathing fast. "Should have heard it."

"It may be trained not to bark," Giannis said.

"What?"

"They may have trained it not to . . ."

Anna said, "Let's go, come on."

She nodded back the way we'd come. The door thumped, tilted open, and a scrawny woman stepped out, a pointy-black pistol in one hand.

"Doan what?" she said.

No sign of the dog—I'd forgotten the sailor babble Leim'eners sometimes used, said, "What?"

"'tal?" she asked.

Capital, I thought, and said, "Yeah."

She said more slowly, "Do you wan'?"

What do you want.

I handed her one of the Fisherle papers. "Is this the Fisherle depot?"

"It ikeook?"

"No, it looks like an empty alley."

"Is at whanit."

"It's not Fisherle? Then why is the address on those legal forms?"

She pocketed the paper. "Um hm. More?"

"My uncle worked for Fisherle. They sent lawyers to his house with these forms, with *this* address . . ."

She extended a hand, kept the pistol aimed at my face, ignoring Giannis. First time a total stranger had pointed a weapon at me.

She said, "Alana."

Just a command, didn't need a translation.

Anna murmured, "Give her the papers."

I drew the forms from my pocket. "What are you going to do?"

She tossed them down a flight of grimy stairs, then said, "Oo ank. No gewho areyou or antyou at. Eave you, right?"

Giannis looked at me. "Did you get . . ."

Anna said, "I think she wants us to leave."

She nodded, motioned the way we'd come. "Right—go."

"I understand," I said.

She relaxed. "Understan. Right. Eave you, go."

"I understand," I said again. "You want us to leave, don't you? Right?"

"Eave, es. Go—right."

"No."

She glanced at Giannis and Anna. "Understan, you?"

"Yes, we understand," Giannis said, and to me, "Nikos, all right, let's . . ."

"No." To her, I said, "Those are ordinary forms with a dummy address, but I don't understand this. Fisherle is a shipping company . . ." She obviously wasn't following, so I said, "A woman at a Pnetian commune, the Lagone Community, told us . . ."

111

"Areyou Lagone?"

Giannis said, "What are you talking about? You went to a Pnetian commune?"

I waved him away, said, "Yeah, we're from Lagone. We found those at my uncle's house."

A pause, then she said, "Dett."

A chill on the back of my neck. "What?"

"Are-ese to Dett."

Giannis said, "He's dead."

"Oois? Dett?" She studied me, weapon still ready. "Yar oo?"

"What?"

"Yar oo?" She pointed to me. "Yar oo—youget Dett ow?"

"My uncle, he was our uncle." I paused, then said, "Father, mother, uncle. Understand?"

"Eliv?"

"Eliv? What's eliv?"

Eventually I discovered that 'eliv' was pigeon 'relative'. Leim'eners were too lazy to speak standard dialect. Still technically the same language, and they were less than 20 kilometers away—apparently Dett had worked at the real Fisherle warehouse in the northern shipyard: the largest, messiest Leim'en dock.

I spotted a horizontal bear at the base of the stairs: the black dog that had been all fangs and foam a moment ago. It waited patiently below. Probably a mimic: engineered way back when to bite and protect and reason, but not to bark. A customized pooch. That, or she'd trained it well.

The woman scribbled an address and said, "Onto afe. Nouldn't shoogo you."

"Yeah, all right," I said, and waved her gun away. "Well, we're going to leave now. Thank you."

Giannis murmured, "Do you know what she . . ."

"Of course not."

We started away, and she called after, "Yougo liwit Grotton."

Grotton.

I stopped. "What?"

She stiffened, gun no longer pointed at me. "Yougo . . ."

"Grotton," I said, "you said—you used his name. What does he have to do with . . ."

"Calm down." Giannis took my arm. "I've heard that: 'Go with the light of Grotton—with Grotton's light'. It's a phrase. He founded Leim'en."

"She said his name." And to the woman, "This is something—what does Grotton have to do with Dett?"

And the Black Room.

"It's okay." Anna took my hand. "It's nothing."

"I want to hear her say it."

"Eelyou . . ."

"Don't start that—you speak standard dialect, don't you?" My voice rose, "What the hell is going on here?"

"Nikos, she doesn't understand."

"She does."

The woman pointed her pistol at me again, clicked her tongue, and the dog crept up the stairs, growling.

"Eave you."

I glared. "Yeah."

"Eave . . ."

"Yeah, I heard you."

The dog nudged her legs, and she let it pass: empty brown eyes and bared pink gums over fangs.

"That's enough," Anna said. "We got what we came for."

"We didn't . . ."

"We got enough. Let's go."

We returned to the tram. Giannis slumped against the door, and Anna released a deep breath, as if she'd come up for air. The tram asked for a destination.

"Okay," Giannis said. "We're ready to go home."

"We have a warehouse address," I said.

"You're serious?" Giannis looked at Anna for support, didn't find any. "We have the name of a warehouse in a rundown section of the docks."

"We have to check it out."

"Why? What haven't you told me? Did you go to a Pnetian commune last night?"

I tried to think of a clever response, when Anna patted my leg: go ahead, he's here now. I was too tired to keep secrets, so I told him. Yes, we went to a Pnetian commune; yes, we found 'Fisherle' written on a crazywoman's wall; and yes, we'd both woken with synchronized night terrors.

"That's why you're not sleeping?" he said at last.

"I promise I'll sleep tonight," I said. Or in five minutes if we didn't get moving.

"Why didn't you tell me?"

"I just did."

"Nikos . . ."

Out with it. I told him about Elena's suicide message and Dett's note. Then, before he could respond, I gave the tram the warehouse name, and we lurched forward.

Anna watched the neighborhood get worse. "Next time, you two come get me. I'll wait in the tram."

* * *

Paper-mache deities guarded the six corners of the intersection of Main Street, Fisher and Bar'ring-More' Road. Cargo trams honked and took turns at the crossroads, and our ride stopped.

"This is it?" Giannis said.

I studied the purple fish-head god and seagull god and crab-claw-shrimp god of the intersection: they were planted in nooks two stories up on the outer walls of the adjacent buildings—crossroad shrines.

"That's the Northern docks?" I said, nodding to half a kilometer of timber and iron storage directly ahead. "Where's the warehouse?"

The road was full of transports—not civilian trams. And a heavy green gate blocked the dock entrance, flanked by a pair of ugly security towers: the perimeter was surrounded by faded green fencing, rimmed with spools of razorwire. Hadn't even had razorwire at the space project. But the project wasn't in Leim'en, was it?

"You think it's in there?" Giannis asked.

I watched a heavy cargo-tram pass through the gap, watched the gate close again. Another transport got in line.

"I don't know."

Giannis tapped the tram switchboard. "It wants to go through that gate. They won't let us."

Anna asked, "Why can't we go around?"

I spoke into the tram speaker. "Go around."

We turned left, tracing the perimeter. Through the perimeter fence, we passed lots of tarped cargo lashed with black cords, a fleet of transports, and lines of identical warehouses. The Northern Docks were an organized sprawl of unclaimed, archaic junk.

As we moved north, activity stopped. I hadn't expected organized blocks of buildings in the docks, but after a few minutes, even the sporadic warehouses were dark with boarded windows, hunkering over vacant lots. The neighborhood on our left got worse too. Shops, offices, temples, and condos turned to 'Warning' signs and clusters of hand-carved deities on the stoops of apartment buildings.

"What is that?" Anna asked. "Why do they do that?"

"I think it means someone died," Giannis said.

"I've never seen that . . ."

"They don't do it in the City, just out here."

Where they're poor, I thought, and turned back to the Northern Docks: overgrown parking lots, half of a building that had probably collapsed in a quake and never been repaired. The barrier fence was pocked and ripped with holes.

I said, "Why would they guard one end so heavily, but leave openings like this?"

The tram stopped. It would have been extremely illegal to wire it to eavesdrop on our conversation, so I assumed we had arrived. I hopped out. Still half a kilometer from the shore, but the air smelled more strongly of salt and dead fish. I went to a man-sized hole in the perimeter fence. Beyond: a parking lot and ten-meter pile of rotting wood.

"You want to just wander around in there?" Giannis called after me. He followed, and Anna locked the doors.

I didn't answer, stepped through the fence-tear, and started across the open lot. Funny that there was this much wasted space. Leim'en was one of the most crammed cities in the world—and here they'd left . . .

A little mound of wood and plastic deities: most fish or birds.

I walked around it, heard Giannis mumbling curses as he followed. Uneven, cracked pavement led to the shell of a warehouse. A faded line on the ground said, '1350 Tidal Flow'. Two-hundred years ago, the water was here, I thought, and I waited for Giannis.

"So," he said. "Is that it? I don't see a 'Fisherle' sign."

I pointed to a moldy board propped against the front door. The words 'Fisherle Shipping' were faded, but not gone.

Giannis repressed a smile. "Good—then we can go, right?"

We walked around the ruined warehouse—piles of ruined plaster and broken bricks—and went to another lot of forgotten ore and timber shipments.

"I realize that she's the first Shan I've seen—you know, talked to," Giannis was saying.

"I don't think she's typical."

"What do you mean?"

"I mean she's an archaeologist, not a soldier, for one."

"Not every Shan is a . . ."

"I know, but she still has that blunt, sort of 'do as I say' mentality."

"I didn't think so."

We wandered around a cluster of abandoned concrete blocks: like old barracks or temples or both.

I said, "So?"

"What?"

"So she's the first Shan you've seen. Do I need to spray you with a hose?"

"What are you talking about?"

"Oh come on, at the restaurant you were all over her."

"I wasn't," he said, put his hands in his pockets. Sharp wind funneled around the crags and cracks in the empty dockyard. "I thought you were."

"I was what?" I said.

"Were going after her . . ."

"*Going after her?* Elena's rites were just—and you think I'm . . ."

"Hey, calm down. Obviously you're not."

"No."

"Okay," he said. "Would it be—I shouldn't call her, should I?"

"She's sitting in the tram."

"You know what I mean," he said.

"I'm just—nevermind. I'm just thinking out loud."

"Go ahead," I said. "Why not?" And thought, You have a one in ten chance to make babies that will live to full-term. "She's Shan."

"You're right," he said.

"Of course I am. You know what that would be like to try to make anything work? She has to go back."

"You're right," he said again. "I know you're right."

We stopped at a boarded building marked *'Depot Stop 118-B6'*. Someone had painted over the sign: *'Saldet H'se'*.

Giannis said, "You don't speak Leim'en, do . . ."

"No."

"Why'd that lady send us here?"

"I said the magic word."

"I don't remember that. What word?"

"Lagone."

The front door was open. All the other buildings we'd seen were locked, long-since condemned. Someone had charted chalk circles and streaky diagrams on the entryway floor.

I frowned. "Smell that?"

"What—piss? Yes, I smell it."

"No, it's like *money*."

"What?" But he followed me in. "You're right."

The air had a sharp, metallic taste, as if I were inhaling a handful of coins. We picked our way through barren plaster hallways with more scrawls on the ground: like engineering notes before a pipeline installation.

What is this? We searched the single-story building. Yeah, it had probably been an office full of clerks and filing cabinets once, now empty. Giannis turned back to the entrance, but I went in the other direction, following the chalk marks. He complained—I told him not to start with me. I would be done in a minute.

The scrawls led to a backdoor and beyond—washed-out in the parking lot—to a paralyzed cargo tram. They'd stripped its wheels and mounted the rusty monster on concrete blocks. The interior was piled with blankets and old garbage. Not garbage, I told myself, someone's home. So why was the money-smell stronger out here?

Movement in the tram.

I froze, and Giannis walked closer, oblivious. Most of the tram-windows had been blasted out, leaving jagged teeth around the edges, in the window-hole corners.

"Hey . . ." I murmured.

Giannis leaned against the tram. He still hadn't noticed the half-covered person on the inside.

"Strange that it smells out here," he said. "Don't you think? Maybe there's a mint nearby . . ."

The tram-person jolted up, rushed to the cargo-door. "Doan whack?" he shouted.

Giannis jumped back. "I'm sorry . . ."

"What do you want?" the tram-man said.

At least he could switch out of gibberish. A gray beard and swollen eyes, but the guy wasn't as dirty as I'd expected. He wore an untucked merchant-suit—with the loopy black neck-tie—and pair of unpolished Leim'en boots. Expensive. Of course, just because he was wearing them didn't mean . . .

"Or should I go back to gutter-talk? You understand dome-speak?"

Giannis: "We're . . ."

I said, "Yeah."

Dome-speak: the Capital dialect. Standard Merr'in. The same dialect they'd been using since the Merr standardized it 1,200 years ago.

"Then what do you want?"

He still had the accent: the Leim'en rush to get sentences out as quickly as possible that had chopped their version of the language into a mess of hyphens.

I said, "What are those marks inside?"

"Chalk marks?"

"Yeah."

"Who—what do you care?" He shook his head as if he couldn't believe I wasn't cowering in fear. I spotted a home-made knife in his right hand, half-concealed behind his back. The blade was a curl of broken glass with a cloth handle.

Giannis said, "Do you know anyone named Dett?"

"What? Dett?"

"Yes . . ."

"No."

"What's that smell?" Giannis asked.

The bum tensed—finally Giannis saw the glass-blade, he fell back—and the bum said, "Don't need you here—leave."

"We're from the Lagone community. A Leim'en woman with a big black dog told us to come here," I said.

The bum hesitated. "What—she did?"

"Yeah, you know who I'm . . ."

"No."

Which means 'yes', I thought. "The woman with the dog paid us off—we're to report for Lagone."

When I paused, the bum said, "Why's the Prophet need you?"

"We're here to report . . ."

"Heard you. Lagone ships its own stock—do you do?"

What do we do? Fair question. "Well, the Prophet can't very well come to investigate himself, can he?"

The bum wasn't impressed. "Sure he can."

He tensed, just like the dog. He could smell that something wasn't right. He asked, "What do you want?"

"We need to see the shipments," I said and thought about it. Were they smuggling Shan artifacts? "They're with Grotton, right?"

That did it, but he pointed his knife at Giannis. "You have a story too, like?"

Giannis frowned. "What?"

"You're the same?"

"Yes. We both . . ."

"You're both from Lagone?"

Before Giannis could screw up, I said, "Yeah. Can you show us?"

He nodded, hopped back in the tram, then popped open a trap door, hanging upside-down to touch the concrete below the tram-belly: too low to crawl under. A child might have a shot.

Giannis murmured, "Do you know what . . ."

"No."

"Just checking."

"Yeah."

We waited for a long moment while the bum scraped and clicked below the tram, and then he returned to the open doorway. "Okay."

We followed him in. The money-smell mixed with hashish and a strong lilac perfume in the cluttered tram-home. A square trap door—one meter by one meter—opened in the middle of the floor, and below, an oily rug had been rolled aside and a round submersible-esque door opened on the concrete to expose a narrow, circular hole.

Another hole.

The bum waited: we were supposed to be expecting this.

"Okay," I said.

Giannis crouched. "Do you have a light?"

"Didn't bring one?" the bum said.

"We assumed you would have one," Giannis said. He was enjoying this.

The bum found a crusty oil lamp and a tiny electric switch-on. I took the electric. Giannis dropped both legs through the floor-hole, eased closer—the bum caught his shoulder.

"What . . ."

"Rope," the bum said, "it's not far, but'll crack your leg, and no other way back up."

I hadn't noticed the plastic rope-feeder attached to the wall nearby. Too much garbage. He dragged a length of knotted rope out, offered us metal clips—luckily we'd worn belts—then tossed the rope-end into the pit. It thumped, not far.

Giannis gave me a 'What are we about to do' look, and I pulled taut on the rope, as if I were testing the feeder.

I asked, "How long since she was here?"

"Don't know, few months."

"Mm." Tried to think of something else to say, some way to ask what we would find at the bottom without actually asking what we would find at the bottom. This didn't feel like black market Shan artifacts.

"Do you want to go first?" Giannis asked.

I thought, Do I look like a walking penis, of course I don't want to go first. The gods only know what—and said, "Yeah."

I took the rope, dangled my legs in the hole and slipped the electric into a side pocket. Oil lamp too awkward, but this bulb wouldn't give me much light. Something occurred to me.

"Giannis?"

"Yes?"

"Spot me."

A moment, and he understood: don't come down. Don't leave this bum and his glass knife with our rope.

"Okay," he said.

To the bum: "How far down?"

"Not too."

I nodded, clicked the belt-clip from my belt to rope, then started climbing. I scraped my hands and tore the knees of my pants on the lip of the shaft, twirled and banged the back of my left leg. Above, Giannis watched through a circle cut-out of dim light.

"What do you see?" he called.

"You."

"What?"

"Nothing."

". . . can't hear you. It's probably a sound vacuum."

Sound vacuum. As I dropped, the money-smell saturated the air: I imagined clouds and tracer-trails of coin dust swirling around me. Darker now, and then I clomped on a pile of loose rope. Ten meters up, Giannis watched through the surface-hole.

"Nikos? What do you see?"

"Hold on," I said and took out my miniature bulb.

"What?"

A pin-prick spray of light, as if I'd hooked a glowfly to a tiny generator. The walls were veiny yellow and rust-orange: copper. The money smell.

This hole, this was . . .

"Can you see anything?"

Part of a copper mine. Black markings up and down the walls, hedged with illegible abbreviations. What do you know about that—copper mines in Leim'en. What was I supposed to find down here, boxes of Shan shark teeth? A narrow tunnel behind me, streaked with more old lines and dashes. No, not old. The chalk marks in the house on the surface—this tunnel couldn't be too old. Twenty years maybe. Then why wasn't it . . ?

I followed the tunnel, stopped at a pile of lamps and half-empty water bottles. The bum left supplies down here. The tunnel abruptly widened, and five meters beyond it opened into a cavern four meters high, but too long and wide for my light. This wasn't part of a copper mine.

The ground: loose stone, mixed with dirt. A free-standing temple was planted in the middle, with a peaked roof and buttressed, leaning walls. An old style, and it was all stone. Low doorway. Supposedly people had been shorter in the past, or maybe it was just easier to build for tiny people.

The temple was one circular room with a detailed sarcophagus built into the rear wall. No trophies or money or—all looted, of course. I drew closer. The air was tighter. Not much ventilation, and it might have been my imagination, but it was harder to breath and when I did I tasted mold and ancient incense. The figure on the sarcophagus was a bearded, bald man in a black merchant-suit—the old kind with the wavy collars and wide sleeves—with both arms crossed on his chest, over a white hook. I'd seen that hook before. Now that didn't make sense. How old was this and who was:

Melus'h Vont' Sakes'i'sh Grotton

Grotton. This was—couldn't be—Grotton. The long-dead explorer-merchant-trader-whatever-the-hell who had founded Leim'en thousands of years ago. Grotton, and he was holding a white hook. A tooth from some animal only found on . . .

Behind me, a shout: "No—gods!"

Giannis's voice, and I sprinted back into the tunnel: shouting above, then a sudden crash. Back at the entrance, Giannis lay on a pile of rope, his right leg twisted backwards. Eyes closed, he took deep, red-cheeked breathes, as if he were fighting back anger.

I said, "What . . ."

Dog barking: something nicked my left ear. The dog-woman and the bum stood overhead. She'd just chucked a glass shard at me, and her dog 'roofed' in the background.

"Ityou nofire!" she shouted, and a shiny blade chicked the wall, past my face.

I grabbed Giannis's armpit, yanked him up, and his fingers snapped to stop me. He yelped as his leg dragged.

"Ah—let go! Let go!"

I kept my grip, dragged him into the tunnel, and a glass-blade bounced past. Why wasn't she shooting?

"Uckin yill—godsear!"

"Screw you too!" I shouted back.

". . . me down, put me down!"

I propped him against the wall, said, "What—did she . . ."

"Just showed up. She told him we weren't from Lagone. I don't even know what we're doing. What can possibly be so—why is this so important?"

"Just lie back. Is it . . ."

"It's not broken," he said. "So what if Dett smuggled Shan relics, why the hell should we care?"

"Yie et! Godsea . . ."

"Shut up!" I shouted back.

"She can't hear you," Giannis said, and he took a few careful breaths. "Get me a long piece of wood or stone, break-off some of that rope."

"Your leg's twisted . . ."

"I know. Go on."

I hauled the rope-coils into the tunnel, overhead something groaned—darkness—then a click-snap, and we were locked in. I held my light between my teeth.

"Do'n 'ave 'or 'igh 'o 'ou?"

"What?" Giannis pressed his leg with both hands. "Don't start talking like . . ."

123

I spit out the light. "Don't have your light, do you?"

"No."

"Here." I left him the rope, went deeper. "Be right back." I returned with two long chunks of stone, a rotten board, two oil lamps, and water bottles.

"What's all that?"

"They left it down here."

"They-who?"

"Don't know, probably the bum and dog-lady. You're sure it's not broken?"

He nodded, took the stone pieces. "I think so. Here . . ." He wound an elaborate brace around his dislocated leg, handed the rope to me, supporting it behind his thigh with a piece of stone. If we pulled at the same time . . .

"No, I'm not going to . . ."

"Nikos—I know how to do this."

"They teach you survival procedures?"

"Yes. Now hold the rope."

I did. He slowly stood on one leg, positioning the brace in an awkward cradle. When he dropped, the momentum—so long as I held the rope— would pop his leg back into place.

"You're sure this . . ."

"It should," he said. "Just hold it—don't pull. Let my weight . . . my weight will snap it back."

"It'll hurt."

He gave me a 'I swear to the gods . . .' look. "Yes, Nikos, it will."

"But it'll . . ."

"Quiet."

He took a breath, closed his eyes.

"Giannis . . ."

Dok.

"Gods!" he shouted, but his leg was facing the right direction. Sweat in Giannis's forehead, and he squeezed my palm hard, laughing. "Gods, I didn't know—if I had known how much that would hurt . . ."

"You all right?"

He massaged his leg. "Oh . . . I think I am."

"Can you walk?"

"Just a minute . . ."

When he'd recovered, we lit the oil lamps, and he limped after me into the Grotton-cavern.

"This is . . ."

I showed him the tomb.

"That's the thing we saw at Dett's house. What did she say it was?"

"A tooth," I said, "from Shan."

"So this is a fake?"

"I don't know."

Giannis nodded, stepped out of the temple, back into the cavern. We didn't need to say it. If this was Grotton's tomb, how in the gods' names could he be holding a Shan tooth millennia before Amith knew Shan existed?

"What do you think?" Giannis said. He wasn't talking about the tomb: we had more immediate concerns. I followed Giannis around the cave perimeter. Solid rock. When we were back where we'd started, I said, "Okay, have to find a way to go up."

"Up? You mean back up the . . ."

"Yeah. If it's locked at the top—doesn't matter. That's the only way down here. Have to get through that metal door."

"How?"

I glared at the tunnel that led back to the surface shaft. "There has to be a way . . ."

"How?"

"I don't know, Giannis. We'll figure something out. It's sitting under an old tram—this isn't a Republican lock, it's a street-bolt, a clunker. Means we might be able to just break it off."

"If we get to the top."

I was already getting tired of this cavern. "Yeah—we don't have a choice, we have to go back that way."

"All right . . ."

The room shook. I dropped my lantern—it smashed, and Giannis went down, but his lantern didn't go out. He was cursing, and I fell into the tomb-doorway: I'd once heard that in big Leim'en quakes, doorways tended to survive—the tunnel collapsed. It fell in a boom of rock that sprayed over Giannis, and bits of the ceiling snapped—stalactites exploded like natural spears, pummeling holes in the floor.

"....out of ..."

I shouted, "Come here! The doorway!"

CHAPTER ELEVEN

His Lives of One-Half

It stopped.

Pebbles continued to drop, like light hail, and Giannis brushed the debris away.

I said, "Are you . . ."

"I'm fine," he said, more frustrated than injured. "That didn't just—what do we do?"

I stared at my broken lantern, thought about the water bottles I'd left in the tunnel: the tunnel was a heavy rock wall. No way to go through it without a wheelbarrow full of dynamite now, which we didn't have and which would probably just collapse the rest of the cave anyway.

"Nikos?"

I remained in the doorway.

"Nikos, what . . ."

"How should I know?" Giannis took a patient breath, started limping around the exterior again. I said, "What? I'm supposed to know how to deal with this?"

"You brought us here."

"I didn't *bring us here*. We came here to look for . . ."

"We wouldn't have come here if you hadn't—it doesn't matter. We have to get out. You left the water in the hall."

"Yeah, I know that."

"And now it's . . ."

"I *know*." I stepped out of the tomb, and Giannis returned to me.

"Well, we're stuck," he said. "There's no way out."

"You looked all . . ."

"I looked, there's no way out," he said again. "We're stuck down here."

"And that's my fault?"

"You wanted to come here."

"Stop it." I went back to the tomb entrance. Think this through. There's a way out, we're not going to die down here. A cave with a temple in the middle of it.

I checked the walls. "Did any of the stalactites break through the floor? Maybe there's . . ."

"There isn't," he said. "I looked."

"Well maybe you should look again. We're going to be down here for awhile."

"Why?"

"What else are you doing? Gods, Giannis, you sound like . . ."

"I don't want to die in this cave."

"Stop being so dramatic, we're not going to . . ."

"Do you see a way out? We're trapped down here, and the only people who know we're here locked us in."

"I get it," I said. He was right: no way out. Some of the ceiling rocks had cracked the floor—the temple-tomb tilted now—but they hadn't smashed through to anything. Maybe nowhere to go even if they'd punched the floor a little harder. Solid rock under us. And above us. And . . .

"How's your leg?"

He shrugged. "It's fine."

"Saw part of that tunnel—almost looked like it got you."

"It didn't."

"Yeah."

He motioned to my broken lamp. "You dropped it?"

"Yeah."

Giannis dimmed his light to conserve oil, then held it up between us. "How much do you think is left?"

I didn't want to think about that. "I don't know."

"It's just dribbles," he said. "Around the bottom, see? Not much." He was right, I didn't say anything, and he said, "Couple of hours."

And then darkness. No. I reached for my electric bulb—not in my pocket. I checked the others.

"What's wrong?" he said.

"My light . . ."

"You lost the electric?" He said it as if I'd pissed on the floor. And I might pretty soon.

"No . . ." But I didn't have it. I checked the doorway, the cavern floor. "Here, bring that in here . . ."

He lit the tomb interior. "There."

I found it at the base of the sarcophagus. "See, now . . ." It didn't work. I banged it against the wall, didn't help.

"What's wrong?"

"Doesn't . . ."

"It's broken? Give it to me." He tested it, then handed it back. "So we have a few hours of light left."

As he limped back into the cavern, I sat on the edge of the sarcophagus, rubbed my face, and tried not to wonder how long the air would last. Yeah. Worry about the lantern, not breathing.

Giannis called, "Should I turn it off?"

I didn't get up. "What?"

"The light, should I . . ."

"No."

"We shouldn't have come here."

Really? I went to sit beside him. The tomb slouched to the side, another quake or a shove might topple it; better to be out here.

I said, "Yeah." Suddenly, we really were about to die.

Giannis adjusted the lantern. "I'm going to turn it off."

Why not? Another quake—a noise—and we would be happy to have the light. No escape right now. He turned the dial, I closed my eyes.

"There are no crates," I said.

"What?"

"I thought we'd find something." Maybe Dett and Elena were Pnetians, and Elena had wanted to die in the ship. There was nothing here. They were all nuts: Kysa, Dett, and my Elena.

"The Fisherle papers didn't lead here," Giannis said.

"Yeah, they did. The dog-woman . . ."

". . . was setting us up."

"Giannis, I've seen 'Grotton' written too many times in the past day . . . they were using his tomb to store or move or do something with something. Grotton disappeared, nobody knows where he's buried."

"Right over there."

"Yeah, I know."

"There's nothing down here." He paused. "Do you think she's still in the tram?"

"Probably."

"Maybe she'll get help."

"I don't—let's talk about something else."

I tried my comm, it didn't work. So we didn't speak. Finally, I said, "You should go back to work. I mean, when we get out."

"I don't think I want to be a doctor anymore."

"No?"

"No."

"Okay," I said. "What are you going to do?"

"I was thinking I'd do what you did. Get married."

"That's not a career." Unless she dies, I thought, and a cold tumor formed in my stomach. I was going to be sick. "I'm sorry we came down here."

"Me too," he said. "Anna will get help."

"Yeah."

I kept my eyes closed, no need to see how dark it was. We sat in silence for a long time.

"Nikos?"

"Yeah?"

"Wake up, it's 7:28."

"What?" I blinked: in my bedroom, and Elena stood in the doorway. She was rapping on the doorframe with the back of her hand. It was too early for that. But I'd been in a tomb under Leim'en, and Elena was dead.

She smiled. "I'm sorry I kept you up with my tossing and turning."

I squeezed the back of my arm: it pinched. Not real, you fell asleep in the tomb. Elena's hair was cut too short, and she had a runner's body. She should have been pretty, but there were purple circles under her eyes, and the way she avoided my stare meant we'd fought last night. I didn't really remember.

"I'm not going today," she said.

Not going—the project; today is her launch. I had dreamed it. It would be fine, of course it would.

"Then why did you wake me up?"

"I'm hungry," she said.

"So eat something."

"We don't have anything, I want to go out." She flipped the bedroom light on. "Come on, get up."

"You're not going?" I said.

"I told you."

"You spent two years training for this."

"I don't care," she said.

"You beat out a hundred other . . ."

"I'm not going."

"Have you told them? Did you call the Director?"

She went into the kitchen. "I will later." I heard her opening cabinets, slamming them too hard. "I'm very hungry, Nikos."

I got up and watched her from the doorway.

"Why aren't you getting dressed?" she said.

"You have to go."

"I don't have to. I woke up with a bad feeling about it."

I went to her, and Elena started pacing. She knew what was going to happen, had planned this all along as an elaborate suicide, but now she had doubts. Still, she wouldn't look at me. "Please get dressed."

"Will you calm down?"

"What's wrong with you?" she said and forced a cold laugh. "I thought rest would make you less obnoxious. I guess you weren't just tired last night."

"Did you take your pills yesterday?"

She stopped. "Shut up."

"Did you?"

"Yes, I took them. Gods, you always do this. If I feel the slightest bit off, you want me to take more drugs so you don't have to deal with it."

"They told you about this: it's perfectly normal to feel nervous before your first flight."

"You're not the one going up."

"Yeah, I know."

"So don't tell me about feeling nervous."

"Elena . . ."

"Elena." She bunched her face into an ugly frown, mimicking me. *"If you just took your pills everything would be fine, Elena."*

"Do you want me to call?"

"No," she said. "I'm hungry, I want you to get dressed."

"You can't just not show up . . ."

"I have a bad feeling, okay?" She met my stare, ready to cry. "Please don't make me go. Don't make me go up there, Nikos."

I guided her to the couch. "It's okay."

"I don't want to go."

I couldn't stop her trembling, so I said, "They went over it, there's nothing to be afraid of."

"Don't make me go . . ."

"Elena, you have to. We've spent two years getting ready for this."

"I'm hungry."

She had become a small child. I said, "You can't eat before the flight, you know that."

"I'm just . . ." She slipped away from me and covered her face with both hands. She used to let me see her cry. "If anything happens . . ."

"Nothing's going to happen. You know that, just up and back down."

". . . it's your fault. I don't want to do this."

Dett's letter had gotten to her. That's why she was crying.

"Come on, let's get ready."

If anything happens, it's my fault. The muscles in my gut clenched.

"Nikos!"

I sat up fast, and my gray-black vision spotted. Giannis was squeezing my shoulder. Still in the cavern.

"Are you all right?" he said.

I was panting, shaking with adrenaline, both fists balled tightly.

"Hey," Giannis said, "did you . . ."

"I can see." 'See' wasn't the right word, but the cavern was more than solid black, as it should have been. Gray-green dust drifted. Giannis's outline was a humanoid smudge. This was what I imagined the deep sea looked like at night.

"You're right," he said, as if he hadn't noticed. "Our eyes have adjusted."

"Our eyes can't adjust." I stood, one hand to the wall. "There's no light down here. We shouldn't be able to see anything."

"You were screaming," he said.

"What?"

"Did you fall asleep?"

I tried to forget the dream. No need to replay that last morning. She had blamed me, and now that she was in an urn somewhere, she still blamed me. But it was her suicide all along.

"Nikos?"

"Yeah, it's okay."

"Was it about the room?"

"No." I didn't need a Black Room to keep me awake. "It's fine." I forced myself to calm down, back in control. "It's brighter over there." I pointed to the tomb. "Look."

We crept in. Not my imagination, it was brighter in here.

I said, "Get the lantern, but don't light it yet."

He did, and I fingered the baseline of the sarcophagus-stand: two opposite corners had been exposed. The quake had skewed the sarcophagus.

"This is wood," I said.

"That doesn't make sense."

"It's wood," I said again and knocked on the corner of the six-foot rectangle that had been under the sarcophagus.

"How could it support the coffin?"

"It wasn't," I said. "Was resting on the edges." I checked the cavern again. "I think the light's coming from the cracks in the wood."

"Are you sure? It's too dark, how can you tell?"

No reason to debate this, so I nodded to the displaced sarcophagus. "Help me move it."

"What? It's too heavy, we won't be able to . . ."

"Turn on the light and help me move it."

He hesitated. "We don't have much oil left."

"We have to see if we're going to do this, don't we? Now turn it on."

He set the lantern in the tomb doorway, turned it on, and hobbled beside me. If we heaved at the top—it couldn't be more than a hundred kilograms . . . heavy, but not impossible.

"Ready?" I braced beside the box, and Giannis winced as he sidled alongside me. "How's your leg?"

"It's fine. Are we ready?"

"Yeah—push."

We heaved, and the sarcophagus scraped its stone and wood base, grinding like an old-fashioned wheat mill.

I grunted. "Harder . . . come on, push . . ."

It tipped on its side, and the elaborate lid cracked in half, fell away from the box. I went to look inside.

Giannis said, "What's he look like?"

"I don't know."

"What?"

"He's not here."

He came to see: the sarcophagus was empty.

"That was anti-climatic."

I grabbed a heavy sarcophagus-block with a triangle-point, then knelt over the wood square.

Giannis said, "You're just going to bash it in?"

"Sure." I smashed the wood—it cracked, again, and on the third try the old boards crashed through. I kicked out the edges: a crawl-space lined with tin, meter-high cylinders. Most had lids, but someone had forgotten to cover the nearest one. It was filled with yellow-green sand.

Giannis watched over my shoulder. "That looks like . . ."

"Yeah."

"Is that glauston?"

I sat on the edge of the hole, one foot on a cylinder. This wasn't a way out, it was a glauston-cellar. Glauston: glowstone.

"Looks that way," I said.

"Don't get so close."

"Why not?"

"It can make you sick." I started to respond, and he said, "I'm not joking. People die from glauston poisoning."

"I wasn't planning to eat it."

"You don't have to, you just have to be near it. Come on, get away from there."

I didn't. "What do people use it for?"

"It can be synthesized for things like x-rays. They're trying to build a power plant near Nerbet."

I'd skipped science classes whenever I could at the Academy. "A glauston power plant?"

"Yes, I don't know how it works, but you can spin it or something to make energy."

"You're making that up."

"I'm not, now will you get away from it, please?"

"Yeah." But I leaned over the edge to see just how long the glauston-tunnel was. "Bring the lantern over here."

"Don't do that," he said. "Nikos . . ."

"There's something else down there, give me the light."

He did, and I slipped down, using the lantern to check both ways. The glauston-cylinders lined the walls, blocking narrow shelves. And yeah, those were skeletons behind them, wearing clumps of rotting suits in the niches. To the left, the tunnel disappeared into black; to the right, someone had arranged a pyramid of unlit candles and stone deities, and the tunnel ended at a distant wall. I studied the shrine. A segmented half-circle was carved into the floor, near the words:

Save us from doubt in our time of need,
Be light in Grotton's sacred room,
Our world is a dream of a dream,
That must come to fire and dust.

Beyond the shrine, it was brighter, and there were no glowing cylinders at the dead end. I crawled to the right.

"What are you doing?" Giannis called. "Stop—where are you going?"

"I smell the ocean."

"We can't just go crawling around randomly."

"Get down here."

He protested for another moment, then dropped behind me.

"Okay," he said, "you're right." He noticed the shrine. "Did you see this?"

"Yeah. What's wrong?"

"Nothing." But Giannis was staring at the prayer and segmented half-circle.

I read the words again. 'Grotton's sacred room' could mean anything, I told myself. 'Be light' implied that the room was dark—enough. "Let's go."

Half-blind in the swinging lantern-glow, I led the way. Huffing and groaning, Giannis crawled after me.

Then he stopped. "We have to get away from these cylinders, we shouldn't be down here."

I motioned to the dead end. "Look, it's brighter there, do you see that? There's light behind that wall."

"Nikos, I'm not going to just follow you . . ."

"What's your problem? I understand the leg, but what is this?"

He tensed. "What?"

"Don't—everything's an argument. You want to die in that cave, then go back."

"You're an asshole, you know that?"

"Yeah, and you sacrificed the world of medicine to help me."

"No, I'm here because you dragged me here so you wouldn't have to go home to an empty house."

We stared at each other. My younger brother, Giannis had probably always wanted to vent—to whine about how he was seconded by our father. Resented me for—what?

I said quietly, "You think this is the place to do this?"

He smiled uncomfortably. "I could hit you with a skeleton femur . . ."

I didn't smile back. "Come on."

We crawled in silence. Eventually we searched a wall marked with itty-bitty carvings. I pushed the lantern closer: it was a curly, ornate version of early-modern Merr'in. Much older than the shrine-prayer, this inscription might have been written just after Grotton's time:

'ter drkess,
Wll b'gode 'nd aloe justt
to' rckone Hostos 'nd
hiss lives ofe one-hlfe.

Vont' Melus'h

I read it again. Vont' Melus'h—the same title I'd seen on a piece of broken statuary upstairs. A moment, and I understood the inscription, "After darkness, will be good and also just to reckon Hostos and his lives of one-half."

Giannis: "That's what it says?"

"Yeah."

"What's—who wrote it?"

"Vont' Melus'h."

A pause, he edged closer. "Gods . . ."

"Yeah."

Vont' Melus'h: it was signed by Grotton. *After darkness.* He wrote this or told someone else to write it or . . .

"This is here to . . ." I pressed my ear to the dirty stone. Sound—and it wasn't stone. "It's a false wall."

Giannis tested it, let out a nervous breath: maybe he would live long enough to awkwardly apologize. "Do you think they wrote on this wall to stop people from . . ."

"Yeah."

"So how should we . . ."

I curled around, braced on a skeleton-shelf, then stomped the wall with both legs. It broke in a dusty cloud and vacuum-rush of fresh air. Two meters down: boggy waves, and directly overhead a sheer ceiling of concrete that extended in every direction, pierced occasionally with pipes—like root systems from a jungle of steam-trees on the surface. I felt as if I were beneath a theater-stage, not under a forgotten patch of the Leim'en docks.

Giannis said, "If we'd been here at high tide . . ."

"Yeah."

We'd be drowning right now. Only question: how to get topside.

Giannis: "Does your comm have a signal?"

My comm. "You remember what it said?"

"Grotton's inscription?"

"Yeah." It had just dawned on me: I'd kicked the words into the harbor—no records.

"Something about considering Hostos's lives."

Half-lives, I thought. That's what it had said.

I called Anna.

She said, "Hello?"

"Are you still up there?"

"Nikos? Barcuc, I called the Leim'en police, but they won't come to this neighborhood. Are you okay? What happened?"

"We're fine, we're under the docks."

"What do you mean 'under'?"

CHAPTER TWELVE

Thirty Kilometers

I gave her the short version—without the dream, the glauston or Grotton—and when I finished she agreed to call the harbor watch to come get us.

When I clicked off, Giannis said, "You didn't tell her all of it."

"I want her to call for help. Do you have any idea how long I'd be on the comm if I'd gone into all of it?"

He didn't, so we waited for an hour until Anna paddled up in some kind of gondola-tugboat, steered by a hired pilot with only one arm. When we'd returned to the tram, I finally told her about Grotton.

She made the tram stop in the middle of a crowded Leim'en intersection. "We have to go back."

Giannis said, "That's not a good idea, they were armed."

"So? We'll buy some guns."

"You think you're back on Shan?" I said. "You can't just buy weapons here."

"I don't care. We'll hire people to protect us—we have to go back there, Nikos."

"No we don't."

We were being honked at from three different directions. Anna glared at me as if I'd just suggested Shan babies grew from rancid meat: son-of-a-bitch. "Why didn't you tell me earlier?"

"I just told you."

139

She told the tram to turn around.

"Anna . . ."

"If Grotton's tomb is really sitting down there . . ."

"We should go back to the Capital," Giannis said quietly.

"I just want to try," she said to me. "Please. Just a look at the inlay on the sarcophagus will tell me whether it's genuine . . . what?"

"That's not . . ." How to put it? "It broke."

"What—how?"

"We had to get out," I said.

Someone had gotten out of a tram behind us and was shouting as he approached the side door.

Giannis said, "I think we're blocking traffic."

Anna shook her head. "You broke the lid?"

"Yeah. That's how we got out, I told you . . ."

"Did you burn the body too—to light your way?"

"No."

"That's surprising."

"There wasn't a body, it was . . ."

Apparently that was my fault too. "What do you mean?"

"The coffin was empty."

A big cargo driver who looked like he might be half-ox, knocked on the door window, and Giannis cracked it down.

"Doan what?" the ox-guy shouted. "Iddleway godsear thoad!"

"Yes," Giannis said. "I'm sorry, we're trying . . ."

Anna ignored the commotion. "Barcuc Nikos, did you break the tomb building too or . . ." When I looked away—the earthquake, not me, but that probably wouldn't matter—she slumped on the seat. "Unbelievable."

"Ofay etou or tofthe oller!"

Anna glanced at the oxe-guy. "Get away from our tram."

Giannis: "Anna, you shouldn't . . ."

"Ousat what tu?"

"I said get the hell back!" Anna slammed one palm to the glass, and the oxe-guy instinctively jumped away. Giannis closed the window, and I grabbed the comm-speaker.

"Back to my house—take us back to my house."

Anna was shaking her head, as if we were really going to be in for it once our parents got home.

"Didn't either of you *think*?" she said at last.

As we left the traffic jam, I wanted to celebrate not being dead rather than respond to a scolding. So I let Giannis answer.

"Nikos is right," he said. "We needed a way out, and we followed the light to the sarcophagus."

"What light?" Giannis told her about the glauston, and she turned to me. "You didn't mention that."

I said, "Yeah, there was glauston."

"Do you understand?"

"What?"

"The shipments," she said, as if it were obvious. "Fisherle is smuggling glauston. Owning it is illegal, it's very dangerous."

"We don't know they're smuggling it," I said. "What?"

Anna was rooting in her pockets. She found her scrap of crazy-person notes. "'The Fire is Buried with Grotton'," she read. "'Fisherle brought it in, we will bring it down'. She knew."

I said, "Why would she call it 'the Fire', why wouldn't she say 'the glauston is buried with Grotton'? What do you build with glauston?"

"Bombs," Anna said.

That startled Giannis: he looked as if she'd just clapped her hands to wake him. Oh no.

He said, "You can't make bombs with glauston."

"You can make bombs with daium, and it's the same thing. I don't know exactly how, but they do it on Shan."

"They make glauston-bombs?" Giannis said.

"Yes," Anna said. "We have to tell someone, this is serious."

"Tell who?" I said.

"I don't know, your Senate?"

Giannis said, "What if someone in the Senate is smuggling it."

As much as I didn't want to, I understood. I sagged against the door. It wasn't—the Senate had committees and inspectors, all kinds of security measures to stop this from happening.

I said, "The bum on top of the tomb said the Pnetians came to check up on it."

Anna didn't understand. "The Pnetians? Like Lagone?"

"Yeah, that's how Kysa knew. And there was a shrine."

Giannis forced a smile. "You're kidding."

"Giannis . . ."

"Pnetians are looney, but they're harmless—why would they do this?"

"I don't know."

"You think the Pnetians run Fisherle, that they're smuggling glauston?" he said. *You think the world is shaped like a dildo?*

"I don't know," I said again, but that wasn't true. "Yes. And Dett knew. He drowned the day before Elena's flight—after he warned her."

"What?" Giannis said. "Now he was murdered or something?" He turned to Anna. "All right, so how bad would it be?"

"What do you mean?"

"A glauston-bomb, what's it like?" Anna shrugged, but she knew. Giannis saw it too. "Come on, what?"

"They've never been used in a war on Shan, they've only been tested."

I suddenly wished we hadn't come here, wished Elena *had* been screwing around. Let someone else deal with this. Giannis wanted more, so Anna told him.

"How large is your Capital, 15 kilometers across in the city proper, with the Senate in the center? The smaller bombs range about one kilometer, the larger ones are close to 30."

"What do you . . ."

"They explode, Giannis. They heat everything to several thousand degrees and blow it all away. And when they're gone, anything that's still alive gets daium sickness and rots."

Giannis was quiet for a long moment. "For 30 kilometers . . ?"

Anna took my hand. "Are you okay?"

"No."

"We have to tell someone," she said.

"We will, I just need to sleep. Oh, I should tell you before I forget . . ." I told her about the Grotton inscription I'd kicked into the harbor. "Does that mean anything, the half-lives of Hostos?"

Before Anna could respond, Giannis started talking about a lecture he'd once heard about how Hostos wasn't really a single person, but a code for the Merr secret police. Ignored him and thought about it:

And I have shown that the Ages must continue, all of them stretched but the last.

That sentence had bothered me before. There have been five ages, defined by those 15-year Hostos-generations.

. . . it totaled to roughly 245 generations of our short-lived.

Nervous-muscle tension in my chest. What had Anna said? How many years was that? I did the math: 3,670. 3,670 years after Hostos until the end of this Fifth Age. He'd been writing 6,470 years after history began. Which meant—what? I added it up, counting upside-down, from the beginning of time rather than in terms of how much we had left. This age was supposed to end in the year 10,140—in another 1,140 years, according to Hostos's 245 generations. What if they weren't 15 years long? It was obvious: he'd stressed it twice. I had assumed there would be a Sixth Age. The Sixth Age was a vague 'to be announced' time period . . . what if he'd meant this—the Fifth Age—would be the last?

What if all the rest were 'stretched' but ours?

Fifteen years—what if Fifth Age generations were only measured at seven and a half? Half-lives. The Fifth Age was supposed to last from the end of the Merr Dynasty to the end of our calendar: 1,840 years. Divided in half: about 900 years. Which would mean there are only another 200 years until the Republic falls and the Sixth Age begins.

That's what this is about? The end of the world is only 200 years away, not 1140? Hostos had just been a man—nevermind Giannis's lecture—how the hell would he have known any future dates? So what if an imaginary deadline changed by 900 years?

Anna stopped Giannis. She'd been scribbling figures on her scrap paper.

I said it first, "It means there are 200 years left."

They both looked at me. Giannis said, "How did you get that?"

"If the generations in the Fifth Age are only seven and a half years long . . ."

Anna: "What makes you say that?"

"The half-lives inscription . . ."

"It's more complicated than that." Giannis was ready to shout us down with another pointless story—to attract Anna's attention—when she said, "You can't just divide 15 by two."

Don't I feel stupid. "No?"

"No." The numbers on her paper were written in some Shan language, not Merr'n, and she said, "Hostos's generational predictions are all based on simple 15-year generations, but that doesn't mean that each is exactly 15 years long, it doesn't end at a wall the way our calendar says it does. The half-life of a generation is the age at which Contonus initiates were branded for the Sun: one month before their seventh birthday. If a child died before then, they would say he had lived not half his life, and if he died after . . ."

"So I was close?"

"What?"

"Seven and a half compared with a little under seven is close."

"Contonus changed with each age, they shifted with the 15-year cycles." I wasn't following, and she forced a smile. "Did you know all of this? Is this a joke?"

I thought about the segmented half-circle. What if the lines represented spokes, like a wheel? Like a calendar. "What—no. Why would you . . ."

"It's okay," she said, and her smile began to fade. "It's funny, and it's clever—that something this simple would change it like this."

Giannis didn't get it either. "Like what?" he said.

"It's all right," Anna said. "Just tell me how you figured this out."

I said, "We didn't figure anything out, I just told you what . . ."

"Stop it. You know what it means."

"I don't."

"You saw the glauston, you knew about the bombs, and you thought . . ."

"We didn't."

"Nikos . . ." She was angry. Pissed at me for frightening her. "If you're lying to me, I'm not going to . . ."

"What does it mean?"

"After today," she said, "it means we have—your calendar ends in five days."

*　*　*

Exhausted, we ate leturns: wheat pockets of greasy fish and white-salt sauce. They tasted better than they sounded, and as our tram retraced the four-lane highway into the Leim'en'a Mountains, the sun went down.

Anna and I slumped against one door, Giannis against the other.

"Where'd the day go?" he asked.

We spent it in a tomb, but I said, "I don't know."

Day Six is just about gone. Anna had explained her arithmetic three times, and I had finally pretended to understand how 'the half-lives of Hostos' meant we had six—almost five—days until the end of the Fifth Age.

The sky bruised, then blotted, and the mountains faded from green-brown to blue, then to dark silhouettes. A part of me rubbed his eyes and said that it was time for bed. The Elena-nap aside, I still hadn't slept.

"He could be wrong," I said at last. They both looked at me. "So what if a guy who died 2,000 years ago says the world is going to end in six days?"

Giannis said, "Five days."

"After today," Anna said.

"Yes, five full days," Giannis said.

I waited for an answer, and Anna said, "He's been right before."

"They changed his numbers after the fact. The Merr altered all of those texts 1,000 years ago."

"We don't know that," Anna said.

"It's the only thing that makes sense, isn't it? How could he predict anything before it happened?" We all knew the obvious line: Hostos was a prophet, the last in connection with the old gods, the Bialu. *They* showed him what was coming.

"I don't think we know either way," she said quietly.

"Very diplomatic."

"It just means the end of the Republic, doesn't it?" Giannis said.

Technically that was true, but here was the problem. If we ignored the Hostos-line that still bothered me—*and the beginning of another*—the scriptural calendar ended. Hostos and the other prophets had described, in cagey rhetoric, each of the past five ages. Not one discussed a Sixth Age, and that's what had Anna worried. Of course, to a cynic it made perfect sense.

Hostos and all the saints of whatever-the-hell were writing thousands of years ago, but their texts had probably been altered numerous times. Most recently, by the Merr and the founders of the Republic of New Amith. Why would the Senators attempt to describe anything beyond their Fifth Age? They wouldn't.

"Then why have a deadline at all?" Anna asked. "Why not say the Republic will last forever?" I didn't have an answer to that, and she said, "I don't think it's a coincidence that you found glauston with that inscription."

We stopped at a checkpoint, and soldiers checked out tram registration.

"I know," I said. "The Pnetians believe it."

"Maybe," she said. "It doesn't matter whether or not the text was changed."

Giannis got it too. "This is insane."

"So the Pnetians found the tomb a long time ago," I said, "and they calculated Hostos's date. They don't believe the gods will return on their own . . ."

Works are a part of salvation. The soldiers let us go, and we rolled through the roadblock.

Anna said, "That's my point."

Very simple, I thought. The Fifth Age was going to end in five days, with or without the gods. I looked out the back window, watched another tram stop at the checkpoint.

"They know too," I said.

They followed my stare, and Anna said, "How?"

"I don't know," I said. "But the Nine Laws passed before we'd even cremated Elena. They're rationing, setting up checkpoints, securing the Capitol . . ."

"This is crazy," Giannis said. "How can you be sure the Pnetians would have calculated the same number you did? They may think we have ten days left or two years."

"Dett's letter," I said. "The timing is right, and Elena's transcript . . ."

"We have to tell someone," Anna said.

Giannis: "Why would anyone believe this?"

I said, "We'll show them the tomb."

"And she's supposed to be gone. She didn't get an extension."

"Yeah." I'd forgotten about that. I was a kidnapper. Anna smiled and squeezed my arm.

"We'll figure it out," she said.

Before Giannis could panic, I said, "If you're right, the Senate knows already. And there should be more glauston, shouldn't there? The government isn't going to fall because of ten barrels buried under Leim'en."

"If they make a bomb it might," Anna said.

"Just one?" Giannis said. He still didn't believe the glauston horror stories. "How big would it be?"

"I don't know."

"Larger than this tram?"

"I don't know, I've never seen one."

As our tram drove through the outskirts of the Capital, we talked about Hostos and bombs and the end of the world. This was putting me in a good mood: nothing like positive reinforcements after a life-shattering tragedy. The Capital thickened into residential neighborhoods, and as Giannis tried to determine exactly how quickly we would die in a glauston blast, the tram stopped.

"What, where . . ."

"We're here," I said and hopped out. Anna followed me up the lawn.

"It's the middle of the night," Giannis called after me.

"Yeah—where's she going to go? The Senate took over her dig. They don't know where she is, and if they find her, she goes back to Shan."

Anna slipped her arm through mine. "Lower your voice."

"We have to sleep tonight—tomorrow we'll decide what to do: who to tell, where to start looking. If you want to go home, take the tram."

"I'm okay."

They waited on the front porch, while I searched for my keys.

"The Director assigned you to the dig," Giannis said. "He's on that Senate committee, isn't he?"

"Yeah." I found them in my left pocket. I still didn't understand why Kysa was sent to the dig or how this connected to the Black Room. Maybe it didn't.

"Doesn't the Director know where you live?"

I put the keys in the door—was unlocked.

Anna pulled me back. "Nikos . . ."

A heavy guy in body armor blocked my entryway hall. He looked bored, and only after the door had opened entirely did he stiffen and unholster a pistol. Giannis scrambled off the porch—the soldier didn't try to stop him—and I froze. Not frightened or even surprised, I watched as two more soldiers came up the sidewalk and cut off Giannis. One of them started screaming and waving a pyck at Giannis, as if he'd stumbled into an open-air market and she wanted to haggle. Giannis dropped onto his belly. I needed to cut the grass, it was getting high: Giannis almost disappeared into it.

"Raise your hands and step away from each other." We did, and the heavy soldier babbled jargon into his comm. Presumably, the target had been acquired.

Giannis was clearly terrified, and Anna looked as if she'd just swallowed a moldy egg, but I felt numb. Hadn't intended this, but I hadn't done much to prevent it, had I? We'd come right home.

They hustled us to a cargo tram three doors down. I don't know what I'd expected, but it hadn't been a lazy, overweight soldier in my living room. We were loaded onto benches in the back of the windowless tram with two of the soldiers. And just like that we were off.

"Where are we going?" Anna asked.

"No talking," the market soldier said.

I gave Anna a sarcastic 'you should know better than to ask that' look, but she wasn't in the mood. "I want to know who you are and where you're taking us."

The heavy soldier said, "We were dispatched by the Junior Consul."

"Are we under arrest?"

"I can't answer that."

The market soldier frowned. "That's enough, no more talking."

But I wanted to play along. "If we're not under arrest, can you hold us like . . ."

"Yes," the market soldier said.

"Good to know."

"I said 'no more talking'."

"And I said 'that's good to know.'" She twisted, and I was suddenly sprawled on the floor. The right side of my skull—just above the ear—was throbbing. My vision spotted. I blinked it away, sat up, and pressed a hand to my face. The market soldier kept her pistol drawn—she'd clobbered me with the butt. Nice.

Anna's knuckles were white on the bench, and Giannis was watching me, fists shaking.

The market soldier motioned back to my seat. "Sit down."

I pressed one palm to my swollen scalp and thought about clever retorts. But there was really no need to get pistol-whipped again, so I returned to the bench. She got her wish: we rode the rest of the way in silence. Finally, they ushered us out—into an alley behind one of the Capital buildings. I recognized the cobblestones and glass towers across the street.

We waited, Anna examined my head, and they walked us through a narrow, carpeted hall, down twisty stairs, to a waiting room with a receptionist and magazines.

Giannis asked, "Where are we?"

"One of the Senate annexes."

The market soldier raised her eyebrows at me, but I pretended not to notice.

Anna said, "Are you okay? How hard did she hit you?"

"It's fine."

"I told you it was a bad idea."

"What?"

"I should have gone back."

Giannis said, "What do you think they . . ."

"Okay," the market soldier said, and they guided us down a hall of bureaucrat-portrait lithographs, past a few fake plants, and finally into a conference room.

The long marble table was full of men in patterned togas—except two seats directly across from the Project Director. At the far end sat a grizzly man I knew was the Junior Consul. The rest were bureaucrats and Senators: I didn't recognize any of them, and Anna was the only woman. The soldiers shut the doors behind us, and the Director stood, pointed to the empty chairs.

"I'm sorry," he said, "we only planned for two." An aide went to get Giannis a chair. As Anna and I sat, the Director noticed my head. "What happened, are you all right?"

"Yeah . . ."

Anna said, "One of your soldiers did that on the way here."

"I'm sorry."

The Consul said, "That wasn't intended."

"What do you want?" she asked.

One of the Senators asked, "Why are you still here?"

I said, "That's my fault."

"I'm sorry?"

"Yeah, I kidnapped her."

Most of them weren't amused, but I scored a couple smiles.

Giannis got his chair, and the Director gave me a 'buddy' look. "You understand what would normally happen at this point, don't you Nikos?"

"This isn't normal?"

"No."

"Yeah, I guess it isn't."

The Consul leaned forward: he was accustomed to being the center of attention, and I was hogging it. "You, ma'am, are the last Shan on this planet—because of your *kidnapping*. You, Mr. Healy'll, and your brother, are subject to arrest. If you're convicted, you'll serve for 50 years."

Hmm. "That doesn't sound like kidnapping."

The Director said, "You stole documents, Nikos. About your wife."

Oh yeah. Giannis was shaking his head—the gods only knew at what— so I said, "Or what?"

The Consul frowned. "Or what?"

"What do you want? Why aren't we in prison?"

"We have a lot to discuss," the Director said.

"Like what?"

"You have to understand that we're on the verge of leading our first wave, really pioneering, the first successful flights. Unless we have an advocate like you, the Senate committee will never even allow a vote."

He was talking about the Project. Why was this so important? I thought about the comm room, the noise Elena had made. "You fixed it?"

"The *Melet*'s problems were just that. We're beyond the kind of basic breakdown we had in the past."

"You know I saw Elena's file—it wasn't the ship." I didn't want to argue about this. We should tell them about the glauston.

The Director remained calm. "It *was* the *Melet*, Nikos. How could you think it would be anything else?"

Biological, I thought. *We're* the problem: we're never meant to leave. It doesn't make sense, but that doesn't mean it isn't true.

He continued, "Years have gone into the new design, we have the best engineers—you know what we have to work with—and they're going to let the funding fall away."

The Consul was nodding. "Karto'u is blocking the vote."

Karto'u? The same Senator responsible for Kysa's job at the dig?

I said, "You're going to send up another one?"

The Director said, "We don't want to let this set a precedent . . ."

"Yes or no?"

"Yes. We are." He started up about the good of the project, the noble endeavor, the race against the Shan that—like it or not—was upon us, may the Gods bless the Senate and her . . .

Anna asked, "What's happening on Shan?"

"We don't know," the Director said.

One of the Senators muttered, "What do you expect?"

Anna turned to him. "What?"

The Senator looked at her as if she were a child. "Do you think your Ckish would deign to tell us what's happening?"

"Have you tried to find out . . ."

"Of course we have." He opened his mouth, and the Consul met his eye: *no.*

The Consul nodded to me. "We want a speech from you to the full Senate tomorrow. In exchange, you and your brother will be granted amnesty."

"What about Anna?"

His expression didn't change. "She's been liberated from her kidnappers and is free to fulfill her duties by returning to Shan."

"What do you want me to say?"

"You'll speak in support of the space project. You'll make it clear that it *must* be renewed. Do you understand?"

How the hell had the Lagone Prophet seen this coming? This speech would violate the deal I'd made to see Kysa. "Yeah."

"Good." He spoke quickly, as if he didn't have the patience for his own words. "We'll provide an escort and soldiers for your protection tonight."

"That's very generous of you."

"Yes, it is."

Giannis and I stood, but Anna didn't move.

"Senator Karto'u?" she said.

The Consul nodded. "Yes . . ?"

"He's blocking a vote on the space program?"

"That's right." The Consul shifted irritably. "Do you have something to say?"

"Why would he do that?"

The Senator said, "It's fairly obvious that . . ."

"We're finished with this conversation." The Consul gave Anna a patronizing look. "You can stay tonight under our protection. He'll do fine, we'll have talking points for him tomorrow. Once he's given his speech, it'll be safe for you to go back." He paused. "Thank you."

'Thank' could easily have been 'Screw'. Thank you too, I thought.

CHAPTER THIRTEEN

The Golden Wall

W e went back outside with the soldiers, and once our tram was moving, Giannis said, "I don't understand."

Anna sat between us, the prick-soldiers sat in another room this time.

"Karto'u is the one who assigned Kysa," I said.

"I'd heard of him before," she said. "He's been in the Senate for six terms. He runs several trade committees."

"So, he chairs trade committees—what does that have to do with anything?"

"His committees are import and site inspections."

Shit.

The tram bumped and turned a corner. Giannis said, "What does that mean?"

Anna put a hand on his shoulder. "Calm down, it's okay."

He slipped an arm around her, still shaken from the meeting. "What falls under import and site inspections?"

Anna was rubbing his arm the way she might console a frightened dog—why was it bothering me?

"What do you think?" I said.

They both looked up: I'd raised my voice.

Anna said, "Are you okay?"

"Yeah." And to Giannis, "You're a doctor, think about it. What would be in that category?"

"I don't know, Nikos."

"Dock warehouses in Leim'en."

Anna said, "You both need to calm down."

"Why didn't we tell them about the glauston?"

Giannis said, "I wasn't thinking about it."

"Neither was I," Anna said. "Why didn't you say something?"

"I don't know."

We sat in silence, and I had time to go over it again: the Pnetians smuggle glauston for a bomb. Out of religious fervor, they decide to blow-up the Republic. No—what about Karto'u? How can the Pnetians get away with all of this? Influence in the Senate, loosening the belt of committee regulation: bribing the inspectors? If they had an influential Senator they wouldn't need to worry about the inspectors, they could plan around them. Karto'u was the link.

"He's a Pnetian," I said at last.

Anna nodded. "He may be. But why do they care about the space project?"

I didn't have an answer. "What time is it?"

Giannis poked his comm. "3:30."

"In the morning?"

He smiled. "Of course."

"We're officially in the countdown." I massaged my face. "Gods, I need to sleep."

Without moving from Giannis, Anna patted my knee. "You kept me up, you know."

"What?"

"I never would have gone to Lagone if you hadn't talked me into it."

"Yeah, sorry about that."

"It's okay. Barcuc knows what's happening on Shan right now."

"He does, does He?"

Anna looked away. "Barcuc's a 'she'."

In other words, I deserved to be sitting by myself. Once I'd rested, I could focus on why the Pnetians wanted to kill the Space Project and where they might hide a bomb. Just too damn late, and I was too damn exhausted, and my head still hurt too damn much—the tram stopped.

The soldiers took posts at the front and back doors of my house, Anna collapsed on the couch, and I laid out a blanket for Giannis on the floor. Then, I stumbled into our—my—bedroom and without thinking about the piles of Elena-stuff that still cluttered it, I popped out my comm and plopped on the mattress.

My stomach growled. Ignore it. I tried, but it rumbled again. Fine: no need to sleep. That's fine. Probably some moldy fruit in the ice-box. Quietly, I went to check: ugly grapes, a mushy apple, but that pear didn't look too . . .

My comm rang.

I stared at it. A buzzing black dot on the counter. Who could be calling?

"Hello?"

"Nikos?"

Anna. I leaned around the corner: the living room was empty. No Anna, no Giannis. She sounded . . .

"What's wrong?"

"Thank you for answering. Did you talk to them? They're trying to reach us."

"Who?" There was blood on my right palm. Not mine.

She said, "Where are you?"

". . . home."

I followed a streak of brown-crimson from the kitchen walls to the living room and out—it led past the bedroom, into the incinerator. From here, I could see the open incinerator door, something was dripping from the ceiling. Not water—it looked like red paint.

"Nikos?"

"Yeah."

"Are you okay? I want to come over."

"Yeah."

"They want us to help them."

What? "Who . . ?"

"The people from another version of our world," she said.

I approached the incinerator, pressed open the door and it knocked against the shower door. Inside, the ceiling was dripping blood into an empty blackness on the floor. This was nothing like the moldy old box we'd found at the Wesler Estate, but somehow it was the same. The Black Room. If I stared long enough, I would go blind. I willed my eyes to find depth.

A voice rasped from the dark floor: *"Are you there?"*

"Yeah," I said.

"My name is Cardinal Giovanni Mercati. I am at Saint Michael's Door, calling to you on behalf of the Holy See and the leader. We are at war and in great danger. Can you help us?"

Didn't follow, but I said, "How?"

"Our worlds have been connected before, but not for a long time. We believe you have a weapon that can help us. You call it a bomb made of glow stone."

I looked away, saw the Black Room imprinted on my vision when I closed my eyes. Glauston, whoever it was was talking about glauston. Goddamn it.

"We are fighting for a purer world," Cardinal Giovanni Mercati continued. *"You can share it with us. Your world is so close when you touch the other side of the Door. Reach past the darkness, and I will guide you here."*

The Door sounded an awful lot like the Black Room. And this guy sounded too much like the Director.

Anna's voice in my ear: "Nikos, we're running out of time."

"I know," I said.

The Cardinal guy started to say more, but now I heard singing behind him, drowning him out. The song again: *"For tomorrow's war, for labor's glory, for peace and for the laurel, for the shame of those who repudiated our Fatherland!"*

I backed away from the incinerator, and my comm crackled loudly. I tried to pull it out of my ear.

Voices shouting on it: ". . . your speech! Thank the gods for what you've done." "An entire world—I can't believe they're all dead."

And that song: *"The poets and the artisans, the lords and the countrymen, With an Italian's pride . . ."*

Couldn't get the damn comm out: ". . speech was so powerful! Death means nothing!"

Knock, knock.

I sat up. Wrong room: I was back in the bedroom, disoriented.

Anna stood in the doorway, one hand squeezing the frame. "Did I wake you?"

I told my pulse to slow. "No." It didn't.

"Can I sit down?"

I made room for her on the bed, and she sat facing the doorway, as if she were afraid Giannis might walk in on us. I was still breathing hard.

"Did you have another dream?" she asked.

My chest was coiled, as if a frightened cat were trapped in my ribcage. I was angry at the dream for keeping me awake, angry at the Black Room or whatever was causing this, and angry at Anna for smelling like Anna.

"Nikos?"

"Yeah, I'm okay."

"You had another nightmare?"

I thought about lying, then said, "Yeah."

"So did I."

"What was yours?"

She said, "The Capital was gone. There was a black—nothing—outside the window."

"I saw it in the incinerator."

"The Black Room?"

It didn't have to be the same source, did it? "Yeah. I heard a voice from it, asking me to give it a glauston bomb. It was from another . . . I don't know. And I heard a song again."

"The Black Room did something to us," she said. "I think maybe some of this happened already, when we were down there. Our minds blocked it out at the time, but I think we touched someplace else. Something happened our brains couldn't handle."

We had established that, but I understood: she needed to talk, wanted to be consoled, so I stroked her back. It felt like a sheet of wood.

She said, "I want to go back down there."

"To the Black Room?"

"Yes."

"Why?"

"I can't stop thinking about it. Remember what we read in your scriptures? Maybe some of our dreams have happened, maybe some are still coming up. That could be how Hostos knew what's coming—he went down there too."

I was too tired for this. "His metaphorical hole . . ."

"Yes."

"They're going to try to send you back to Shan."

Her shoulders tightened. "I think Hostos went into the Black Room."

"So what?"

"I've been thinking about this," she said. Anna was speaking faster now: if we kept talking, we wouldn't have to face anything else. "I think it opened for us because I'm Shan, and you aren't."

"Then it wouldn't have opened for anyone before the last 30 years."

She shut the door and started pacing. "Two days ago, I wouldn't have believed this, but what if your uncle's artifacts weren't smuggled off Shan. We could have landed much earlier. Very intermittently. Why isn't that possible?"

"I don't know." And I thought of Grotton's tomb. "There's something else." I told her about the Shan-tooth carved into his sarcophagus and the Pnetian shrine-poem.

She stopped pacing, hands folded over her chest. "Why didn't you tell me this earlier? You know what, it doesn't matter. Are you sure it was the same tooth?"

"Yeah."

"There are probably a hundred objects that look like that."

"It was the same."

Anna took my hand. "They're going to send me back. And I don't know which is worse—Shan, the voice from the Black Room, or your religious zealots."

"They aren't mine. And the voice said we could go there, wherever he is. It sounded like he was in danger. That's why he wanted me to give him glauston bombs, to help them win some kind of war."

"Do you trust him—it, whatever he was?"

I thought about it. "No. But I don't trust, that's not really my thing anymore. Not since the launch that . . ." I caught myself staring at a lithograph of Elena on the opposite dresser.

"I'm sorry," Anna said. "Is that her?"

I said, "Yeah."

"She was young."

"Yeah. Let's not talk about it, okay?"

"Okay. What are we going to do?"

"I don't know."

"You're really going to speak for them tomorrow?"

"Do I have a choice?"

She stared at me: *what about Seg'v?* How had Anna gotten so close? That dream—we'd both been dreaming again. Anna was thin, with swollen-sleepless eyes and too-white skin, but my body reacted, and she felt it. We were too close, and she kissed my lips. Her tongue tasted like cinnamon-smoke and oranges.

She said, "I'm sorry . . ."

When she pulled back, a moment's hesitation: was that, are you, onto the bed, and as we, as I—and I kissed back.

* * *

When we finished, neither of us spoke, and we lay sideways—naked— on the mattress. She was twirling my hair with one finger, I tried to memorize her body: fragile neck, tiny breasts, stomach and that catch of red hair between her legs—the color of her eyebrows.

When I opened my mouth, she kissed me. I couldn't remember the last time—with Elena it had been a long time: months before the launch. Mechanical and metabolic; exercise, not sex. This had been the first since—in a long time.

I said, "What do we—do you want to do?"

"What do you mean?"

"We didn't use any . . ."

She shrugged. "You're worried about that?"

"I don't know, it seems like . . ."

"The chances aren't good anyway," she said.

Nothing says romance like abortion-talk after orgasm. "Yeah, sorry."

"Thank you," she said.

"What? I'm the one who should say that."

"With everything, I was afraid you'd break my teeth if I kissed you."

"You were?"

She grinned. "No, not really."

I closed my eyes, but she was wide awake. How many hours had we been up now?

I said, "We should sleep."

"You realize the sun's about to rise."

My bedroom-shades were tightly drawn, but that wouldn't keep the light out. "No . . ."

"It's true."

"Do you think he heard?"

Anna sat up. "What—why?"

"I don't know, I was just . . ."

She started rummaging. "We should get dressed."

"It's still dark out."

"Not for long."

She was right.

* * *

After breakfast, the Director arrived. My left eye was twitching again. I'd gone several days now without sleeping. I probably had Anna's glassy stare; she didn't look at me, she looked at a point on me, as if I were out of focus. Maybe I was.

We let Giannis murmur about how we needed a plan and after today there would only be four left, when the Director interrupted. He only wanted me. While I was escorted to a tram, Giannis and Anna remained under guard in my living room.

Once we'd boarded the tram, he said, "You don't look well."

"Thank you."

"Would you like me to get you something—I can speak with someone—to help you sleep?"

"I'm fine."

The Director handed me a small stack of typed note cards. I closed my eyes. I would beat the nightmares with ten second naps.

"Nikos?"

"Yeah?"

"You should take a moment to go over the cards."

I looked at him, concentrating until he came into focus. The tram felt distant, as if I were watching someone else pretending to be me.

I tapped the note cards. "Talking points?"

"Yes. Go ahead and look over them," he said again. "We won't have a great deal of time once we arrive. The Consul was forced to call the session earlier than we had anticipated."

I pretended to read the cards, fantasized about a warm, comfy bed, and finally asked, "So why are you doing this now?"

"The Space Project is essential to our most basic aspirations. Human curiosity . . ."

When he finished, I asked, "If they keep the Project—how long until the next launch?"

He smiled. "When we're ready."

* * *

Clerks, the bureaucratic equivalent of tram mechanics, rustled past in a steady, frantic flow of togas, folders and clipped documents. We were waiting for my introduction, for a long anti-project speech to wind down. It had been going for over two hours now, the craggily voice echoing out of the main Senate chamber—the Drann—into Nzrgh Hall to my ears.

"It shouldn't be long," the Director said.

"Yeah."

"Your speech, it shouldn't go on too long. Why don't you review the cards again."

Because I don't want to, but I said, "That's a good idea."

"I need to trust you to follow the script."

"So trust me."

"We have fixed the problems with the previous ships—with the *Melet*—and you should know, more than anyone else, just how vital . . ." Applause echoed: the craggily speech had ended. "Keep it short," he said, and we started walking.

Clerks herded us into Nzrgh Hall. I'd never seen it before. A wide curl of oil paintings of severe men in dark togas hung over a bustle of less-impressive real-life politicians—Senators, aides, and a pair of unarmed soldiers in armor—and we stepped into the open doorway to the Drann.

Terraced seating fanned around the central tribunary benches and rostra. As I was ushered down the center aisle, the Director continued to murmur encouragingly into my left ear. Half-full, the Senate chambers' seating was split into six sections—three on either side. Looking out from the front of the room—as I did now—the two right-center wedges were dominated by Senators in the stripes of the old nobility. Behind them and in the far-right section massed a patchwork of darkly colored Corporation leaders and guild board members. On the left, more corporates, mixed—as they moved left—with the shoulder-sash farmers and an agricultural mix with toga-patterns I didn't recognize.

Of course, the first two rows in every cluster of benches were reserved for proconsulars and Shan ambassadors. Still, based on their seating it was obvious where the proconsuls had started. Only one consul—D'us'lle', the prick from last night—was present, the other front seat was piled with folders. The entire Drann was faced in marble with a dome depicting fire and men with axes, tearing apart a golden wall: a whimsical reminder of the Merr Dynasty. Nevermind that a good chunk of this room had ancestors who had gotten rich during the Merr. And maybe that's the point, I thought, as the consul introduced and motioned me to the rostra podium. The Merr were gone because these men's great-great-grandfathers became rich: men want money, and once they have it, they want power. The two weren't mutually exclusive.

"Thank you," I said and took the podium. The low rumble of conversation slowly stopped as the half-empty room of half-interested Senators paused to watch, the way they might a dog fight or a boat race: something mildly entertaining could happen.

"Thank you for your time, and I appreciate your courtesy, Consul," I said, wondered if I should continue with a stream of worn-apologies. The Director's raised eyebrows at the back of the room said no. "My name is Nikos Healy'll and I devoted years of my life to my marriage and to the New Amith space Project and Cosmonaut Program." Funny, I should be nervous. I'd never given a speech. "Now both are gone. My wife, Elena, was a cosmonaut who died in the *Melet* launch. She burned alive inside the ship."

The Consul had turned to listen, a hand covering his mouth and reaction. The Director was losing his color: I wasn't following the cards.

"I listened to her die in the comm room, I've lived with her death for weeks, and I'm scared. How many times have you heard that it's too hard, too expensive, too far?" The room quieted. "That painting on the ceiling isn't a piece of meaningless history—it's what we're trying to do. They built a wall to keep us out of the Palace grounds, let us gape, assured us we should stay out—it was for our own good, they said. The Merr kept us out—for 1,200 years they watered their gardens, marched their soldiers, and bred their cross-eyed Kings.

"We should have stayed out. Shouldn't we? We should have listened and obeyed their decrees, and when one of us died trying to get inside, we should have learned a lesson: know your place." Know your audience, I thought, and said, "We should have been content. Why weren't we? Were we ungrateful? Didn't we appreciate our benevolent monarchs with their laws, appointments, and wealth? Didn't we know it was for our own good?

"After all, each time we climbed the wall, they caught us and burned us alive in public gardens as a demonstration of their goodwill. They were chosen by the gods, weren't they? A divinely ordained family—one family—to govern an empire of 200 million. Were we wrong?"

I waited for a shout of 'no'—it didn't happen—then said, "Or were they? That wall—their golden wall—wasn't built by the gods, it was built by political criminals, by radicals. But there were other men who said 'no'. These men didn't see the wall. Why? Because it wasn't there.

"But now they've built a new one—and this is clever—because it doesn't stand out or shine, and it isn't made of gold or jewels, but of air. You can't go that high. Why not? The punishment's death. But there's no answer to the question 'why': because there is none. The why is in our hands, the hands of the project and the people who have given their lives to climb. My wife was one of them. Now she's gone—but the wall isn't. Don't be distracted—there is no law here, nothing that says we can't go up. Only we can say that. And we only have to look around to know that we don't have to.

"Tear it down, don't leave the wall for your children to face. It's our time, our choice, and heaven won't wait."

CHAPTER FOURTEEN

A Business Transaction

I realized I was done. No applause, but the moment I stepped away, the chamber roared with voices, and the consul shouted over it, "Mr. Healy'll's speech was recognized as a speech in favor—thank you, Mr. Healy'll. Do we have a speech in opposition. Yes, Senator Keem'll, please approach the rostra."

In the hall, I was surrounded by clerks and a crush of Senators. The Director held my shoulder.

"Thank you," he said.

"Yeah," I said, and he cleared a path down the hall.

". . . a career in public speaking?" someone shouted.

The Director found an empty office that could have doubled as a 'pretentious library' stage-set.

"I have a few things to take care of before we go. Someone will bring you lunch, but I advise you to keep the door locked."

"Why?"

"Because we're in the Senate building," he said. "It shouldn't be more than a few hours."

He left me on an uncomfortable sofa. With the detailed gold inlay, this couch might be worth more than my house. I wondered whose desk that was at the far wall, decided I didn't care, and someone knocked. Lunch: a clerk with a roll-sandwich of ham, lettuce, and a spicy yellow sauce. I thanked him, took a few bites, and tried to sleep.

Another knock.

"Come in."

The clerk had locked the door on his way out, so I went to let him back in. A Senator in a criss-cross dark green toga—some kind of agricultural pattern—waited in the doorway. Behind him, the hall was a constant flow of government lackeys to and from the main Senate chambers.

"Your name is Nikos?" the Senator asked.

I didn't let him in. "Yeah."

Scrawny, with a slight northern accent, he looked more like a vegetable salesman than a Senator. "That speech was improvised, wasn't it?"

"Most of it."

"My name is Senator Karto'u. How did they convince you to make that speech? After what they did to you wife . . ?"

"That's a good question."

Not really; they have Anna and Giannis. His threats were subtle, but I knew the Director and how important the Project was to him. That made him dangerous.

"You realize they want to launch immediately, the moment the resolution is passed."

"I'm sorry—what do you want?"

He frowned. "Are you all right?"

"What?"

"Your nose . . ."

He offered me a handkerchief, and I dabbed blood. "Yeah . . ." I sniffed it back, held the cloth to my nose. "Thank you."

"I won't let them. Regardless of your speech, I want you to tell your consul it will not pass this week."

"This week?"

The week ended in four days.

"Yes," he said. "Tell him exactly that, will you?"

"And after this week . . ?"

He backed into the crowded hall, shrugged, and called, "We'll see, won't we."

A soldier jostled him. Karto'u shouted and dropped to the floor. The bureaucrats were gathering, and I stepped to the edge of a massing crowd.

Kato'u had fallen into a puddle—blood was soaking the back of his toga and pooling on the marble tile.

"Senator Karto'u," someone said, and a clerk knelt beside him, grabbed the back of Karto'u's sleeve. "Murder!" he shouted, face flushed. "Get a doctor!"

Karto'u saw me and crawled toward my feet. "Nikos . . ."

He clasped my hand, yanked me close. I'd never seen anything like this before: he looked so frightened, like a dog trapped in a rail track.

" You will be responsible for what happens," he said. "When all of this is gone, and they have the power again . . ."

A clerk pushed me away. "Get back!"

But Karto'u didn't let go. "Forget what you saw, bury it."

"Get back!"

The clerk shoved me into the crowd, and I stumbled back to the office doorway. I had watched it happen. The hall was a mob of frantic clerks, all shouting at once.

"Nikos." The Director was at my side. He noticed the gory stains on my hands and clothing. "Come on, it's time to go."

Rather than ask what had happened, he hustled me out a rear exit, to a tram, and when we arrived at my house, the Director said, "You did very well today. I'll see what I can do to repay you. We may even get some kind of a deferment for your Shan friend."

I stared at him. A soldier opened the door for me. What did the Director want? A 'thank you', a 'high-five'? Just like Elena's funeral—I wanted to laugh. Karto'u had been assassinated by a random soldier in a busy hallway. Powerful people wanted to keep the Project alive. It had been quick and casual, like a business transaction. Bump, bump, knife-goes-in, bump.

"Nikos?"

So absurd. I couldn't help it, I smiled.

The Director grinned back. "What?"

"I've used up my quota. Can you send alcohol tonight?"

"Certainly, I'll see what I can do."

"Thanks."

I got out, the soldier slammed the door—the Director's tram drove away—and I was escorted up my front lawn. Gods, the sun was already setting. Five days left, and I'd wasted one entirely. There was another soldier on my porch. I tried to joke with him, but he wasn't in the mood. They let me in and locked the door behind me.

Anna and Giannis sat together on the living room couch. "There you are," Anna said, but neither of them got up. So I sat on an adjacent chair. They'd switched off the monitor when they heard the door. She asked, "How did it go?"

"Fine."

Giannis nodded to the door. "How long are they going to keep us here? What else do they want—you did what they asked."

They'd been crammed in this house all day, and it showed. Giannis's leg shook rhythmically, and Anna didn't look entirely conscious.

"We may be able to leave tomorrow," I said. "I'll talk to the Director." When that didn't get a response, I said, "Karto'u was stabbed."

Anna straightened. "What—how?"

"I saw it happen, but I don't know. It was a crowded hall, and ..."

"They *stabbed* him?" she said.

"Yeah."

"How—is he alive?"

"I don't know."

"How did you know it was him?"

"We were talking right before it happened. He wanted me to tell the Consul that the Project wouldn't pass this week."

Giannis frowned. "This week?"

"That's what he said."

Giannis said, "There are four days in this week, after today."

"Yeah."

"You don't think they know ..."

"How could they?"

They finally noticed my clothes and blood-smeared hand.

Anna tensed, ready to start bandaging. "Barcuc, I'm sorry, I'm so tired I didn't see. Are you hurt?"

"It's not my blood." That didn't help. "I told the Director to send us liquor."

Anna was confused. "Liquor? Why?"

What kind of a response is—Giannis said, "It's a good idea."

"Thank you."

Anna was shaking her head. "You want to get drunk?" she said it like 'you-want-to-saw-off-your-what?'.

"Yeah." I went into the incinerator room and glared at myself in the sink mirror. Gods, I felt as if I were holding a breath in my ribcage, and I wasn't. Alcohol wasn't going to help. The tension wouldn't go away. Back in the living room, I said, "I changed my mind. I'm going to eat something and go to bed."

Giannis was disappointed. "You don't want to . . ."

"No."

Anna played along. "You need to sleep."

"Yeah. Goodnight."

They said 'goodnight', I ate an apple, then locked myself in the bedroom with a glass of water. Glowering with Elena's things would make me miserable, but I couldn't focus. Needed to sleep. I curled on the bed, closed my eyes, and tried to think positive thoughts. Sleep, don't dream. It wasn't working. Time passed. I thought about the Pnetians, Karto'u's stare, the song from the Black Room, an imaginary daughter I never had, and suicide. Wasn't that what Wesler had chosen? He'd set fire to his mansion and roasted with it. Why? Lack of sleep probably.

Gods, that damn room. It had branded some chunk of my brain, and I couldn't erase it. After a long time—after I'd woken twice with cold-sweat dreams I didn't remember—someone knocked.

"Yeah?"

"Are you awake?" Giannis—that was the kind of imbecile-question he would ask.

"What do you want?"

"Can I come in?"

"No, go away. I'm trying to sleep."

"Please open the door . . ."

I sprang up and slapped the door hard with both hands—I heard him jump. "Go away. I'll see you in the morning."

The rest of the night was worse, and in the morning—when Anna rapped lightly from the other side—I took a long time getting up. I opened the door.

She looked sick, and her expression said that I did too.

"You didn't sleep?" she asked.

"No."

"I want to go back to the Black Room today."

Without speaking, I went to the incinerator room, pissed, then staggered into the kitchen.

She followed. "You're bleeding."

"No, I'm not."

"Yes, look at your shirt."

"I didn't change it, it's not . . ." But she was right. There were red splotches around the neck of my shirt.

"Your face is smeared," she said. "Here." She cleaned it with a wet paper towel, and I took a ten second nap. "This is strange."

"So my nose is bleeding . . ."

"Giannis is too. And there's a sore on one of his hands—like a rash."

"Show me."

She did: sure enough, Giannis's left hand was swollen, the skin crusty and raw.

"What is that?" I said.

"I woke up with it," he said. "It was bothering me yesterday, but not like this."

I noticed his upper lip. "Your nose was bleeding?"

"It's okay now."

"What's happening to us?" I asked, but I had a pretty good idea.

"I don't recognize this," Giannis said, inspecting his hand as if he'd found it lying on the sidewalk. "It's obviously some kind of rash. The nosebleed is probably just a coincidence."

I looked at Anna. "You know what this is, right? From Shan—you told us about glauston."

She straightened, suddenly defensive. "I've never seen it personally."

Giannis said, "What—you think this is some kind of glauston sickness, Nikos?"

"You said that people get sick from that stuff."

"Not like . . ."

"Did you touch it with that hand?" I asked.

"How could it do this?"

"Did you?"

"I just moved one of the container lids."

I asked Anna, "What's going to happen to us?"

"I don't know."

"Is it going to kill us?"

"I don't. Know."

Her serious 'the-hell-are-you-looking-at' expression was too much. I laughed and sat beside Giannis. "So did they bring the liquor?"

He pointed to the hall. "It's in the kitchen."

I patted his shoulder. "Will you calm down? We're going to be fine. Right Anna?" She ignored me, so I said, "Right. Are you ready to go?"

Giannis: "Go where?"

"Anna wants to go back to the Wesler site." I nodded to her. "Am I right?"

She said, "I want to see it again."

"It doesn't matter," Giannis said, "they won't let us leave."

"Let's ask." I went to the front porch. A new soldier was perched on the steps, smoking a cigarillo. He didn't look exhausted, which meant they'd switched shifts recently.

"How is it?" I asked.

"Good." He took another drag, offered it to me.

"Thanks." I sucked the hot smoke into my lungs, blew it back out. It burned the back of my throat, but it felt good. I gave it back to him. "So what are we doing today?"

Day Four in the countdown to the end of the world.

"Sorry?" he said, as if I'd mumbled, and I hadn't.

"What are the plans for today?"

"Do you need something?"

"I'm just wondering when you'll be ready for our trip out." He started shaking his head, and I said, "After my speech, the Consul agreed that—when you're ready, of course—we would be allowed one trip out of the house. You didn't think we would stay indoors all day, did you?"

He continued to smoke, considering that, as if it weren't really important. "That's not my understanding," he said at last.

'Understanding' was a big word, I might need to offer him a glass of booze.

"Do you want a drink? They brought us some last night, but we haven't had a chance . . ."

"No thank you."

Polite too.

"You can just let us know when you're ready," I said and started to go back in.

"I'm sorry, it's not going to happen."

"Just give the Consul a call. Don't worry about your immediate superiors—he made the change late last night—just go straight to him. I promise, he'll say the same thing."

"Are you all right?"

"What?" Oh yeah, I look shitty, right? "Yeah, I'm fine."

"Do you want me to call a doctor?"

"No, I've got one—my brother's here."

He hesitated. "Where do you want to go?"

CHAPTER FIFTEEN

Feel What?

With the Shan evacuation, Anna had said that the Wesler site—and the Black Room—would be investigated by the Senate. But, as far as I could tell, the only people who might be using it were none-too-subtle kids. The lawn was a mess of plastic wrappers, beer bottles, and the occasional flap of discarded clothing.

Flanked by a pair of soldiers, we picked our way through the front gates: the inner yard looked like an abandoned circus. Sagging tarps and neglected machinery cluttered the dig, as if the corps of techies and archaeologists had all suddenly run for their lives without even hiring a maid or cleaning servant.

I murmured, "It closed, right?"

The Black Room—she knew what I meant. "Yes. After you left."

As Giannis and the soldiers meandered behind, Anna and I went straight for the dirt-tunnel.

"There's nothing here," Giannis called.

"Yeah," I said, picking up the pace. We had to see it before they made us go back.

The smoking soldier began to complain about being brought here and how absurd it was that all of this expensive equipment had been left out in the open. 'They' were sure lucky it hadn't rained. I'd insisted we bring the liquor, but no one had wanted to carry it—Giannis left the bottle in the tram.

I followed Anna into the tunnel. None of the generators were on, so it got dark quickly.

She asked, "You didn't bring a light, did you?"

"No—wait . . ." I found the broken electric from Leim'en. A model of cleanliness, I still hadn't changed my clothes. I fidgeted with the light.

"How long do you think we have?" she said.

"I don't know. As long as he stays up there and distracts them, I think we're okay." The electric flickered on. Why couldn't it have done that at Grotton's tomb? "There . . ."

Anna steadied herself on the wall—I followed her stare: the room was open.

She said, "It . . ."

"Yeah, I noticed that."

I stepped inside. The exotic-fungus-room hadn't changed. I saw the same sediment-lined walls of ancient writing and tasted the same mildew, flowery-mold smell. The spores were happy to have air again.

"I don't understand," she said and followed me in. "It was closed, that's why they left . . ."

"It likes us."

White-flash, and I slipped—not out of—but deeper *into* my skull. I sank further: no room, no light, no Anna. I was paralyzed, except that—I was in a padded room of jostling dials and buttons. It was shaking too quickly for my vision to follow. On the right was a circular window with white puffs, like . . .

Gods.

. . . clouds. Upside-down clouds and a brown-green landscape below. This was the *Melet*—no, it wasn't. I had studied the *Melet*; I knew the configuration of gears: 1,2,3 over the dash panel and a pull-tube on the left. This pull-tube was on the right, and these gears were spaced out differently. The room was too big to be the *Melet*.

Someone was praying. Overhead, a man was strapped-in, his eyes squeezed shut and knuckles white as he held a llore block between his hands.

". . . fortune and memory, that you will watch over and protect the generations to come, in this paradise of plenty, I pray." He glanced at a monitor with giant white blobs on a starry backdrop. "Elle, wife of Rosantre, daughter of Meelay and Jessa, traveler of the Republic and patron of song, that you will watch over and protect the generations . . ."

The Director's voice crackled on a dash speaker: "Mr. Ante's'? Are you . . . loud enough . . . can you adjust to . . . not receiving that . . ."

As I watched, the cosmonaut's face twisted—veins and perspiration appeared on his brow—and his arms spasmed. The Director never participated in launches.

"Gods protect me," Ante's' said, watching the monitor. "Gods protect me—save me." Jaw clenched, he winced, and I understood: his body was heating up.

The ship jerked hard, and I slammed into the wall. I was really here. The cosmonaut saw me.

"You're . . ." He choked, cheeks flushed. "Save me!"

Crackle and the Director said: ". . . all right? Can you . . . without giving away . . ."

"Please!"

I grabbed his strap buckles—*snap, snap*—then the other ones.

He jolted when I touched him. I unbuckled the last strap. And—what? I couldn't just jump out. I pulled him up, one arm around his back.

"Save me . . ." he murmured, "save me . . ."

He convulsed, his skin darkening, his fingers coiled like talons in my shoulder.

The Director: ". . . need to confirm . . ."

"Save . . ."

I felt Anna beside me again. She touched my wrist, like a guide. And we were in a grass field. The sky was a clear blue, the kind of color they told you to imagine in relaxation classes. I dropped the guy in the grass, and he trembled—in shock—huffing and gasping, then I slumped against an overgrown table of stones.

He said, "You . . ."

"Yeah."

He jerked into a sitting position, watched me. His skin was sunburnt, as if he'd fallen asleep at the shore. A blister bulged on the back of his hand, and he glowed bright red everywhere else.

"Praise Rosantre, blessed be your name . . ."

"Not me," I said, looked around. We were in the outskirts, just a kilometer, maybe less, from the Capital. I recognized an out-of-service windmill nearby, and the road to Leim'en beyond.

"I was a coward, I wanted to burn . . . did you see?"

"What?"

"You will be replaced," he said. *"They're coming."*

I was back in the room with Anna and the mold. She exhaled, as if she'd been holding her breath.

"Nikos?"

"Gods."

"I'm going to tell you what I saw and then I want . . ."

"I went into a spaceship, saved a burning man, and left him in a field outside town." When she didn't respond, I said, "That's it, right?"

"Yes."

"You saw that?"

"Yes. I kept you in the ship until you had him, then I found a place to set you down."

I waited for more, then said, "You 'kept' me there?"

"I don't know how I saw it, but somehow I knew the ship was going up, so I put you on it . . ."

"They launched another ship—that's what that was, and you put me on it?"

"Yes."

The Director had already launched a second *Melet*, and I'd saved the pilot. But why had the Director monitored the flight? That never happened. "How did you know *I* wouldn't burn?"

"You were still here. Neither of us left this room."

Nevermind that that didn't make sense. "That was some kind of dream. We fell asleep or were hallucinating . . ."

"Do you really think that's all it was?"

"What else could it have been? How could we leave the room and be inside the room at the same time?" I glared at the walls. "This is just a place."

"It felt . . ."

"They all feel real."

"Okay."

I said, "The Director was talking to the guy, Ante's'."

"I don't . . ."

"That's breaking tradition," I said. "The Director wasn't in the control room when the *Melet* went up—it's been a tradition for the Program Director to stay away during the launch since before I was born."

Anna didn't understand. "Why?"

"He's supposed to pray." Something else was bothering me. So what if the Director was there? "I'm sorry, I don't know what . . ."

She held my hand. "It's okay."

I began to pace. "Either we're going crazy or this isn't just a room."

"Or both," she said.

"Yeah, well—I want to know." I searched the ceiling for a sign and found more fungus. "We have to go out the south road, toward the pass in the Leim'en'a Mountains."

She nodded. "How do we do that?"

"We have to tell them something." The soldiers. "We have to give them some reason to let us leave the city."

"What?"

"I don't know. What did we just do—we just moved a person from one place to another: out of a ship to an empty field. And I wasn't affected by the atmosphere, I was fine."

"What was he looking at on the ship's monitor?"

"What?"

"He was watching something," Anna said. "He said he wanted to burn . . ."

Like Elena, I thought. "What if they only send people who want to . . ?"

"What?"

"People who are ready to die?"

"I don't understand," she said. "That man was watching some kind of space display, wasn't he?"

"I don't know."

"They didn't have one on your wife's ship?"

My wife's ship. I shook my head.

"He saw something." Anna was convincing herself, but that didn't mean she was wrong.

They're coming. Why was the Director so eager to send up another ship? Why did the calendar end in four days? The Pnetians were building bombs, and we still hadn't heard from Shan. And don't forget the people in another world who want those bombs too. It was too much.

"We have to get out of here," I said and started for the tunnel.

"You want to leave the Black Room again?"

"Not the room," I said, "the Capital. We have to leave right now."

Giannis waved from the tunnel exit. "There you are—are we ready?"

"Yeah."

He stopped me. "What happened?"

"We need to go."

"What's wrong?"

"We have to get out of this city right now."

He smiled, as if I were a dim-witted child. "They won't let us."

"I don't care." I shrugged past him. "Come on."

The smoking-soldier waited on the surface with his spear-like pyck in one hand. Ignoring me, he studied the Wesler mansion, as if it had just popped out of nowhere.

"Where's the other soldier?" I asked.

"Inside." He thought for a moment, then told me to get Anna and Giannis. "I can't watch all three of you if you're down there."

"You mean 'protect us'."

He wasn't in the mood. "Get them."

Once they'd come up, the soldier told us to lead the way to the mansion, so we went up the lawn.

"We heard someone screaming," the soldier said. "You've had a chance to look around—Fanc'l is searching the house now, and once we've found him, we can leave."

That didn't fill me with confidence or inspire me to be first in line. Apparently, Fanc'l was soldier #2, and he'd vanished into the house.

"Wait," the soldier said at the entrance. He tapped me with the pyck— if he pulled the trigger, I'd be hit by a shot of poison. "How many rooms are there?"

"I don't . . ."

"Fifty-two," Anna said.

"Why don't you call him?" I said.

"I've tried," the soldier said. "He isn't responding on his comm."

"It could be broken," I said, "have you tried . . ." –Oh, I don't know—". . . physically calling for him?" I cupped both hands around my mouth, and when no one objected, shouted, "Fanc'l!"

Nothing, and after a few more yells, the soldier poked me again. "Let's go."

I went first, Giannis and Anna right behind, and the soldier—still smoking—brought up the rear. When Wesler'll had cracked, he'd set fire to his mansion, and half the building burnt to the ground. However, what remained had been just enough for a reconstruction by the new owners. They'd thrown up new rooms and bandaged Wesler'll's scars with wallpaper and rugs. Before leaving the estate as an archaeological dig, the owners had also covered everything in transparent plastic sheets, as if they were afraid Anna's team would track mud on the carpets and encourage dogs to jump on the furniture.

The entry-parlor smelled like foreign dust, and the sheets made me think the house was in mourning. A giant piano, two couches, and an armchair were all bolted down and draped, and enormous plastic coverings hung from the ceiling to the floor on all four walls. They didn't quite fit— the sheets were too loose and wavy.

I stopped in the middle of the room: there were three doorways, and through one, a stairway rose to the second floor.

"Which way?"

The soldier indicated a random doorway, so I continued, my feet crinkling on the plastic-covered floor. Where had they gotten all these tarps? Or, more precisely, where had their servants gotten them? Through a second, smaller parlor, we passed a plasticky dining room, then entered the outer kitchen. The heavy stoves and counters were insulated by wraps in preparation for a major geological event.

The soldier motioned to the back of the kitchen. "What's that?"

A bowl? No—there was something non-plastic on the floor—a pistol. We froze, and the soldier grabbed it, checked the magazine. It was identical to the pistol in his holster.

The new pistol in one hand, the soldier awkwardly adjusted his pyck with the other—yeah, technically, a pyck could be used one-handed, but not without experience this guy obviously didn't have. He didn't want to be here, but he couldn't just leave his companion or offer the gun to one of us. So, he did the sensible thing and stuck the new gun in his pants and ordered me to search the rest of the floor, then returned to the stairs that led to the second floor.

I did, and as I mounted the stairs, Giannis murmured, "The gun doesn't make sense."

"Nope."

It had occurred to me too: no soldier would abandon his pistol, and an attacker wouldn't leave it behind. The stairs ended at a vulnerable landing that split into three similar halls. The soldier paused on the top stair, readied his pyck, then chose a hall. We passed rooms full of unrecognizable plasticked furniture. Finally, the hall turned left, and I stopped. A soldier lay face down seven or eight meters away, a pyck beside him.

The smoking soldier leveled his pyck at the empty hall and stepped in front, eyes on the discarded weapon. There were no doors between us and the body. As the soldier crept closer, the plastic walls ruffled on both sides. There was no breeze, and the soldier paused, spat out his cigarillo.

"Fanc'l . . ." he said, his pyck trembling. "Get up, Fanc'l."

Fanc'l didn't move, but there was no blood, no sign of a struggle.

Anna grabbed my arm.

"What?" Then I followed her stare to a lump in the plastic on the left wall, in the vague outline of a person. The soldier hadn't noticed, and he approached Fanc'l, five meters away. Now Giannis saw the shadow too, he opened his mouth, then looked at me: *what do we do?*

Anna said, "We have to . . ."

"Wait."

"Nikos . . ."

"Just wait."

The soldier was four meters away, and the figure behind the plastic remained absolutely still. Say something. What if it's a statue, what if it isn't a person?

Giannis murmured, "Doesn't he see?"

"Shh."

"I'm going to say something."

"No, just . . ."

But Giannis shouted, "There's someone . . ."

The floor broke under the cigarillo-soldier. Giannis's warning gave him time to spin, and he caught the edge of the hole with his pyck-hand—the spear pointed straight at me—and yelled something between 'waa' and 'whoops' as he lost his grip. The soldier fell, his pyck twirled, and a pellet hit me in the stomach.

Something smashed on the first floor, and I heard the soldier groan as if he'd just given birth, then Anna and Giannis started talking too fast. Somehow I'd fallen onto my back and Giannis was yanking off my shirt to inspect the wound.

Anna hovered behind him. "You'll be all right. You'll be fine, Nikos."

Giannis concentrated and did something with my stomach. "Does that hurt?"

"No."

"What about that?"

"No."

My gut and groin had gone numb and when I told him, his 'concentration' face hardened into one I hadn't seen before; probably his 'give-me-that-scalpel-I-am-not-going-to-lose-this-patient'   face. Except he wasn't a surgeon.

Anna turned, but I couldn't move to see what she was looking at, and a woman said, "Is he all right?"

Anna said, "What are you doing here?"

"I got out . . ." I'd heard that voice before. "And I came here last night."

I asked, "Is that the crazy Lagone woman?"

Anna nodded. "Kysa, yes."

Giannis wrapped an arm around my back to haul me up. "Help me, we have to get him to a hospital."

181

Kysa: "What happened?"

Without looking at her, Giannis said, "He got hit with a pyck—help me, Anna. We have to try to get him to a hospital as quickly as possible."

They hoisted me up, jostled down the hall, nearly dropped me on the stairs, and had to stop for a breath at the front door. The tram was a good 35 meters away. Kysa wanted to help, so she grappled with my feet. I couldn't feel my chest or thighs.

After he'd dropped me in the tram seat, Giannis crouched by my face. "Can you feel that, Nikos?"

"Feel what?"

Not even a smile, and he asked Kysa, "Where's the closest hospital?"

"The Brevda hospital, it's about ten kilometers away. There's a monastery clinic around the corner, but today's a holiday, it won't be open."

"Let's go." The tram started moving.

"It won't be open," Kysa said. "The hospital is only . . ."

"No," Giannis said. He had become a general at war. I'd never seen him like this, and suddenly I respected the fact that he wasn't just my little brother. It'd be a shame if I died in the next few minutes. I felt detached—the pyck's poison coo'ed into my DNA's ear: 'It'll be fine. Just let it happen.'

A pyck fired toxins that were notoriously lethal in 2 – 30 minutes. I'd already lasted ten, and the antidote was a joke. Leave it to the Shan to invent a poison that killed in ten minutes with an antidote that required 20 minutes to deliver.

The tram stopped, and Giannis jumped out. I remembered waking up a month ago with my left arm entirely asleep and handling it with the right, as if it were someone else's appendage. Though I was paralyzed, my face, fingers and feet still tingled—the rest had disappeared.

Anna straightened, watching Giannis. "No, don't . . ."

But apparently he did. I heard glass breaking, then shouting, and Giannis appeared in the tram door.

"Ready? Help me with him—one, two, now!"

They jostled me across a sidewalk, up three steps, and into a hall that smelled of rubbing alcohol. A doctor-in-training tried to stop them, but

Giannis wasn't listening. They propped me against a stone wall: the monastery entryway was a marble hall of unlit candles and periodic shrines.

The monk doctor said, "We are not liable for this. You cannot leave him here."

"Aester kit," Giannis said. "Where is it?"

"Has he been . . ."

"Yes. Let's go—where is it?"

Giannis hurried the monk away, and Anna crouched beside me, stroking my hair with one hand. Kysa watched from the opposite wall.

"It's going to be all right," Anna said.

"Yeah . . ."

Her touch felt distant, as though she were rubbing my scalp through a wool cap. Anna was more frightened than I was. The poison had mellowed me out; I didn't believe I was dying, someone had slipped a downer in my drink.

"I'm sorry," she said.

"Stop, I'll be okay."

"I know, I know."

I couldn't feel my toes. "I didn't see, is it a big monastery?"

"Not really, no." She looked for Giannis, then leaned close and murmured, "I'm so sorry, Nikos."

"For what?"

"You deserve better, you know that?"

The fingers on my left hand were gone. I said, "You didn't shoot me."

She kissed my forehead, her eyes and nose red.

I said, "It's okay." But it came out 'somay'. My tongue wasn't behaving, and that just made it worse. Anna stroked my hair more frantically. Gods, I was exhausted. All the sleep I'd missed rolled together in a single wave—I felt it coming.

Giannis shouted, "Okay!" He hustled over to me, pushed Anna out of the way and adjusted a syringe. "Nikos? You can hear me! Open your eyes!"

My eyes aren't closed, I tried to say, but that wasn't entirely true. My eyelids were lead, they'd gotten too heavy—I wasn't strong enough to hold them up.

"Hey. Look at me. Stop that and look at me." Giannis slapped my cheek hard. "Hold open his eyes—do it now!"

I tried to blink them shut, but Anna pried open my eyelids, and Giannis worked on a vein in my right arm. The world blurred.

"You watch me, Nikos. Don't go to sleep. Watch me."

Screw that, I thought. I didn't have a mouth anymore. Just let me rest.

"Good." To Anna, "Talk to him. Make him stay awake." As Giannis fumbled with an armful of vials and needles, Anna pressed her face to mine.

"Please," she said, "Nikos, don't . . ."

"*No.* Tell him a story," Giannis said quickly. "Once there was a man named Nikos. And he decided to go into an old house with his brother, his Shan friend, and a soldier."

Original story, I thought.

"And they looked all around for another soldier. Nikos, do you hear me? I said they looked all around for a second soldier . . ." He was speaking from the end of a tunnel, his voice getting more frantic, and Anna shouted something. My body exploded in pain-tingle, as if I'd been dropped in a pool of steel pins. I heard someone groaning, then lurched onto my side and vomited. That was my groan.

Anna held my shoulders. "Are you okay? Can you hear me?"

"He's up," Giannis said. He collapsed to the floor, limp and surrounded by medical instruments.

I spat some more, then looked up at a kid in a brown, monk's robe. A throwback to the Gumay Period, monasteries still insisted on ridiculous costumes for their doctor's-in-training. Giannis had worn one for years.

"Thank the gods," the kid said.

I slumped against the wall to catch my breath. Lightheaded, I waited for the pinpricks to recede.

Giannis grabbed a needle-box with a pair of plastic pouches attached, then laughed nervously. "You're very lucky I'm a good doctor."

I was panting. "Yeah."

"You were out for about five minutes."

"I was?"

"Yes."

Anna remained at my side. "We thought you'd gone."

I forced a smile. "No such luck." Then noticed that beyond Kysa, the ground glittered. Someone had broken the stained glass in the monastery's front door—I frowned at Giannis. "Did you knock first?"

Kysa helped him up, and Giannis fidgeted with the needle-box.

"We should probably go," he said.

I asked the monk, "Is there an alarm?"

He nodded.

"Then yeah, you're right," I said, and Anna guided me to the broken exit. I slipped on the glass, and Giannis caught my fall. On the way up, he murmured, "You're getting old."

"You too."

CHAPTER SIXTEEN

No Panicking Yet

Without paying for the broken door, we returned to the tram, Giannis said that I needed to go to a 'real hospital', and I said, "Yeah, but not here."

The near-death goodwill began to fade, as we argued, finally agreeing on a larger, renovated monastery where Giannis was licensed to work just south of the Capital. The tram started moving.

I met Anna's stare. She was thinking the same thing: *we have to get the cosmonaut. I have to know I didn't dream that.* If we followed the south road past the Monastery, we should bump into that abandoned windmill. I just hoped the cosmonaut would wait.

"You fixed me," I said to Giannis. "Why do I need to go to a hospital?"

My blood could still be infected, and there was the slim possibility that one of them had been poisoned too. I didn't understand how, but Giannis assured me that we all needed to be tested—even Kysa, who looked half-asleep in the back seat.

I motioned to her. "You're coming too?"

Giannis said, "Nikos, sit back. Will you calm down? Gods, your heart stops, and the next moment you're ready to jog around the neighborhood."

"I don't trust her."

"Relax."

"I'm fine, let go of me."

"Just don't overdo it right now."

Which means what? Shut up and stare out the window? Don't ask Kysa why she attacked the Consul's soldiers—he fell through the floor, but the first one had been incapacitated. She was a Pnetian.

Kysa looked at me. "I wanted to see them again."

Anna asked, "Who?"

I said, "The people in the 'other worlds', right? The alternate versions of New Amith."

"Yes."

"How'd it go?"

"The room was closed."

I said, "That's too bad."

Giannis gave me the same look my childhood tutor had. "Nikos . . ."

"She's lying," I said.

Kysa was confused. "What?"

"It was open." *What the hell.* "I don't believe any of that—your poetry, what you say you saw in the Black Room—I think you made all of that up." I hadn't survived the pyck to screw around. "It was open—Anna and I went inside."

Before Giannis could start, I told them what had happened. The burning cosmonaut, our heroic rescue, even his melodramatic *'they're coming'*.

When I finished, Kysa said, "We should go back."

The rest of us disagreed. We had to leave the Capital, find a hospital-monastery, and then prove that we'd really dropped a cosmonaut into a windmill field. Kysa stopped arguing. What choice did she have? Outside, the afternoon sunlight was too sharp, but I watched the neighborhoods pass. New Amith Capital was the opposite of Leim'en.

The old Merr Palaces had been built in the middle of a corn field, encompassed by disparate villages and fiefdoms leftover from the Gumay Period. When the Merr fell, the Republic of New Amith appropriated the palatial ruins, and a city of bureaucrats had grown around it like mold, absorbing all of the independent townships in a continual swell of highways and suburbs. Seven-hundred years later, many of the Capital neighborhoods still clung to their centers and old markets.

The Visakin Road—the southern highway—rose above the complicated mixture of planned and organic boroughs. On the right, we passed the outline of a stone fortress, long-since overwhelmed by market strips and tourist offices, and on the left, a line of monoliths. Hundred-meter high red-brick towers, the Tellen complexes had been built in the empty lots between the suburbs. They provided free housing with complimentary meals and wine to the lazy and artistic.

Finally, the Capital was gone in a prairie of weedy ruins. The Visakin Road split into Vis and Kint. Kint drifted west through the Aem Mounds, then southwest for one-hundred kilometers of hilly grass-ruins to the Durges River and the east-west villages of Desspre' and Jun. Vis sliced straight to the southern pass across the Leim'en'a Mountains. If we didn't take the pass, it continued to the outer airstrips and factory districts of Vis'ke: an old mining town for owners who didn't want to pay Capital taxes. Somewhere in-between the mountain turn-off and Vis'ke were windmills.

We took the Vis to a quiet hospital, where Giannis talked our way into the rear offices and began to draw blood. Kysa had been terrified that someone in the hospital would know she was a runaway, so we left her in the tram.

Giannis did Anna's blood first, she was fine; then checked himself, also normal; and then he pricked my arm. He swabbed it with a cotton ball and rubbed the cotton on a slide that went into another machine. Giannis looked through a scope and spent several minutes adjusting it. Neither his nor Anna's blood had taken this long. My knees felt weak, and I slumped onto a plastic chair. Anna looked more nervous than I was.

"Come on Giannis—what?"

"You're fine," he said. "Hold on . . ." He put a different slide in the machine, then went back to mine. "I think this is broken."

"Me too," Anna said.

I asked, "Why?"

"You're fine," he said again, distracted by what he saw.

"Let me see." This time he didn't argue. In the scope, I saw a random pattern of blood cells in a vague loop.

He put in a different slide. "Now look at this."

I did: it was the same. No—there were subtle differences in the number and sizes of cells, but they'd coalesced in exactly the same pattern.

"How did this happen?" I asked.

Giannis glared at the slides. "I have no idea. I think we should try a different machine."

I let Anna take a look, and she asked, "Whose is this? You two? You *are* related, don't strange things sometimes happen with siblings . . ?"

"No," Giannis said. "The first one was Nikos's blood, the second was yours."

Anna smiled. "I have the same blood as someone from New Amith?"

"It isn't the same blood . . ."

"Then what is it?"

"I don't know," Giannis said.

I stared out the window at the half-empty parking lot. Our tram was still there, but so was a new one. Big and black, without windows, it looked exactly like the tram the Consul's soldiers used. And it hadn't been there when we'd arrived. I had the mad impulse to jump out the window and scramble across the lot to our tram: there was a clear path; the government tram had blocked the main entrance.

"Look," I said, and now they both saw it.

Giannis said, "They couldn't have found us."

"Yeah, they could have."

"You're being paranoid, it's probably not for us."

"Even if it isn't," Anna said, "they may have our descriptions."

"No panicking yet," I said. "I think one of us should try to walk out the front door." When they objected, I said, "You don't think it'll attract attention if we go out the window?"

"They're probably in the hall," Giannis said. "The moment you open that door . . ."

"I said 'no panicking yet'." To Anna, "What do we do?"

"I think you're right," she said. "One of us should try to walk out."

If they'd found us, Anna was the reason. *Yes, we're looking for two men and a Shan woman . . .* It didn't help that Anna was 20 skin tones whiter than every other person on New Amith.

I smiled at Giannis. "It has to be one of us."

"Odds or evens?"

"Odds."

One, two, three—I held out two fingers, he held out three. Five was an odd number. Shaking, Giannis went to the door.

I said, "If you want me to . . ."

"You chose odds."

"Just walk to the tram so we can see you."

He left, and I unlocked the window: no sense being unprepared. We waited.

"I think that machine is broken," Anna said.

"Mm."

"Nikos?"

I was watching our tram. "Yeah?"

"Why did our blood do that?"

"It was the machine."

"I think so too," she said. "Your brother probably wasn't . . ."

"How long does it take to walk outside?"

Anna stepped beside me—still no sign of Giannis.

"He'll be out in a minute," she said.

"Yeah."

As we waited, I tapped the window. My gut clenched. Calm down, he's fine. My tongue tasted sharp and acidic, like heartburn or adrenaline. He should be out by now. Why won't my pulse slow down?

I asked, "How long should we wait?"

She massaged my shoulder, but it didn't help. "Just be patient."

"He should be out by now."

"Nikos, I'm sure he's . . ."

Two soldiers escorted Giannis to the government tram. They'd bound his wrists behind his back, and when one slid open the side door, the other shoved Giannis inside.

Anna said, "Oh no."

"Yeah."

Footsteps in the hall behind us, and I heard a whispered conversation through the door. The two soldiers remained outside the government tram, their backs to us, and I hoisted open the window.

Anna grabbed my arm. "We can't . . ."

"Yeah we can." I patted the window ledge. "Come on."

Someone knocked, the doorknob turned, and Anna clambered out the window. I heard the door open, planted one foot, and was right behind her—we ran for our waiting tram. Twenty meters away, and the two soldiers didn't turn. Fifteen.

Behind us, someone shouted, "Stop! Hands up—stop!"

At ten meters, one of the idle soldiers saw Anna and reached for his pistol. Nine, eight, seven.

"Stop!"

Behind us, I heard a snap, and something hissed past my left leg. Six, five, four. Snap-hiss, and now the two soldiers in the parking lot raised their guns, screaming orders at the same time. They'd shoot us down when we paused to open the door. Anna reached the tram, and Kysa threw open the door—I lunged in after Anna, and the doorway dinged and tocked as bullets ricocheted away.

Anna: "Close it!"

I slammed the door, and it jostled in more gunfire. I yelled at the tram, "Go south!"

And we were moving, a government tram right behind us. How the hell had they turned around so quickly? I hadn't even seen the soldiers jump in. Anna crouched on the opposite seat, and I squeezed the door handle with one hand. Gods. Why were they shooting at us? My jaw clenched, and I couldn't stop trembling. Stop—just stop, we made it. Something knicked the rear bumper, and the tram swayed. Because of the soldiers at the estate, they must think we attacked them. I closed my eyes, choking the door handle as hard as I could.

". . . do we do?" Anna shouted.

"What?"

"We can't outrun them."

The tram jumped again.

"I don't know." Out the rear window, I watched the government tram gain. They had Giannis in there. My alcohol bottle sloshed and banged against the wall.

"We have to do something—we can't go faster."

Back on the southern highway, the government tram was going fast. What were they going to do—ram us off the road?

Anna said, "They're going to ram us off the road!"

Yep.

The government tram slammed into the back. Our tram skittered and swerved, but the auto-control corrected the turn. They hit us again.

Kysa looked more confused than frightened, and when our tram shuddered again, she said, "Shouldn't they try to take us into custody alive?"

"You attacked them," I said. *Crunch-slam.* "I don't think they care."

"We have to give up," Anna said.

"No."

"Nikos, she's right. If they can't take us alive . . ."

"No." The tram banged and swerved, and I cracked my head on the wall again. "They'll take us back to the Capital—we have to get away from the city."

Anna crept to the rear window. "The bumper's almost gone." The government tram rammed us again, something snapped and broke. "There it goes."

"Get away from the window!"

Without the bumper, they could smack right into—the nose of the government tram bucked the rear windshield in a spider web crack. I grabbed Anna's arm and yanked her away. Each time they hit us, we drifted across the road more dangerously, and I spotted a roadblock ahead.

Kysa shook her head. "We're in trouble."

"You think?"

The rear windshield smashed in a jagged circle. Glass sprayed through the tram, and this time the government tram didn't back off to build more speed: it kept its snout pressed through the broken window. If they turned, the momentum would drag our rear wheels—we might flip. The roadblock was 40 meters away.

The government tram started to turn: the remaining glass snapped and exploded away. Thirty meters from the roadblock.

Anna said, "We're going to die."

That's the spirit.

Twenty meters.

I opened the side door. The road flew past, but we were close to the grass shoulder.

Ten meters from the roadblock, the soldiers waved and shouted at us to stop.

"Okay . . ."

Our tram's rear wheels lost traction, our tram lurched, and Anna dove out the door. She held my arm, so I slipped after her, catapulting across a rush of speeding cement and hard grass. The road clipped my left shoulder, then the side of my face, I somersaulted down a shallow embankment and plopped on my back. My left arm began to throb, and I heard something heavy crunch, then a fast screech of metal and a series of satisfying crashes.

"Nikos?" Anna limped beside me: how was she already up and about? "Are you okay?"

I sat up. My left arm and right ankle hurt, but neither had the vision-blot-nausea that I associated with broken bones. I'd broken my right arm as a kid. Twice. Anna helped me up, and I winced.

"What's wrong?" she asked.

"I think I just twisted my ankle, bruised my arms." We went up to the road. "It could be worse."

Both trams had flipped onto the checkpoint's tangle of sharp wire and tire tracks. Ours seemed to have smashed in half, spilling debris across the highway that had tripped the government tram. It lay upside down, its wheels still spinning. I didn't see any soldiers.

"What's that noise?" Anna said.

"The hissing?"

She nodded, and I spotted the government tram's pinned hydro-balloon. They were supposed to be unbreakable, but it was definitely leaking. Stalled tram-traffic already appeared in both directions.

I went for the government tram. "Giannis is in there."

Anna tried to stop me. "It's leaking, you shouldn't . . ."

"We can't leave him."

"Wait."

"I just have to . . ."

The tram exploded.

CHAPTER SEVENTEEN

The Glass Sky

We found Kysa on the shoulder, shaken but uninjured. Anna wouldn't let me search through the wreckage or wait for the fire and rescue teams to arrive.

"There's nothing you can do."

So we left the road and hiked through a neighborhood of apartments, across a tarred parking lot to the porch outside some kind of abandoned machine factory.

"Okay," Anna said, and she sat. "Let's think about this."

I didn't want to huddle on a dirty stoop, so I kicked rocks and thought about Giannis. Why had they knocked over our tram? Didn't the government pricks know that they couldn't just plow through an overturned tram?

"That was so stupid," I said. "Why would they do that?"

"It's over," Anna said. "We have to decide what we're going to do right now."

"Maybe he got out. He could have jumped out—just like we did."

Except that they were holding him captive, and we hadn't found him or anyone else on the roadside.

Anna said, "Please, let's try to figure out what we're going to do."

Kysa said, "I'm sorry about your brother."

I tried to think of something disparaging to say, then just sat beside Anna on the stairs. "Why is it dark already?"

"It's getting late," she said.

I wondered if the end of the world was scheduled for midnight or noon—before or after the last day?

"I don't know what to do," I said. "I give up."

"What?"

"I'm too tired, and there's just too much—we can't do anything." As the adrenaline left my bloodstream, my body ached. I was done.

"We're not far from the Leim'en'a crossing," Anna said. "That means we could still find the field where the cosmonaut . . ."

"Go ahead."

"Don't do that."

"Anna, Giannis just blew up. I know you had a special bond with him too, but he was my brother."

She looked away. "I don't think we should stay here."

"Then go."

"You can't just give up."

"Why not?"

"You know why."

"You mean I can't give up because the world's going to end in a couple days?"

Kysa said, "Why do you . . ."

Anna cut her off, "We have to know whether or not we really moved that man to an empty field, that's important."

"I don't want to talk about this anymore."

"Will you come with me?"

I pretended to think about it. "No."

"Why not?"

"We've already had this conversation."

She took a deep breath, searched the concrete for something to clobber me with, then nodded to me. "You're coming along."

"What?"

"We're going to find that windmill. Now get up."

I couldn't really believe that Giannis had been obliterated in that tram explosion, but it was a legitimate excuse to be difficult.

"Aren't you tired?" I said.

"Of course I am. But we have to move."

This conversation was exhausting. When she helped me up, I didn't struggle, and when we started walking parallel to the distant highway, I watched the ground. It was impossible to sleep and march simultaneously, but I was determined to try.

Four hours later, we found the windmill.

"This is it," I said.

We stood exactly where we'd left the cosmonaut.

"Are you sure it wasn't over there?" Anna said, and she pointed to another empty patch of grassland.

"I leaned on this pile of stones."

It was too dark to tell one ruined clutter from the next, and the grassland was full of overgrown masonry. So no, I wasn't sure, but that was definitely the windmill, with the curl of highway and mountains in the backdrop. We were in the right area, but the guy was long gone.

Kysa said, "I don't see anyone."

Why was she still following us around?

I shouted a few times, didn't get an answer, and Anna joined me. We watched Kysa wander.

"We should let her go," Anna murmured.

"I didn't realize she needed our permission." I slouched on a crumbling wall. "Are we done?"

"I really thought he'd be here."

"Even if it worked, that was twelve hours ago. Why would he still be here?"

"It's after midnight," she said.

"I know." I cupped a hand around my mouth. "Kysa!"

She waved, and I suck a breath to yell again.

"He's here!" she shouted.

We went to see: Kysa was right. Thank the gods it was after dark. I recognized the outline of his flight suit, no need to lean close enough for the features. I couldn't see the flies, I just felt them in my hair. Anna examined the body, then led us away.

She said, "Someone cut his throat and left the stone in his hand."

Naturally.

Kysa asked, "You saved that man?"

Anna looked at me. "What do you think?"

"I don't think it did much good."

"We brought him here, and someone killed him . . ."

"With a pointy rock?"

"Yes."

"Then that someone left him and the rock in this field?"

"He's dead, Nikos. Someone opened his throat—didn't you see?"

"How would anyone know he was here?"

"He could have called. He may have a comm—I'll check." She returned, shaking her head. "They could have taken it."

"You heard him, he said he wanted to die."

"Nikos . . ."

"You heard him."

"*Okay.*" Anna tensed. "It's not important now . . ."

"Suppose a flight is successful," I said, "and the cosmonaut comes back and tells everyone that he saw something important on the screen." She waited, and I continued, "What if the Pnetians know what he's going to see, and they arrange for suicides to go up. So either way, the cosmonaut dies."

She was getting tired. "We have to go back to the city."

"Because he killed himself in that field over there?"

"Yes. It means the room moved him."

"We moved him, remember?"

"That's my point," she said. "That room isn't just a room."

No, I guess not. I nodded to Kysa. "What do you think it is?"

"I'm not sure. We've all been inside," Kysa said. "And it changed each of us."

"It didn't *change* me, I just can't sleep." I paused. "Wait: you went inside with Wesler, right? And then—what?—he stopped sleeping?"

"Yes."

"And then he burned his house down?" She nodded, and I asked, "Who else went down with you?"

"His mistress."

"And she was Shan, right?"

"Yes."

You need someone from Shan and someone from New Amith to open the Black Room. That's why it hadn't opened for Kysa the last time. And that's why Dett had collected Shan artifacts—the same reason Grotton had been buried with a tooth on his sarcophagus.

The Shan had been coming here for centuries, and the old gods required one of each to operate their Black Room. What did the cosmonaut see before we saved him? Maybe the pain was too much, maybe he couldn't walk. *He said, 'They're coming.'* Because of the Black Room's design, we couldn't comprehend it. Isn't that what Kysa had suggested at Lagone? I'd seen more than my eyes could register, and that's why I couldn't sleep. All time and space existed simultaneously in that old room.

Or maybe they didn't.

I still didn't understand the Space Project. What did Elena see on the *Melet*'s monitors?

"Nikos . . ."

Anna and Kysa were watching the sky—I looked up. There was something wrong. Where were the stars and the moon? It was sheer black. The longer I stared at it . . . that's going to be there when the sun comes up.

Anna touched my hand. "What is that?"

I glanced at the cosmonaut's body and had the feeling he was laughing at us. *I know something you don't.* The horizon flashed white, then a beautiful red-orange. Light reflected off the sky.

"Gods."

The glow spread. The ground rumbled and snarled with a delayed crash, as if a table of 1,000 kilogram plates had been knocked over.

The sky was a ceiling of dark glass—half-reflective black—and it was moving in a slow circle. The glow snapped and flared, throwing shadows and lighting bits of empty land.

Anna said, "That explosion came from the north."

We should have more time, I thought.

Anna sagged against a rock pillar. "Barcuc."

So that's what a glauston bomb does. The horizon burned. I needed a moment to sort this out. Kysa stared at the fire-glow, hypnotized. If you ignored the obvious death and destruction, the light was pretty.

"I know how you feel," Anna said.

You want to surrender, I thought. And now I have to say something inspiring.

"You're the last Shan on New Amith."

"Probably, yes." She shook her head. "If that was glauston, there will be fall-out. We don't have to stand in the explosion to be hurt."

"I know."

"We can't go back."

"Yeah. But we have to."

"Nikos, if we walk into that . . ."

"No one else can use the room, Anna. We have to stop this."

"You're unbelievable," she said. "A moment ago, you were ready to . . ."

"*Look up.* Do you think that'll go away on its own?"

"You want to move the sky?"

Very dramatic. "No, I want to move what's blocking the sky." And throw the Pnetians in a pond somewhere. I looked at Kysa.

"You knew this was coming."

Kysa shook her head, but I advanced on her. "You believe what they believe: we have to burn this world to end the Fifth Age, right? To bring the gods back?" I pointed up. "Okay—*now what?*" We were too slow to stop the bombs but I could still break her nose. "You wrote about Grotton and Fisherle—*you knew.*"

Kysa just stared back. "No . . ."

"Don't lie to me right now."

Anna tried to stop me. "This doesn't help us."

"She came from Lagone." To Kysa, "What about the room? How does that connect, why were you there? Were you supposed to watch it all along? That's why you went to work for the Weslers in the first place?"

A massive cap of dust-smoke was rising in the distance. Elena and my brother were both dead, and I was too pissed to conceive of my own mortality. At least if I were dead, I wouldn't be forced to stay awake. A flit of genuine terror choked my stomach, faded. What if I ceased to exist? That's been done, relax.

"We don't know that the room will work," Anna said at last.

"It has before."

"No. I mean—*that* is larger than the cosmonaut you pulled out." She was staring at the glass sky. "And we don't even know what it is. If the Pnetians smuggled glauston . . ." She glanced at Kysa. "Maybe they're the good guys."

I started for the road. "Yeah, maybe."

"You're going to walk?" she said.

"It looks that way."

"You won't make it."

Very encouraging. I stopped, tried to make her feel guilty. "You're right. I need you with me."

"We have to try to stay alive," she said.

"No, we don't."

* * *

Kysa lagged behind. Anna wouldn't leave her, and I was too tired to fight her right now. Maybe later. Even through a makeshift cloth face-mask, I could taste the smoke. Kilometer-wide torrents of iron-black smoke rolled across the road. It was almost sunrise, and on my right—to the north—the horizon spattered and flared a silent red-yellow. The Capital was roasting.

Ahead, an old man was walking away from the smoke. I pulled the cloth from my lips and coughed on the cinder-drift air.

"Are you from the Capital?" I asked the old man.

"Yes."

"What happened?"

"I don't know. My sons live there."

I hacked up a mouthful of dirt. The man was coated in ash, and so were we.

"Sorry," I said.

The man said, "My comm doesn't work. There's something in the sky. What did we do wrong?"

"Nothing."

We walked away. Smoke caught in my chest, like an itch, and every other second I coughed half-heartedly into my cloth. The wind and the masks kept us from speaking. We passed isolated homes and barren olive fields. I didn't want to think about it, so I closed my eyes and pretended I was asleep and dreaming about the end of the world, not real. The Republic had existed for 700 years, it wouldn't disappear in a night.

Ahead, the road was clogged with trams. All four lanes were jammed in the same direction: south. People ambled on the roadside, smoking, drinking, watching the traffic.

When we reached the mess, I called, "How far is it blocked?"

One guy stopped, a bottle in his hand. "I don't know. Far." He walked away. "What do you think?"

An elderly woman in a stalled tram waved out her window. "The provinces are all gone, you know."

"Yeah."

"The Shan destroyed all of them."

"Shan?"

"Of course. They're in the fields there . . ." She noticed Anna. "You did this!" She started pointing wildly. "She did this—stop her!"

"Don't look," I said.

But the woman was drawing attention, and someone shouted, "She's Shan! They're supposed to be gone—what's she doing here?"

How they could spot a Shan through the dust, I didn't know, but I pressed past the crowd, clearing a path for Anna. A rock went over her head.

"Don't stop."

"Nikos . . ."

"Don't run."

Watching the ground, I walked faster, Anna and Kysa right behind.

"Why is she going that way?"

"The Shan did this!"

Someone tripped Anna and she fell into me, catching her balance on my shoulder. Kysa was cut-off in a sudden mob. Their trams clogged with dust, the people were drunk, high, and terrified. Someone lobbed a stone that landed at Anna's foot. But they didn't have the nerve yet.

Someone called, "Get away from her."

They were talking to me: they wanted a clear shot. Anna grabbed my shoulder, her breathing rapid and irregular—as if she were afraid I might step aside. I tried to push through, but a circle of people closed.

A man with hot whiskey-breath yanked my arm. "Let go of her."

I shook him off. *Think.* "The Shan didn't do this." They weren't listening. A rock missed Anna's leg, but they were throwing harder. "How will this help?" I shouted.

Anna had dropped into a defensive posture, using me as a wall against the bulk of the crowd. A big guy shoved me, and I pushed back.

"You're with her?" he said and grabbed my arm.

I twisted away, and a rock bounced past Anna's face.

"Please," she said, "Nikos . . ."

The big guy caught my wrist and someone else hit me from behind. I lost Anna.

"Nikos!"

Say something. Stop them.

"Please!"

I wrestled, but they dragged me into the mob. *Think.* I heard a smack, and Anna yelped.

"No!" she screamed. "Don't—please!"

Think.

"She's pregnant!" The hands loosened, and I slipped free, pushed back to Anna. Anna pressed a hand to her bloody forehead, then grabbed my palm.

"She's a pregnant woman!" I said again, "and she isn't even Shan—her father was a Senator!"

The mob began to quiet, and I pulled Anna away before they could change their minds.

"What's wrong with all of you?" I said, forcing my way through the crowd. "We're trying to find her first born, now help us or leave us alone!"

They let us go.

". . . should have said . . ."

". . . didn't know . . ."

Kysa joined us at the roadside. The traffic continued, and when the mob was behind us, I checked Anna's head. It wasn't a deep cut, but it was messy. Blood dribbled down her face, already coated in filth and dust. I cleaned the wound, then wrapped it in a piece of my shirt.

Anna was still shaking. "You saved my life."

I smiled. "Yeah."

She kissed me. "I'm so sorry."

"It's okay." I nodded to Kysa. "You don't have to come."

"Yes I do," she said.

The room's in your head too, isn't it? I thought and kissed Anna again.

"Come on. We should keep moving."

Anna wouldn't let go of my hand. "You're a very good liar, you know. They all believed you."

"How do you know it isn't true?"

She patted her belly. "It isn't."

"There's a chance . . ."

The western horizon flashed, blackened with smoke, and there was a rolling thunder-echo. I was suddenly glad that I wasn't here alone. There was nothing more depressing than watching the end of the world by yourself.

Anna said, "That wasn't the Capital. That was another city."

We weren't close enough to see what the bombs had done; so far they appeared to be scattering swarms of dust and crazy people.

Anna said, "The Fifth Age just ended."

"No," I said. "We still have 30 hours." When she gave me a look, I checked my comm. "And ten minutes."

CHAPTER EIGHTEEN

Glauston

We reached the outskirts of the Capital. The landscape was ringed with pocked farmland and smoking Tellen complexes. All the barricades, checkpoints, and roadblocks had been blown away. The center of the city was still a haze, and as we walked, the air became a heavy mist of filth that scratched and tickled my throat. We had reached the edge of the blast. The hulk of a burnt tram appeared through the drifting smoke, and I tasted a rotten smell, like dead fish or forgotten eggs. Not fish. We hiked through a cratered field of orange trees, paused to eat, and ignored the bright lumps of clothing in the yard.

"The house," Anna said.

Good idea, I thought, and we headed toward the house. It was unlocked. A cluttered two-story with broken windows, the interior of the house was soiled in ash. All the food was gone, and the plumbing didn't work. Anna collapsed in the living room, and I paced.

"Does your forehead hurt?" I asked.

"Yes."

Kysa rooted through the empty pantries.

"There's no food," I called.

Anna murmured, "She's not looking for food."

"What's she . . ."

"Weapons."

I coughed. "I'm glad one of us is planning ahead."

Anna relaxed on the couch, raising a dust-cloud. She looked like a rug someone had hung in the sun and then beaten out. I felt that way too, but if I sat I wouldn't be able to get back up. Kysa came into the living room empty-handed.

I said, "Nothing?"

"No."

"If we keep moving," I said, "by tomorrow afternoon, we should be there."

Anna smiled. "You want to walk all night?"

"Do you have something better to do?"

"Help me up."

I did, and after another brief search, we left the house and returned to the highway. A pack of dogs galloped along the roadside, barking and wrestling over scraps of meat and bone. Someone shrieked like a human alarm from a nearby villa, and we entered one of the village suburbs. All the signs were gone.

A woman in body armor was picking through the rubble that barricaded the road ahead. She looked at us curiously, then grabbed a pyck she'd planted nearby and shouted, "What do you want?"

"Nothing."

Keeping my distance, I wandered through scorched front lawns, my shoes crunching on glass and slivers of warped metals.

"You're going the wrong way," the woman said.

"Thank you."

Anna said, "I told you so."

I wasn't familiar with the southern suburbs, but it was just as well. The skeletal village thinned, then became kilometers of ruined villas and farms. The crops, factories and mansions had been stomped into craters, glass-blisters and charcoal debris. The air hung in a cloud of ember-dust that smoked and blurred the destruction, making it look even worse.

The smoldering trams became lop-sided hulks, then crouching mounds of metal, then drifts of steaming bits. It was getting worse, and at the remains of a turn-off for one of the belt highways that circled the city, I paused.

"Do you feel that?"

The air *tingled*, as if it were charged, still hot with an ozone smell. My exposed hands and face—cough, cough—began to itch and burn.

Anna said, "We're breathing it right now."

"Yeah."

Glauston. The beltway ramp was a slope of bruised cement and discolored rocks. We could climb and follow the ruined road that circled the city and avoid the city center on our way to the Estate. That would take us right by my old neighborhood.

"Let's go around," I said.

I scraped my hands and knees as I climbed, then paused halfway to cough some more. My fingers itched. I scratched my cheek—that just made it worse.

Anna screamed, "Barcuc!"

I spun, almost fell. A horse waited at the base of the slope, watching me with huge black eyes. It had crept up behind Anna, and now she backed away with Kysa. Torn harness straps dangled from a ripped tow outfit, and the horse stomped, snorted.

"Gods, you scared the . . ."

"It poked me with its nose," Anna said.

Snort, stomp.

"Yeah—what?" I said.

The horse whinnied, tossed its head.

Anna said, "Go away!"

The horse stomped again.

"What do you want?" I said.

Another neck toss. It understands.

"What?"

It cantered away, paused at the roadside, and nudged a pile of lumpy clothes with its hoof.

"Yeah, I'm sorry about that . . ." It whinnied again. "What? I'm not coming back down . . ." *Snort, stomp.* "Yeah—we heard you. A lot of people are dead, you should get out of the . . ." Whinny. "Okay." Stupid, but I picked my way back down.

Anna said, "What are you doing?"

"It wants to show me something."

"It's a *horse*."

"Yeah, I see that."

The horse waited by its dead master.

"Okay," I said. "What?" When I didn't get any closer, the horse huffed: 'stop screwing around and look at the body'. I eased closer. *Snort.*

It was idiotic, but I looked down: half of a charred man, both legs and one arm missing, the man's skin had burnt and flayed off, though some of the clothes had fried into his flesh—wait.

Behind him, a three-meter box had overturned in the ditch, coated in ash.

"What is it?" Anna called.

The horse stomped once, tossed its mane, then galloped away. I watched it go.

"Nikos?" She came to see, Kysa right behind. "It's a box."

I went to investigate. A coil of severed wires ringed the edge. Some kind of fuse.

The air smelled like burnt hair and chemicals, and as I stared, Anna said, "Get away from it." She pulled me back to the road.

"It's another bomb, isn't it?" I nodded to Kysa. "It is, isn't it?"

"I don't . . ."

"Yeah."

We climbed back up to the beltway. It wasn't terribly inspiring. Sections had collapsed and what remained was a path of craters and endless wreckage that rolled and piled in the wind like sand and scrap metal. My hands had swollen in an itchy rash, and when I coughed again I couldn't stop.

"Take a breath," Anna said. "You have to breathe."

Really? I retched, tasted bile, and spat a wad of yellow. Nice.

Anna told me to take a slow breath.

I sniffed, coughed again. "Why?"

We continued walking.

* * *

That night, the air glowed.

207

We would reach my house in a few hours. From the beltway, the Capital was a depressing smudge of ruin, blurry firelight and emptiness. Most of the suburbs were simply gone. And in the yellow-green glow of smoke and dust, the landscape looked like a memory of a memory or a cheap lithograph: as if it were underwater.

The itch became a burning, as if I'd rubbed my skin raw or been sunburned—and it was spreading. Irritating. Anna had it too now, and the splotches looked worse on her bright skin. Nausea and the occasional dry heave left a stale, acidic taste on my tongue. And my eyes hurt. But I was too tired to whine or complain. And anyway, the city had it worse.

My nose was bleeding again. I sniffed back the blood—tried to hide it—which didn't help when Anna noticed.

"You're going to die before we even get close," she said. "We should . . ."

". . . stop having this conversation."

Dong.

We paused. The bell rang again. We walked to the edge of the road and looked down on the blown-out remnants of a temple. Somehow, the bell-tower was completely intact. In the glow, we watched a pair of men stacking bodies in a pit. Some were still moving. Each time they tossed a body, the bell rang.

Anna tapped my arm. "Come on."

I didn't move. "What are they doing?"

"The crematorium is probably broken."

"But they're not all dead."

"Come on."

We walked away. The artificial lithograph-glow faded as the sun rose, but the 'overcast' sunlight didn't cheer me up. Dust-smoke gray and yellow, it made me nauseas. We split rations we'd found on a pair of dead legs, and the highway turned. We'd tracked the perimeter of the city center, and the destruction and dust-glow receded, but the wind picked up. Craters became rubble became charred corner walls and then the outlines of buildings. Smoke rose from temple pipes on the left: that oven was working.

An hour later, we entered my neighborhood. Most of the houses were half-houses, their roofs, windows, and at least one of four walls blown away. Mine was missing two. But the lawn god was still there.

"Nikos."

Giannis stood in the doorway.

CHAPTER NINETEEN

Third Rites

S hit. I was asleep or hallucinating. He wore a bulky coat and hat and had lost hair. Pinkish scabs covered his chin and cheeks—from scratching a pebbly rash. He coughed.

"You're dead," I said.

"Not yet."

Anna ran up the stairs. "Oh no."

I just stared at him. "You look like . . ."

"You too," he said.

"Yeah. Squatting?"

He cleared his throat with a messy noise that meant something was wrong. "They brought me here."

"I saw the tram blow up. You're dead."

"There were two trams," he said. "I struggled, kept mine from following."

"I didn't see two trams."

Anna said, "What difference does that . . ."

"I'm going crazy. I don't believe he's here."

"What do you want me to do?" Giannis said.

Anna said, "Nothing—come inside. You need to sit down."

She guided him to the rubble inside, and I followed, Kysa behind me. Something rumbled in the near-distance.

"Where were you when it happened?" Anna asked him.

"Here. They brought me back here."

"Help me," Anna said to me, and to Giannis, "Does the plumbing work?"

"No."

We went into the kitchen, and Anna cornered me. "What is the matter with you?"

"He's dead . . ."

"He's not—he's right there: look."

I did. She was right. Giannis started choking and spat a mouthful of blood. He was alive, but he wouldn't be for much longer. *Yes, your brother's miraculously alive, but he'll be dead in an hour.* I had been surprised by how quickly they'd been able to chase us, the soldiers must have had one tram blocking the entrance and another nearby to stop a getaway.

We found some water in the icebox.

"How do you feel?" I asked Giannis.

"Terrible." He accepted the water. "Why'd you come back here?"

I told him about the cosmonaut's suicide.

"We moved him with the Black Room," I said.

"Okay. So?"

"So if we could move him, we might be able to . . ."

"I thought you just wanted to leave."

"I did."

"So you wouldn't get this."

'This' meaning what had happened to him.

"Yeah."

"The air is poisonous, you shouldn't have come back."

"We're almost there."

"Today's the last day," he said.

"Yeah."

"So does the world end at midnight?"

"I think it's already . . ." I looked up. The roof was gone, and I watched a spread of fiery dots arc across the blackglass sky overhead.

Kysa said, "What is that?"

"I have no idea."

211

The dots grew like streaky meteor bits. A ball of fire landed on a house across the street, and what was left of the building erupted. I could feel the heat on my cheek. Giannis winced. The flames spread, and another fireball dropped further up the street.

I said, "I don't believe this."

It was raining fire.

"If we're going to go," Giannis said, "I think we should go now."

"You're probably . . ."

The back of the house turned to flames. I'd fallen against the front wall, and the fire billowed, spewing a soup of dark smoke. Anna helped Giannis out, but I just watched the inferno spread, mesmerized as it ate my house. Flames chewed up the walls and snarled along the floorboards toward me.

"—ikos!"

Get up. I couldn't breathe, and the air was too hot. Blind, I grabbed something and stood. I sucked a breath that scalded my lungs and knocked me over.

"Where are you? Nikos!"

I ran from the living room to the kitchen: the back wall was a mass of flame, and through the doorway I saw my bed burning—covering my face with a shirt, I started grabbing things: papers, clothing, shoes, trinkets, and when a hot board smashed past my head, I hurried to the front lawn and dumped the armload on the grass.

Anna was hysterical. "Thank the gods! I was afraid . . ."

I pushed past her and went back in.

"Nikos!"

Back to the bedroom—the doorway was a square of fire, and I tried to press through: too hot. Something exploded in the kitchen, sparking shrapnel. Anna grabbed my shoulder hard and yanked me outside. I doubled over, coughing, and she blocked the front door. A piece of the wall fell.

I said, "That's my stuff in there . . ."

"It doesn't matter."

"It does. I'm not going to just let it burn!" When I ran, she hit me hard, and I dropped back to the grass. Giannis was choking uncontrollably, while useless-Kysa watched. "Stop it," I said. "Get out of the way!"

"It isn't your stuff," she said.

"Anna, I'm going to . . ."

"It's not yours."

"Of course it is."

"No." She kicked the pile I'd brought out. "This is your dress? Your necklace? These are yours?"

I tried to stop panting. She was right. It was all Elena's. I hadn't saved one piece of my own.

"It was too dark," I said.

"It's okay," she said.

I started to tell her to go to hell, then she winced and examined her burned palm. Anna's skin was smeared black and gray with soot and dried blood. What was I doing?

"Let it burn," she said.

Third rites: burn the belongings of the deceased.

"Yeah."

I helped Giannis to his feet, and we all went into the street, away from the burning houses. The sky twinkled with fire specks.

"You shouldn't have hit me," I said to Anna.

"No?" She sounded surprised.

"Of course not."

"You wanted to get yourself killed." She pointed to Kysa. "Make yourself useful and help us carry him."

Kysa took Giannis's other arm.

He said, "It's a long walk, I don't know if . . ."

"You will. We'll race, if you don't keep up."

The entire suburb was burning: lawns of flame and houses turned to skeletal ovens.

A smile. "You'd win."

Yeah, what else was new. Anna met my eyes: *you're welcome.*

* * *

213

It took another seven hours to reach the Wesler Estate. Seven hours of corpses, endless fire, continuous coughing and a frightened woman in the street who had . . .

"Taley?" To me, "You're Taley?"

"No."

"Taley, you can't leave me here without a knife—what if I get hungry? Who's going to cut out the bones?"

We had kept walking.

As the suburb thinned, the fires struggled, smoldered, then became burnt-black grassland. There were no more fireballs in the sky. We were out of food, water, and when Giannis collapsed, I panicked.

"Stop—open your eyes!"

Anna said, "He's okay, just give him . . ."

"Look at me!"

Giannis fought to breathe, confused. "What's wrong?"

Finally, pasture farms and desolate fruit groves became private villas. The fire hadn't come this far. The grass was just discolored with ash, but Giannis was getting worse, we all were.

My nausea was constant now, but at least there was no blood when I vomited. Take solace where you can.

Anna said, "There." As if we wouldn't recognize it behind all the trams.

Government trams clogged the streets, and a small army loitered around the main gate.

Anna said, "What is this?"

Kysa and I helped Giannis closer, and now he saw the soldiers. "Where are we? What is this?"

"They must know," Anna said.

"Yeah."

"I mean they must have somehow . . ."

"Yeah."

As we approached the Wesler estate and its limp perimeter fence, one of the men shouted for our names. Wanted to yell, 'Captain Suck-My . . .' but gave him my real one instead. They waved us onto the Wesler lawn. The dig tents had burnt to a yellowish mush that layered the ground and stuck to my boots like chewing gum.

Even more soldiers guarded the tunnel entrance, and Kysa froze. The mansion was gone. Crumbles of black stone stood at the four corners, but the rest was scattered across the lawn like lazy brown garbage, all wood flakes and glass.

Before we could reflect on the mess, the soldiers ushered us down the ramp, through the tunnel, and to the Black Room. Except that—clogged with ceiling lamps and packed with soldiers, techies, and men in dark togas—it wasn't black at all. I spotted the Director half-asleep at the far wall.

He jolted when he saw me, noticed Giannis and shouted, "Water—they need water. Bring rations too, and everything we have to treat the poison."

He gave Giannis a cot and shook my hand as if I'd just pulled his dog from a freezing pond. "Thank the gods. How did you—it does not matter, does it? You are here now."

"Yeah."

They brought water, and I took a long drink that made me choke. We sat around a cluttered table in the center of the room, and the Director watched me anxiously, as if I might disappear at any moment.

"I cannot tell you how much this means," he said.

"Thanks for the water."

"Oh not at all." He pointed to the walls. "Do you know why it is so crowded in here?"

Is that a trick question?

Anna asked, "Why?"

"There is no glauston in the air."

She glanced around, as if checking for herself. "What do you mean?"

"Somehow, this room acts as a buffer against the glauston sickness." He nodded to Giannis. "So while your brother is already in bad shape, he won't get any worse just breathing." Anna started to protest, and he said, "It's true, believe me. They do not know why, but we are safe in here."

The way he was grinning—I asked, "What happened?"

"What happened?"

"To the city?"

"A glauston bomb detonated on the steps of the Senate."

But I already knew that, so I asked, "What about the sky?"

"They don't know."

'They' again. "Well why are you here?"

"They were originally looking for you. Then they realized the air was safe."

Anna frowned. "I don't understand. Why would you look for us . . ."

"Don't you think we have flight recorders on our ships?"

Ah. They saw us lift the cosmonaut out of the ship, and we were under guard at the time, which meant they could determine exactly where we were when it happened.

I asked, "Why do you have so many soldiers?"

"They're not mine," the Director said.

"Where is he?"

"On the surface—comms do not work in this room."

"The guy died, you know."

"Who? Mr. Ante's'?"

"The cosmonaut, yeah. He killed himself—just so *they* know."

"Nikos, do you think any of us want to be in this situation?"

He was avoiding an answer. I said, "*This*—whatever's in the sky—arrived on Shan a week ago, didn't it? And now it's here. Was that the reason for the urgency? You couldn't see it from the ground . . ." It clicked in my mind. "You weren't just looking inside the *Melet*, you were looking *outside*. You were supposed to pray, but you were watching from another room, weren't you? The *Melet* had some kind of recorder, and you saw them coming." The tseon lenses in the missing Appendix to Elena's file . . . "That's why we've been acting like we're at war since Elena went up—but you needed to launch another ship to know how much time we had. And Ante's' showed you."

The Director smiled, as if I were a child. "We have to make decisions sometimes that are not as simple as . . ."

"Who is *we*?" I wanted to hit him. "That was Elena too?"

Anna rubbed my fist. "Okay . . ." She said quietly, "Stop."

"Please," the Director said. "I am glad you're here, I really am. No one wanted this to happen, but I look at your return as a sign that we will end stronger than we began."

He was making me sick to my stomach. Maybe the original ships had been launched to compete with the Shan, but the Space Program had nothing to do with competition anymore—we were launching ships, burning people alive, because our telescopes didn't work. The Director had probably seen the glass ships years ago. The apocalypse the Pnetians had foreseen in the scriptures, he'd glimpsed through tseon lenses hidden on manned rockets. If I didn't step into the hall, I was going to hit him. I excused myself, stood, and the Consul stepped in.

"Our luck is back, isn't it?" Then he noticed Kysa and called to the soldiers, "How did she get down here—lock her up now!"

Frantic, Kysa turned to me. "Please . . ."

The soldiers slammed her against the wall, clamped her wrists behind her back. The Consul said, "Senator Karto'u and his allies were traitors, and this woman is part of it. We've know who she is. Search her."

At some point, Karto'u had become too dangerous, and the Consul had assassinated him. But it hadn't made any difference, had it? It only took one person to plant a bomb.

They found a blade under Kysa's shirt, then knocked her to the floor.

Anna winced, grabbed my arm.

"He's right," I said.

Anna looked away. "She's . . ."

The soldiers dragged Kysa into the hall. She was crying quietly.

"Good," the Consul said. "How long have you been here?"

"Not long."

"You understand what we have to do?"

The Director said, "I haven't gone over this with them . . ."

"We don't have time." The Consul clapped his hands, as if someone had just unveiled a delicious pig. "The Republic is gone. Our Senate was annihilated in one stoke, and I have just learned that there have been attacks as far as Bis-Run. A glass cloud covers the entire planet, and we-are-paralyzed." He lowered his voice, as if he'd rehearsed this delivery, and had just reached the second, more emotional segment of the monologue. "They killed without any warning. They burned men, women, and children alive. That blast is rotting our bodies and fouling our air, and it will not end until we are all gone.

"Whoever they are—and I do not believe that matters—it is our duty, our responsibility to defend ourselves, and to fight back." If this had been the Senate, it would have drawn a few partisan "Aye's!" He paused, then said, "But how do we fight them? How can we kill what blocks out the sun? We do not have to: we only have to *move it*. Send them away. No—I see your answer. How can you expect us to do that, it's impossible." He pointed to the Director. "We've seen you do it. We know you used this room. You will move them away exactly as you moved that cosmonaut, and then you will draw all power into one place so that stability can be restored."

I waited, but he wanted an answer. "All power in one place?"

"Yes," he said. "If communication and law diminish through the Republic, New Amith will break into a thousand pieces and we will return to the Bloody Nations." He meant the Gumay Period. "You will make them leave, whoever they are, then you will bring all weapons here. You will make it clear that we still have a reigning Consul and that until the crisis has abated, he is in command."

He. I stared at him. "That's impossible."

The Consul tensed. "Why?"

"How could we find every weapon and stop everyone who might . . ."

"If you can move anything anywhere, then it is not impossible. It will take time, that's all."

"When will the crisis end?"

He shook his head. "I think you misunderstand the situation. This is not a negotiation. You *will* do these things. We are in real danger, and you are obligated to help us."

"What if we can't?"

"You will."

Anna said, "No, he means what if the room doesn't . . ."

"I know what he means."

I wondered how many soldiers he had here, then asked the Director. "What do you get?"

"It's not about that," the Director said. "We are in crisis."

No better time to split open the system and plant yourself in the center of a new one. When I still didn't agree, a soldier went to Giannis's cot.

"I *will* save the Republic," the Consul said. "If you refuse to help, your brother will be executed for treason."

Giannis was only half-conscious, but now he stirred. No, go back to sleep, I thought. Treason, huh?

"Yeah."

"You will help us?"

I met Anna's stare: *they don't know.*

"Okay."

CHAPTER TWENTY

A Slow Death

Five minutes later, Anna and I stood in the center of the Black Room. Curled into a fetal position, Kysa was kept under guard in the hall, and though they'd carried Giannis out, the soldiers hadn't bothered to strike any of the tent partitions: the room was a mess, the mold-smell replaced with body odor. The Director and Consul watched from the doorway.

Anna said, "Are you . . ."

"Yeah."

Keep pretending, I thought. You don't know what you're doing.

"Okay," the Director said, and he gave me a 'whenever you're ready' nod.

I murmured to Anna, "Can we just do this whenever . . ."

"I don't know."

Nothing happened. They waited, I tried to ignore their stares, then said, "This might not work with an audience."

But they didn't want to leave. "Are you trying?" the Director said.

How the hell should . . . "Yeah."

They hissed and whispered, but refused to leave

"The other times it just happened," Anna said.

"Yeah."

"I'm worried about Giannis."

"He'll be fine."

"If we can't get this to work . . ."

"I don't know."

"You're not worried?"

"Of course I'm worried. What do you want me to do? We should try to concentrate or—stop thinking about other things."

"Okay."

It didn't work—at first.

"Let's try again," I said. "Remember when it opened the . . ."

The room blurred, like a two-dimensional painting sliding to life.

I heard Anna: ". . . there's another . . ."

Presence. My senses didn't register. *Everything* was out of focus: vision, smell, touch, taste. I was in a dream-coma between consciousness and nightmare.

". . . Anna . . ."

". . . okay."

The room went black. I floated in a void that sucked and pulled at a metal cloud orbiting a blue-white ball. The ball was New Amith, the clouds were crescent moons, fingernail clippings. From above, they looked like blackglass ovals. Ships.

I said, ". . . inside."

A muddy room. Long and high, the walls were wet muck that dripped from the ceiling like paint. I didn't leave footprints as I went into a second room. A totemic head, dozens of meters tall, was planted in the center of a circle of rabbits. Like a quartz mountain, the head rose to the ceiling. Without a nose or ears, it had four red eyes—each larger than me—and a lipless jaw.

". . . Anna?"

". . . I see it."

There were more doorways, but I didn't want to wander. The ship was large enough to cloud the sky—there could be hundreds of kilometers of bunny-head rooms. I went into a third room, planted with grass and spiky-branched trees. A meaty pig flicked its ears and munched on a patch of grass.

The tree bark was crowded with writing, old menst. The miniature letters looped in spiral rows from the roots all the way up.

In the ship, I said, "Could be kilometers of . . ."

Someone said, *"Trees."*

A 'man' waited behind me, dressed in a black toga. Hairless with big brown eyes, his skin a yellowish green—as if it had been preserved in a jar—the 'man' smiled.

I said, "You . . ."

"Yes. What you expected?"

Its mouth moved, but didn't mimic the sounds. 'Yes' should have stretched, with more vowels.

I should have been frightened. "This is . . ?"

"Lost things," he said.

"What do you want?" He waited, as if he hadn't understood, and I said, "What . . ."

"What do you think I want?" he said. *"Music."*

Now I didn't—was he talking about the voices I heard in the Black Room? The ones singing about youth and people I didn't know? "Music?"

"Yes. Three-hundred million songs about war. Wouldn't that be beautiful?" Behind me, the pig chewed more loudly. *"It is good to see you,"* the Bialu said. *"I remember some of the things that brought us here. The smell of gooserain, other things that are also gone. Peace-conflict. Ae."* I didn't answer, and he said, *"You asked. That is what I want. But I can't have that, there are only nightmares now."*

"I don't understand."

"I have been more than you ever will. And I want you to help us. Together, we can be even more."

"How?"

"Revenge."

"You want to hurt someone?"

"Yes."

In the Black Room, I said, ". . . do you understand this?"

Anna: ". . . of course not."

With the Bialu, I asked, "What do you want me to do?"

"Something is coming," he said, *"far away in space, but it will be here soon. You will stop it."*

"How?"

" You will send it away. And then you will become our prophet in a new golden age. You will rule your people, as well as the other two entangled realities. Doesn't that sound interesting?"

I wasn't following. "What is 'it'? What do you want me to move?"

He turned to the enormous idol-head in the next room. *"I don't know. Somewhere, a dam broke. A locked door opened. And they are what was on the other side."*

Very poetic. "Something's coming after you?"

"Yes."

"And you want me to stop it?"

"Yes."

"When do they arrive?"

"Soon. This is why you were created: to stop them."

Why I was created? The Bialu didn't want us to leave New Amith and the Black Room: that's why we burned? I couldn't think that this being had somehow fiddled with the entire history of New Amith so that I would one day step into the Black Room with Anna.

"I don't believe you."

He squinted, as if I'd gone out of focus. *"Reach out to a blue star nearby. You'll see it. The danger is near that star."*

"No." The pig nudged the back of my legs, and I steadied myself on the old menst tree.

In the Black Room, Anna said, ". . . Nikos, what are you doing?"

"Why should I do this?"

The Bialu said, *"Do you understand?"*

"I understand. I said, 'no.'"

"We will find someone else."

"Find someone else then."

"Your world is gone. Your people will die if we don't intervene. That's obvious. I know you care."

Intervene? He was threatening me. I should have cowered and cringed, but I didn't. The Bialu—if that's what he was—could somehow save us from glauston-sickness and more bombs.

I asked, "What will this danger do when it arrives?"

223

"Chain a dog to a fence and release parasites over its entire body. They are not the chain or the vermin: they are what follows. Disease and worse."

A slow death. "Yeah, okay," I said. "I need time—give me time. And stop."

"Stop?"

"Stop the glauston poison, stop the bombs."

The Bialu chortled, like a man choking on a paper ball. He was laughing. *"You blame me?"*

"No." I blamed homicidal Pnetians. "But you can fix it. People don't get sick in this room—you can intervene."

"When you help us, we will intervene."

"I'm not a prophet," I said. "I don't want to be. You picked the wrong man to use—I don't believe in the gods."

He hesitated, as if he were waiting for the punch line. Is that a joke . . ?

"This is larger than you," he said at last. *"I have lived for too long to play whatever game this is."*

"Yeah, me too."

"I will not help until you agree."

In the Black Room, Anna said, ". . . we should do what it wants."

". . . no." To the Bialu, I said, "I'm not a slave."

"You are a product."

"No."

"You will do as we tell you or you will become extinct."

In the Black Room, Anna said, ". . . what difference does it make? Nikos, I'm going to put you near the blue star. I see it."

". . . no."

The Bialu said, *"This is not complicated. Your ancestors understood."*

"I'm not Hostos." To Anna, ". . . okay. Bring me back."

She did. The Director and Consul tittered and whispered, oblivious.

"What was that?" Anna said. "What did you do?"

"You saw what happened."

"Nikos, I'm going to put you back."

"No, you're not."

"We have a chance to negotiate, and you can't make that decision."

"That wasn't a negotiation," I said. "I was wrong."

"About what?"

"I said this wasn't meant for us. That it's like putting a dog in a flight simulator—it's the exact opposite: it's like putting a Vermouse in a landfill."

"Stop it." She grabbed my arm hard, and glanced at the tunnel. They still hadn't noticed us. "Are you going to tell them?"

"Yeah."

"We have a chance to end this right now. We should go back."

"No."

"You're unbelievable."

"Do you trust it?"

"I don't think we have a . . ."

"Of course we do." She didn't release my arm, and I said, "Stop that."

"What is this?" she said. "What's your plan?"

"We have to fight back."

"We have to use the Black Room . . ."

"We will," I said, "when we tear their ships apart."

Anna looked as if I'd painted my face bright pink: *are you mad?*

"There are *thousands* of ships," she said, "we can't fight them."

"We can. Let go of my arm." She did, and I rubbed it. "Nice hold."

"You're making a mistake."

"No."

"I believe him."

"It," I said.

"I believe *it*."

"I don't. And anyway, it doesn't matter. I don't trust it as far as I can kick it. So let's find out how far that is."

The Director and Consul approached.

Anna murmured, "They've almost finished Shan."

"You don't know that."

"It worked, didn't it?" the Consul said.

I stared at Anna. Somehow she had sensed the Bialu ravaging Shan. They hadn't come to barter. What if it was the other way around? They didn't build the room for us, they built us for the room. We were supposed to be their slaves, isolated on different planets until—for whatever reason—we stumbled into their machine. And *wham*—they arrived. What were our limitations? Could they switch it off if we turned the room against them?

"What happened?" the Consul asked.

I told him.

When I finished the Director said, "You won't send them away."

"We went into the Bialu ship . . .

The Consul stopped me. "For a technology like this to exist in society, we must have laws. Imagine if the first person to invent gunpowder had refused to share that knowledge with anyone else. My point is that you have the ability to use the room—the device. That's all. You do as we say, but you don't decide what is or is not important. Am I clear?"

What was he afraid of? That I would toss him into the ocean somewhere and make myself Consul? Anna had been thinking the same thing. I said, "Yeah."

The Consul said, "You were not in a position to negotiate, you didn't have the authority, but I respect your approach to the situation."

He knew damn well that I had refused to negotiate because I was stubborn, not out of respect for his sovereignty, but I said, "Thank you."

"Now, however, the situation has changed. Now that I've had an opportunity to review our options, you can negotiate." When I didn't respond, he said, "The Bialu want to impress us. But, I see no reason they would lie to you about an external threat. And if *they* are threatened by some distant enemy, the Republic is threatened too."

The Republic is gone because of glauston bombs, not because of a distant door somebody forgot to lock in outer space.

But I said, "I agree."

"You will negotiate with the Bialu," the Consul said. "You'll do as they ask, and *then*—after you've moved their enemy away, whatever it is—if they refuse to help us, we can discuss a different course of action." To Anna, "Do you understand?"

She said, "Yes."

To me, he said, "I have doubts about leaving this in your hands." But you don't have a choice, I thought, and he continued, "But I do not think you would consciously hurt the Republic. You're smart enough to see what's happening and the damage that's been done. Do you think we should negotiate?"

No. "We don't have a choice."

"You don't think we should try to send their ships away?"

So wily. But he was treating me like a clueless dog. Say 'yes', and it means that not only would I try to punish the Bialu, I might just take control of New Amith. This was dangerous. At a certain point, the Consul's fear overwhelmed his ambition. What percentage chance did he need? I wondered. At what point would he cut his losses, shoot me in the back of the head and bury the Black Room?

"We can't fight them," I said at last.

"But if you could?"

"We can't."

He stiffened, as if I had tried to nip his hand. "Okay."

Bingo. 'Yes' means I'm rebellious, 'no' means I'm lying. So I'd pretended to be a realist: *why fantasize about the impossible?* It sounded good, and I was suddenly just a sensible guy trying to stay alive. Which wasn't true.

"Are we ready to try again?" the Consul asked.

Just like that. When I hesitated, the Director walked me to the nearest wall. "You're doing very well. After everything that's happened, I'm impressed with all you've done."

What exactly had I done? I'd realized the Pnetians were smuggling glauston just in time to watch the Capital explode. Giannis was dying because I hadn't gone out, as I should have, and now the Director was *impressed.*

"I haven't done anything," I said.

"This room only works for you and the Shan woman. That in itself . . ."

"It's a coincidence." I watched the Consul question Anna, his left hand crooked at the side of his toga. "What is he giving you?" I asked.

The Director said, "Nikos, our way of life is under attack."

Our way of life has been kicked to the curb and bludgeoned to brink of death, I thought. "Yeah."

"You don't look well."

"I don't feel well."

"You'll be remembered for this. Our Consul won't forget." When I didn't answer, he said, "This is a chance to atone."

"Atone?" At first I didn't get it, and then understanding snapped like a rubber band inside my skull. "You're talking about Elena." Slow down. "You think I can make up for what happened to her?" My heart was pumping too hard.

Anna looked over, and the Director said, "She was sent up to confirm this, after all."

"To confirm what?"

"The Bialu ships."

"You knew they were coming from the tseon lenses, why would you need . . ."

"We didn't know *when*."

"That's why she's dead." I was getting upset, but not angry. It was so absurd. "Why would you need a person in the *Melet*?"

"The same reason we needed Mr. Ante's' in the *Pret*, to guide the ship back down and confirm what we've seen. Elena knew."

All that bullshit about discovery for humanity's sake, maintaining a sense of wonder or competition with Shan—they just wanted to confirm what *we already knew* from the recorders. One extra layer of flammable proof. That the Bialu were coming.

"The Shan knew?"

He nodded. "The Ckish did, yes. But it's more complicated than that."

Of course it was. Elena had known she would burn and that she would literally see the gods—even if they were on a fuzzy monitor—before she died. Her transcript meant exactly what it said.

The Consul called, "Are we ready?"

"I'm sorry," the Director said to me.

"You confirmed that the Bialu were coming years ago—in the earlier launches? All of this was about *when*. That's why she's dead."

Smiling, the Consul stepped between us. "We're ready when you are, Nikos."

Kysa was restrained in the hall, Giannis coughed, and Anna met my stare: *I know*. For Elena, I thought. He knew how to motivate me.

"We're ready," the Consul said again, and he waved to the soldiers. They held Giannis at gunpoint. Giannis was dying of glauston sickness and they wanted to shoot him. It felt surreal and almost funny, like a fever dream. I wanted to laugh or set him on fire. They didn't leave this time.

I closed my eyes, as if that made a difference. My flesh itched and burned, and my mouth tasted like old blood and bile. I imagined that Anna could hear me. We're going to turn on them, I thought. Right now: for Elena.

CHAPTER TWENTY-ONE

The Sixth Age

The room slipped out of focus, but this time we didn't leave. There were two of me; one real, the other a blip-ghost that flicked from place-to-place when Anna transported me.

The Consul said, "Is it working?" He saw both of me, and his soldiers were frightened.

The real me said, ". . . yeah."

Anna moved me from one end of the room to the other, as if loosening her joints—warming up. I was like a ship that she could steer; a stone she could toss across the water.

The Director was backing up to the tunnel, and the Consul shouted, "No! Watch him—hold his brother! Nikos, go to the Bialu. Negotiate—just as we discussed."

But Anna didn't pull me out. She'd seen my crazy stare.

"Nikos," the Consul said again, "you will do as I say or your brother . . ."

"No. You will do as I say. You're no longer in charge. Everyone needs to drop his weapon or we'll find out how well you can swim. How's that sound?"

The Director ran, and several soldiers started to follow—the Consul went to the guy holding Giannis. "Shoot him! Do it now!"

I didn't have to touch anyone to move them. I could grab them by thinking about it—no, 'grab' wasn't right. It was as if they responded to me—the same way a tram followed the directions we gave it—not the other way around. Their bodies just weren't in the Black Room anymore because I asked them not to be. Instead, Anna took us to a bright blue ocean on the other side of the world. No land anywhere in sight. This was marginally better than tossing them into space or the center of the sun, right? They were suddenly floundering in the ocean, the Consul and all of his soldiers. They could swim, barely, and a few nearby sharks noticed. Good enough. Get out of that jam or become a piece of meat; either way, it wasn't on me anymore.

Anna returned me to the Wesler lawn to block the Director from escaping. He was frozen at the mouth of the tunnel-hole. He'd cut his leg in the run from the Black Room and was trembling, as if the ground had just vanished. It might.

"Nikos . . ."

"*For Elena?*"

"I'm sorry."

I didn't believe that. "New Amith is done."

"You're right." He looked at the shell of the Wesler mansion. "I see that. We were not strong enough to fight the evil . . ."

"This has nothing to do with *evil*, it's the end of the Fifth Age. It's time to move on. And *they* didn't do this—the Pnetians did. Elena was one of them. They waited until they had enough bombs, then they stomped our little Republic into the ground." But I still didn't really know why.

"I wanted to save them, Nikos. That's what the space program was about, that's always what we wanted." How damn noble of him. When I didn't respond, he continued, "The device—that Black Room—is dangerous. You should understand that, before you use it again. I believe it does more than simply move things from place to place. Did you see anyone in it, people from another world?"

"What do you know about it?"

"I know what she told me, a woman called Aelia. They have a version of this device in another world. We are connected to them by it."

I'd heard that name before. Where? I was too tired for this. "So it links us to other planets or worlds or something," I said. "I don't care right now."

"It is more complicated and risky to use the device than we understood at first. When you activate it, I believe *they* may see it too."

"The other-world people? Somewhere somebody notices when we move things around with the Black Room? So what?"

"Aelia told me—"

"Was she one of them? Whoever 'Aelia' is, she came from another world?"

"No, she was one of us, but she knew that the device would work for you. That's why you were assigned to the dig."

Aha. That's why I recognized the name: back when all of this was starting the Director had mentioned her in passing. "And?" I said. "Where is she? Maybe it's all the glauston poison in my brain, but this sounds a lot like you're stalling. Is she here?"

"I don't know where she is . . ."

"That's enough. Go away. I don't ever want to see you again."

He started to protest, then stumbled past me. "Thank you."

My first selfless act. We returned to the Black Room. Just me, Anna, Giannis, and Kysa. I untied Kysa, and before anyone could speak, I asked Anna to put me in another Bialu ship.

The Black Room faded into a metal cavern. Hundreds of meters high, walls too distant to see, I'd entered a jungle of humming glass pipes. I passed through the rods like a phantom after-image in a cheap lithograph, half-real.

I was supposed to negotiate, so where were they? The vast Bialu boiler-room-jungle-gym was empty. After exploring kilometers of metal and plastic, I found a side doorway and a sculpture garden. Marble men-Bialu posed, dramatic and bare-chested, hugging mortal wounds. One was missing an arm, another had half-fallen with a shard of his skull blown away, and a trio of scarred figures mourned a pile of marble carnage, complete with immaculate intestine coils, organs and a dead leg.

As Anna moved me toward another doorway, a toga'd Bialu stepped into my path.

"You made these?" I asked.

"Yes."

"Why?"

"That's the wrong question."

"What's the right question then?"

"How did they die. We were proud before our first real war. We went looking for others in the vastness, and what we found humbled us. It changed us. You have no idea. It was the first time we were ever cold."

"Lucky you. It's cold here all the time. This is about the enemy I heard about earlier?"

"Yes."

"Your enemy—whatever they are—are the ones who brought 'the cold'? The ones who were behind the locked door or the dam or whatever?"

"We call them a disease. We don't know what they are. But before your sun was born, they brought death. And we had to run. You have no idea what it's like to watch the world end and keep going."

I kind of did, but I said, "And they . . ."

" A second home, but they found us. Then a third. This is a disease that cannot be killed. There is no salvation or hope. We cannot fight them, so we began to work on a trapdoor: you. The product that would evolve to use the device. Both hidden so they wouldn't find it."

"To fight them," I said.

"To isolate them, so that they can never return to harm us in the life of the universe. Curing a cancer isn't about violence, it is about removal."

"They hurt you."

"Yes."

"And now you want me to save your third home . . ."

"Our third home is gone. We are all that survived. Of 17 million ships, fewer than 4,000 survive."

Seventeen million of these ships couldn't beat the 'disease'. And here was one, blocking out the sun with the gods only knew how much weaponry onboard.

"You want me to send the disease away?"

"Yes."

"Then what?"

"You will become our prophet, and we will begin a golden age."

Prophet sounded a lot like puppet. "What kind of 'golden age' is this supposed to be?"

"We will make music together, Nikos." Music again, and now it knew my name. Of course it did. *"We will use your power to rebuild. We can take more worlds than can be counted. You must realize how important you are."*

"You want to 'take' worlds? You're talking about conquest. More war."

"You will serve alongside us. There's no other way."

Something occurred to me, and I asked, "You made the Black Room, this device?"

"We made you."

That wasn't actually an answer. It said it made us, designed us to use the Black Room, but not the Black Room itself. "Do other people, somewhere else, see when we use the Black Room?"

"The device is like a tendon connecting muscle to bone. When you stretch, it pulls tissues to hold them together, to maintain its structure. Some of the device you can see, some of it touches other worlds. When you use the device, it is as if the entire joint were moving."

The Bialu should have been talking to Giannis, he was the doctor after all. I wanted to leave the Black Room. Bury it. I understood what the others had done. Hostos, Grotton, even Wesler. The Black Room, this device, drove everyone mad. No one should know about this. Except that now *they* were here. I couldn't turn it off. We would be their tram to plunder. Their *product*.

Pain.

I felt my body in a kick of heat, and driving pain through my belly. I heard screaming, felt the Black Room again. I was standing beside Anna: Kysa had driven a knife into my belly—no, not mine. Anna's belly. Anna was hunched over, shaking, blood starting to soak her shirt.

Kysa said, "Nikos, you can hear me; Anna, you can hear me. Do exactly as I say. Bring the Bialu here—to this room."

Anna said, ". . . I won't do that . . ."

Kysa twisted the blade, and Anna cried out, fell to her knees. Kysa pulled out the knife, raised it to Anna's throat. Anna clutched her gut, bleeding heavier now. Maybe I could get to her in time. "Bring the Bialu here," Kysa said, "or I will kill her."

"How is killing her going to help you?" I started for Anna, and Kysa jabbed the knife into Anna's throat—I stopped. If Kysa pressed just a little harder, Anna's neck would slice right open.

Anna was trembling uncontrollably, tears streaking her cheeks. Her forearms were all bloody from holding her stomach. She couldn't stop the bleeding. It was starting to pool around her legs. Gods, she was going to die. No—she wasn't.

"Don't hurt her," I said. Stupid thing to say.

"Bring the Bialu here, Nikos," Kysa said.

"I can't. You hurt her. Anna is the one who puts me where I need . . ."

"I can . . ." Anna said. She gasped, her neck rigid against Kysa's knife. "I'll try."

Don't, I thought. But she did, and I was back in the Bialu room.

The toga'd Bialu seemed unimpressed to see me again. *"Are you ready to begin?"*

"I'll tell you how we're going to begin," I said. "You're going to save a Shan woman named Anna who is being held at knifepoint in the Black Room or none of this is going to work. How's that?"

Distantly, I heard Kysa say, "Bring it here. Now."

I felt the cold knife driving into my neck and a deep burn in my stomach. Somehow using the room was tapping me into Anna's body, blurring us together. Terrific. Pain spotted my vision, hard to focus. Damn it.

"Bring our god here, Nikos."

"Listen, if you don't help me," I told the Bialu, "this woman . . ." Knife going deeper, and I could feel my pulse in the blood of my—*Anna's*—guts. ". . . is going to kill the Shan woman, understand? You must see this. You won't be able to use your device—your trapdoor—at all, if she dies. Please . . ."

The Bialu just stared, like a cow. *"Yes we will."*

My head jerked up, as the knife went into Anna's neck.

I could feel the Bialu in the ship overhead and also the Black Room. All I had to do was give it a nudge, and the Bialu would be down in the room with us. Ready?

Anna said, "No."

I was back in the Black Room, no Bialu. "Anna, please . . ."

Kysa's patience was gone, I saw it. In an instant she would—

Another voice: *"I can help you. All you have to do is ask."*

Not the Bialu, but I recognized it. Shouldn't have been able to understand it, but I did. It was the voice from my nightmare.

Kysa and Anna heard it too. Even Giannis sat up. "What is that?" he asked. "Do you hear?"

"I am at Saint Michael's Door. I see you."

Kysa was looking around, as if there were more soldiers hiding in the walls. "Who is that?"

"Give her to me," the voice said. *"Send her across with a bomb."*

Anna met my stare, and I could read her eyes: *we could do it.* Somehow, she could feel the other world.

"We can help each other," the voice said. *"This can be the beginning of a holy alliance."*

Help an alien god conquer the universe, bring that monster down to this room for a crazy woman, or give a glauston bomb to a faceless voice from another world. None of it was ideal. But okay.

"We can't let a new age begin like this," Anna said. "I'm sorry, Nikos."

Anna jerked her elbow back into Kysa's nose.

Pain made my vision spill. I felt my—*Anna's*—throat open, and a cold snap as I was separated from her. Kysa was picking herself up from the far wall. Anna fell forward, bleeding out from her open throat. She gasped at me, lips going blue. Didn't think it would, not going to . . .

Sure you did.

CHAPTER TWENTY-TWO

Aelia

I tackled Kysa, and Giannis went to Anna, fumbling to take off his shirt, trying to tie it, wrap it around her throat—too much blood. Kysa was stronger than I thought, and she flipped me against the wall. But I had her wrist. She jabbed the knife, aiming for my torso, and I blocked with my free forearm—the blade went straight in, a shock of pain. But I didn't care. Twisted her wrist and slammed her into the wall, then pinned her with a knee on her neck. She was spitting and kicking, scratching at me.

I said, "Stop it!"

"They're *ours!*" she yelled. "This belongs to us—everything we've done is right! You don't understand any of it."

I was done. I punched her square in the face—never done that before. The impact jostled my arm, hurt my knuckles and ratcheted her head back, stunning her.

"They're not your gods, they're nobody's gods. They're some king of dumb aliens running from a disease. I don't care if they created us, I don't care what they did."

Kysa was weaker now, said, "We brought them. We created a new age."

"You blew people up. You ruined this—you *ended* everything. You didn't create shit."

She stopped fighting, my knee still planted on her neck. "Maybe," she said. "But you broke the sky."

"Nikos . . ."

Careful not to shift my weight, I looked over my shoulder at Giannis and—Anna wasn't moving. Bare-chested, Giannis was still messing with her throat, using his shirt like a wet rag to mop at Anna's open throat. Her eyes were open, staring at the ceiling. It wasn't registering, not really.

"It's broken now," Kysa said. "The sky is broken."

I grabbed her knife and got off her. "Be quiet."

Giannis said, "There was nothing—it was too deep and she lost too much blood."

"How could it happen that fast?" I went over to hold Anna's hand, feeling for a pulse. Dumb, but I felt like this was what I was supposed to . . . "Anna?"

Kysa started to move, and I said, "If you stand, I will kill you." She stayed put.

I set Anna's limp hand on her bloody lap and backed away from her, pointed at Kysa with the knife. She was frozen, watching me.

"Someone could have stopped this," I said. "Right? Anna brought you here, remember? I wanted to leave you, but she brought you. And you stuck a knife in her to try to—what? Help me to *understand* this."

"The gods are here," Kysa said quietly.

"Really?" I approached her slowly, playing a little with the knife, trying not to think about—nope. "Are they? I don't see them. I see you. I see your knife, and I see my dead friend over there. You cut her really fast— fast enough that we couldn't stop you. I don't think you're going to die like that. I think you're going to feel it for longer. *Understand?*"

Gianis said, "Nikos . . ."

"What? You know how many people have died? You really think one more is going to matter? You think anyone will care?"

A voice, *that* voice, said, *"I care."*

I stopped. "You do?"

"I do, because she has hurt you. She is weak, she is wicked, and like vermin she should be expunged."

I said, "I like this guy."

Giannis came over to me, coughing. "Let me take the knife."

"No, I'll hold onto it. Kysa, what do you think? Should I give you to them with a glauston bomb? Maybe they can solve this for us?"

"You can't," Kysa said. "With the albino dead, you can't."

"You can," the voice said. *"And the leader will remember you. Our alliance can begin like this. As you said, we will solve this problem for you. Send her through Saint Michael's Door to Rome."*

Rome. "How about that?" I said. "That's perfect—isn't that what you said we should be called, Kysa? Didn't you write that?"

Kysa started to scoot away toward the doorway. "I don't know what I said . . ."

"You wrote that on your cell wall, remember? At the Lagone Community. Voice from Saint Michael's Door: can you hear me?"

"I hear you."

"Your home is called Rome?"

"Rome is the name of this city, the capital of the Italian Empire and a part of the Third Reich."

I didn't follow, but I didn't have to. "And if I give this traitor-woman to you . . ?"

"We know how to deal with vermin."

"And the bomb, what would you do with the bomb?"

"Study it, use it to end a terrible war and preserve our way of life."

"That all sounds pretty reasonable." I saw Anna out of the corner of my eye. She was too still, like a rug. An Anna-rug. I asked Giannis, "Why shouldn't I do this?"

Kysa said, "It's not possible now."

Giannis said, "This is—I don't know. This is too unknown. Even if it works, what if you do it wrong? What if you move a bomb and it goes off?"

"Good point. I should test it first on someone else."

"No, Nikos—listen to me. We don't know what this is or who this man is."

The voice: *"My name is Cardinal Giovanni Mercati. I am a representative of the Holy See and caretaker of our most valuable relics. This—Saint Michael's Door—is a part of my ward. I am not a soldier, I am a scholar. I believe in truth and divine justice. I believe that God has brought us together now to see this through. I believe that you can save not only the Church but our leader and the Reich from danger. I believe, Nikos—you are called Nikos?—I believe that you are*

239

connected to us, that you are a good person. This is not chance, this is divine intervention, fate."

Divine intervention was right. Giannis and Kysa were both watching me, silent. I knew Giannis's 'you-aren't-seriously-going-to-jump-off-that-rock-cliff-without-looking-down-are-you' look.

"The time I broke my leg, you pushed me," I said.

Giannis frowned. "What?"

"I didn't jump on my own. I wanted to, but I didn't. I needed a push."

"I didn't break your leg."

"I know," I said. Kysa started to interrupt, and I asked the voice, "Who is there with you?"

"No one."

"If I somehow send the Pnetian woman to you, what will you do if she attacks?"

"One of the leader's aides is here, she will keep us safe."

So he lied. Just like that, there was something else going on here and—wait.

"She? She-who? What's her name?"

"Aelia."

Now he had my attention.

I closed my eyes. I had to try this. Giannis shouted at Kysa not to move. I reached out like before, tried to, and—nothing. Breathe slow. Remember how it worked before: Anna was in your head, you were in hers, and . . . I could feel the Black Room and past that, if I stretched—like shifting the weight of my mind from one foot to the other—I could feel further. The Capital, the planet, the Bialu ship overhead, the frozen void of space, and on and on. It was really kind of mystical, but also strangely hyper-normal. It was as if I'd put on reading glasses for the first time or suddenly found my balance on a bicycle. The damn thing *was* meant for us and we were made for it. And then, reaching out—not reaching, so much as changing my point of focus, like looking from something nearby to something far away—I could feel a curtain, staticky and frizzling with color, energy—something bizarre and charged and lurking all around, between and through the cracks in the air and our bodies. This was the other world. It was hovering in space, it was gyrating *through* my body totally unseen, unfelt. It was there. Everything was so simple.

"Nikos," Giannis said, "are you all right?"

I said, "No."

He was on to something. Let's not try with a bomb, let's do it different the first time. I nudged Kysa through the curtain and went with her: we were in a stone vault lit with sick white electric bulbs. A severe, red-faced man in a black suit watched me, his eyes widening as we came into focus. Another Black Room—*their* Black Room. Saint Michael's Door. Behind him, a sharp-eyed woman was smiling, her arms crossed over her chest. She was beautiful, and in that instant—I *knew* her. That made no sense. But the way she looked at me, relieved to see me, some kind of unspoken understanding in her expression, as if we shared a secret that I obviously already knew. Except I didn't.

"It's wonderful to meet you," Cardinal Giovanni Mercati said, and he nodded to Kysa. "You must be the traitor."

The sharp-eyed woman, Aelia, came closer. "Hi Nikos." She handed a small pistol to Mercati. "I'm sorry about this."

Mercati said, "This will be a compact between us. We will handle your traitor, and in exchange you will bring us a bomb."

Except now that I was standing here, part of me still back on New Amith with Giannis, they looked so—Cardinal Mercati might as well have been the Consul. This wasn't different, they were just frightened people like us. Looking for a bomb.

"No."

Mercati said, "Do you understand what I'm asking?"

"I said 'no'."

That seemed to make Aelia happy. She came over to me. "He's right, you know. You are still a good person." She reached into my pocket—I said, "Hey . . ."—and she took the red-tipped pen. Totally forgotten about that—how would she . . ? "It's really good to see you again, Nikos."

I just stared as she took a pad of paper from her pocket.

Mercati was getting irritated. "The leader may tolerate this kind of nonsense, Aelia, but here I am in charge." To me, "Do we have a compact or no?"

Aelia ignored him, flipping open the pad of paper, past several pages of scribbles, until she came to a page that was partially empty.

At the top, it read:

Nikos forgets the fires of Paris; Nikos forgets everything he knew on Earth; Nikos even forgets our life together.

Nikos has a new life on New Amith, and he finds love.

Something else was scratched out. Wait. It was written in the same ink as the red-tipped pen, the same as Elena's note about a dead child we never had.

"What is that?" I asked.

She started writing a new line. "We used to be in love," she said. "Then things happened, and now we're here. You always wanted a different life in an earlier time. Your wish is about to be granted."

She wrote: *Nikos forgets New Amith . . .*

"What are you talking about—I've never seen you before."

She didn't look at me. "You saw me at the funeral for your wife, Elena. I told you everything would be okay."

The sentence: *Nikos forgets New Amith, forgets me and all of this, and he is alive on Earth one-hundred years ago . . .*

I said, "The things you wrote didn't happen."

"Because I wrote them, yes." She paused. "I still love you, you know. You're depressive and frustrating, but you're . . ." She kissed my cheek. "I am sorry about this."

She finished the sentence: *. . . in a simpler time.*

And I was.

For awhile anyway.

END OF BOOK ONE

AELIA

Or

THE FIRST GODDESS: PROPAGANDA & REMEMBRANCES

THE GREAT YEAR CYCLE: BOOK TWO

E.W. Park

FOX POINT BOOKS

PROLOGUE

This is propaganda. Sure, there is some truth in it, but don't kid yourself: history is a pack of lies. It's like a clock that tells the wrong time with perfectly-running gears. So where did this story come from? The short version: it was written by superstitious zealots, followers of the monarch they called "the first goddess," after the last world war. The first goddess is, of course, more commonly known simply as Lady Summer. The manuscript was rediscovered in the old vaults under the University of Sepanul about 50 years after the Red Peace. My colleagues and I spent some time digging through it, comparing our research with details in the book, and do you know what we found? These are some damn fine falsehoods. Whoever cobbled it together did their homework. We know there were at least three contributing authors over more than a century. I won't bore you with the details, all of which will be published in my forthcoming work, *The Sins of Experience: A Treatise on the Discourse Surrounding Mortality in the Summer War, 1456 – 1580*, available at print houses throughout Sepanul.

Casual readers should remember that this is a work of fiction. Our understanding of the period before the Crash has improved significantly in recent years, and it's important to remember that although the characters in this story may resemble real historical figures, they are, in fact, *characters*. The edition you hold in your hands has been gently edited by scholars of the University of Sepanul, myself included, and we have tried to retain as much of the original spirit of the manuscript as possible. Here and there, this may make for misunderstandings, but that's life, isn't it? You feed guests with the food you have.

One other brief note: before the Crash, little was known of the multiverse. This makes for anachronisms, some of which we have updated. Just remember, when this book was written, no one knew anything about other versions of the world with wildly different outcomes: a universe in which the Nedals (or "Neanderthals" as they're sometimes called) went extinct prehistorically; a universe where the city of Amith was called Paris; a universe—as absurd as it sounds—in which humans never evolved the ability to manipulate the molecular configurations of the elements. Crazy, right? I could go on. But that would pre-empt my own forthcoming book; instead, let's just get on with it. Consider yourself warned.

CHAPTER ONE

"The world is coming to an end, you know."

"It's good to see you too, mother." Aelia forced a smile and guided her daughter, Junia, through the sidewalk crowd.

It was an important day: the Kavesfaer military parade had the streets mobbed, tomorrow was Junia's seventh birthday, and it was also the day that Aelia would first speak to the gods. The parade stretched further than she could see, with plenty of pomp to go around. Red flags blustered outside every insulae apartment building, and red ribbons were tied to trees, streetlamps, hell, even overhead gutters. The olive-skinned Sogjuks might be in the city to commemorate their victories of the Great War, but no one in Amith would mistake Kavesfaer for a Sogjuk celebration. This was all about Amith, and there was no getting away from the color of blood. Crimson zeppelins even hung in the sky like painted clouds.

"I can't hear my own thoughts," Behlain said. "Parades were never this loud when I was your age—it's going to damage Junia's hearing."

A corps of Sogjuk soldiers marched past with muzzled attack dogs. The crowd cheered a Gredan tank that resembled a red dung beetle carrying a turret.

"How are you?" Aelia asked.

"Tired," Behlain said. "We should have a civilized conversation at my home in Vultani."

Behlain forced their way through the crowd. Away from the press of unwashed body odor, liquor and sugar-grease stench, until they found a graffitied courtyard where naked children splashed in a copper-sparkle fountain. Water sprayed from the mouth and fingers of a statue of a pregnant woman in a toga, her belly straining below engorged breasts. The air overhead was crowded with laundry lines and dripping window-box air conditioners. People laughed, whistled, and shouted to one another from window-to-window across the alley in thick center-city accents, completely ignoring the nearby parade. Aelia wasn't in the mood to wander backstreets—they were supposed to meet her husband, Cael, in a few minutes—but for now she humored her mother.

Junia picked up a crumpled paper and showed it to Behlain. "Grandmother Behlain, what does it say?"

Behlain made grumbly noises and told Aelia, "You see? The world *is* ending." And then to Junia, "You shouldn't pick up trash, dear. Even if it's true trash."

Aelia took a look at the paper: it was a pamphlet with seven colored circles at the top, over the words, *The Prime Planets in Cancer.* Below, a crude illustration of a tidal wave and the words, *The Great Year begins with an Unstoppable Deluge.* There were flames, too, with more ominous-ish predictions: *Honor the gods. When the Eagles Leave, Our World Will Burn.*

"It's just a silly piece of paer," Aelia said.

Behlain nodded to Junia. "Do *you* honor the gods? Has your mother taught you about the Great Year?"

"That's enough," Aelia said. "Let's go watch the parade."

"Mommy, I *know* about the Great Year," Junia said. "Is it coming soon? Domitus said it will happen if people forget the gods."

"The gods are fine," Aelia said. "We offered to them today, didn't we? And not just once: we honored them when you woke up and also when you hung the Kalends wreath. Don't worry about the gods, little bluebird."

Aelia tickled Junia, and Junia burst into surprised laughter. "*Mommy!*"

"And no more worrying about the Great Year, okay?"

"But Domitus said the barbarians in Asia . . ."

"No worrying about Domitus either. He doesn't know everything."

Junia charged a flock of pigeons, and they burst up, dodging clotheslines and open window frames to the top of the alley. Smiling, Behlain said, "They have me on three lozenges for my back pain, and I take two more pills for these headaches. But what do the doctors know. All they care about is money."

Aelia said, "Thank you for coming, mom."

Behlain rolled her eyes. "It's the eve of her seventh—of course I'm here. But maybe you'll get lucky and I'll die of stroke in this heat." She laughed at the uncomfortable remark, as if it were a joke. No way it was a joke. "The Dalenbl policy will pay double before my 55th birthday next Febred."

Aelia knew she was her mother's only friend. Carbo's other six wives had moved out with their children after he died last fall. This left Behlain alone with Carbo's old clothes, photographs, and nonsense Great Year pamphlets. From her career as a Hukon attorney, Behlain still received monthly stipends from the main Dalenbl courthouse. She had plenty of money, but she never spent it. How much, Aelia wasn't sure, but it hardly mattered. Getting Behlain to move out of the eighth floor insulae apartment in the Hukon where Aelia had grown up wasn't about money. It was about her mother's dumbshit stubbornness.

Behlain launched into a lecture about the value of self-sacrifice, and Aelia cut her off: "It's time to meet Cael. Come on, Junia."

Junia asked, "Mommy, who is that lady in the fountain?"

"You don't recognize her? That's Lunda."

"But Lunda is the moon, not the *water*."

"The moon stirs up the water to create life, bluebird. Without the moon, there would be no tides, and wouldn't that make the night still and dark?"

"I'm not afraid of the dark," Junia said.

Behlain said to Junia, "Your mommy was *my* bluebird when she was your age. Did you know that? And I used to give her presents sometimes. She doesn't remember it, but I did." Behlain handed Junia a wrapped case, the size of a cigar box. "Go ahead, open it!"

"Mother, we have to go," Aelia said.

Junia tore off the wrapping: a box of colored chalk. Smiling wide, she said, "Domitus doesn't let us play with his chalk!"

"Now you have your own," Behlain said. "Here, let's see if they work . . ."

Aelia felt her blood pressure rising, as Behlain knelt in slow motion, grumping and moaning about her hips, to help Junia draw colorful squares on the pavement. Pleasant passive aggressiveness, that's what it was. *What? I can't give my granddaughter a present of sidewalk chalk?* That's what she would say, with arms flailing and caricature loudness, if Aelia protested. Behlain and Junia drew a sequence of connecting boxes, and then Behlain very very slowly found a rock. Hop-jump. By the gods, Behlain was pushing it. Yes, let's play a game right now, when we're supposed to be meeting Cael. Perfect idea. On Junia's first jump, Behlain tickled her, and Junia shrieked in laughing, mock-terror. All right, that was cute. Aelia couldn't suppress a smile. Maddening, but damn cute.

"*Aelia.*"

Behind her, the fountain statue had changed. Lunda had her hands on her hips now, water coursing down her legs. The sound of Junia and Behlain playing drifted away behind a faint buzz, like the residual noise from electronics that Aelia normally tuned out. It was growing louder. Had it been there all along?

"*Aelia,*" the statue said again. "*I am with you. I look over you, I protect your child. But you must do something in return.*"

This wasn't real. Statues didn't talk. Aelia was frozen. It was a trick, some kind of animatronic thing, an automaton.

"Who are you?"

"*I am Lunda. Goddess of the moon. And you were right, you have honored me. That is why I am here.*"

The buzz didn't stop, loud in both ears now, as if some kind of device were being amped up. "What do you want?"

"*You will travel east,*" Lunda said. "*You will leave Gredan and go into the Sogjuk Empire. You will find the man who calls himself Marin, the ruler of the Tartar Horde. You will take your daughter to him. She must go there, Aelia.*"

This was insane. Behlain and Junia were oblivious, they hadn't noticed. Why weren't they looking? The gods might be real, but not like this.

"No," Aelia said. "I don't understand."

"*You will take . . .*" The statue stammered and then repeated, "*You will find the man who calls himself Marin, the ruler of the Tartar Horde. You will take your daughter to him. You will take your daughter to him. You will take . . .*"

Aelia backed away and said, "I will not!" Behlain looked up, startled: the statue was frozen again. It hadn't moved. A triangle of red jet fighters roared overhead, the sonic boom—*thud, thud, thud*—followed by scattered applause from the nearby street. The wind-rush blew charcoal smoke from the sidewalk grills.

"You will not what?" Behlain said. "Aelia?"

"Nothing." She was shaking. "We should get going. I told Cael we would meet him."

Behlain pulled herself up in a slow-motion huff. "If it's easier for you, I can go home."

"Don't be silly," Aelia said. "This is fun."

Clutching her chalk-box as they returned to the parade route, Junia said, "Mommy, I'm hungry."

Behlain asked, "You didn't feed her earlier?" And then, before Aelia could respond, Behlain told Junia, "You'll have to wait, dear. It's too expensive to eat here."

Back on the Doudre, Aelia took Junia to get in line at a steaming meat stall. Don't think about the statue. Am I losing my mind? It was some kind of trick, a mechanical joke or something. Behlain planted herself a little ways away, hands on her hips. How dare I feed my daughter when and what I choose to feed my daughter, Aelia thought. Silly, but true. When it was her turn, Aelia bought them all steaming drabens—wheat rolls of pork and spiced onions—and large plastic water bottles. And yes, it was expensive. But the good kind of expensive. It got her mind off the nonsense in the alley. But what if it was real?

"I'm not hungry," Behlain said.

In the parade, wheely Sogjuk artillery cannons and Gredan horseback lancers passed. The lancers wore silver feathered helmets and carried shiny rifles atop horses weighed down by ridiculous-looking black and green armor. Aelia led them along the parade route north, away from the east-west Doudre Road, into the mansion blocks of Calfe. The draben might have been overpriced, but it was delicious. Junia finished hers before they had even crossed the Doudre, and now she gestured with her empty wrapper at a pair of caldets in the street ahead. "Mommy, *look!*" Aelia couldn't remember the last time she'd seen a caldet in person. Ten meters tall and covered in scruffy brown fur, the caldets looked like giant, overweight horses. They were guided on chains by a crowd of serious-looking handlers, and all of them—the caldets and the handlers alike—

seemed deadset on looking as grim and bored as possible. They seemed to be oblivious to the crowd, the drums, even the soldiers and other armored vehicles

"They stink—ew, Mommy!" Junia said as they passed. She was right, the caldets smelled like a mob of unwashed cattle or a pack of wet dogs matted in damp fur. It wasn't great.

"Come on, let's keep moving," Aelia said.

"Where exactly?" Behlain said.

Not going to get into an argument, Aelia thought. She kept them moving, along the multi-laned Mivous Loop. Supposedly the road tracked the ancient perimeter of a famous long-gone Roman camp. And long-gone was right: these were rich blocks now, lined with iron and copper gates outside big row houses. Black-orb cameras kept watch, rather than starving Roman soldiers. Through one fence, Aelia saw a driveway mosaic of a woman reclining with a handful of white grapes. A bit of a cliché, but it probably looked cool from the upper windows of the marble house.

"This is hopeless," Behlain said. "We'll never find Cael in this crowd."

Junia dropped her chalk and let go of Aelia's hand to grab it. The crowd cut her off. Junia was gone. Aelia's heart stopped. "Junia!"

There she was: Junia jumped back through the crowd and took Aelia's hand again. "Tweet, mommy!"

"Hold my hand, bluebird. It's too crowded for you to run off."

On a concrete island in the middle of the five-way traffic circle in the heart of the Mivous Loop, more people crowded around a red-marble temple to the Divine Julius. One side of the temple was covered in scaffolding and tarps, some kind of repairs or renovations. The rest of it was all bare-chested, muscular friezes depicting Romans and Gauls locked in mortal combat. In impressive, but cartoony style, the temple commemorated the site where Caesar had supposedly camped more than one-thousand years ago, during his last Gallic campaign. The building had been constructed around an ancient oak tree that rose through an open hole in the roof. The significance of the tree was a bit unclear, something to do with the resilience and strength of life—or maybe just the importance of trees, most of which the Romans had levelled, after all.

Aelia spotted Cael with his oldest wife, Tes, with the crowd around the temple. Tes's three-year-old daughter, Jean was planted on Cael's shoulders, and their second daughter, eight-year-old Alvra, was there too. No sign of Cael's third wife, Subeia or her son, Domitus.

"We'll never be able to cross the Mivous Loop," Behlain said. "With the parade and all of these people, it's hopeless."

The parade curled east around the Julian Temple toward the torch-rimmed dome of Vumin's Temple. Looking past that—east, beyond the mansions, temples, and marble rooftops of Dalen's Forum—Aelia saw the glass towers of Netzi Hill. They always looked out of place to her, like bulbs of toothy crystal jutting up way too high. Police sedans barricaded the edge of the parade route, their lights flashing red-white-red. Cops in red vests were managing an impromptu crosswalk for anyone interested in going over to the Julian Temple, and Aelia led her mother and daughter across.

When Cael saw Aelia, his face brightened. He lifted Jean down from his shoulders and went to clear a path for Aelia. "How do you like these diesel engines!" Cael said. He kissed Aelia quickly and then pecked Behlain on the cheek too. "Hello Behlain, you look well. Did you have any trouble finding us?"

Behlain let out an exasperated laugh. "In *this*?"

Junia ran over to show Alvra and Jean her colored chalks. Tes was supervising the girls, but Aelia couldn't make out what they were saying in the thunder of drums and passing trumpets. That was all right. She was steady again, the statue hadn't happened. Somehow she had slipped into some kind of daydream. This was the normal world.

"This is too loud for the children's ears," Behlain told Cael.

Cael nodded, still smiling and holding Aelia's hand. "No argument here. Junia, did you see the calstads?"

"They *stink*!" Junia said.

"Definitely!" Cael said, laughing. "Like big wet dogs. Maybe we should get one as a pet?"

"*Daddy!*"

"What, you wouldn't like that?"

"Subeia isn't here yet?" Aelia asked.

Tes came over, rolling her eyes in full-on gossip mode. "Where is *Domitus*, you mean. What that boy gets away with is ridiculous."

"He's almost thirteen," Cael said. "It would be strange if he weren't a little difficult now—I was difficult like you wouldn't believe at his age."

"The older your children get, the more they'll forget basic respect," Behlain said. "Just you wait. They forget completely who it was who gave them life in the first place." Nevermind that Behlain had never given birth, Aelia thought. Twenty-two years ago, her husband, Carbo, had discovered Aelia in a basket near the Vetrim docks on his walk home from the plastic works. It wasn't as unusual a story as it sounded. Aelia looked eastern, and most immigrants from beyond the line came west in desperation. Babies complicated already over-strapped poverty. Aelia knew that she was probably meant to drown as a child. That was almost certainly what her parents, whoever, whatever they were, probably had in mind. Except they couldn't do it. They went the basket-route instead, dangling that little glimmer of hope that maybe some pious or barren Amith native would take pity on the little eastern doll. And Carbo and Behlain had.

That was twenty-three years ago. She'd been out of Behlain's household for nine years, since she met Cael at Namesh Market, when she was thirteen. Young—certainly younger than him; Cael was twenty-one at the time—but not crazy. The older they got, the less the age difference seemed to matter, as if she were gaining on him. Like he was aging down and she was getting old before her time. Every anniversary, she did a little ritual: a look back at where they had been one year earlier. How good was their marriage, how happy were they, how often did they have sex, what were their dreams—that kind of thing. And every year, all but one—there had been a hard year about five years ago—every anniversary but that one, she realized that she loved him more than she had the year before. Crazy to think. He'd brought her north, out of the Hukon, to a house with new clothes and fresh water in the pipes. Sounded silly now, but these were the things that defined her life, that had given her Junia. Material life, improvements that made it possible to not worry about money all the time, and a man who cared about her. Love that grew over time. Maybe that was the point of the tree in the temple behind her.

"Daddy," Junia said, "look what grandma Behlain gave me!"

"Those are nice chalks, Junia—very impressive."

Behlain nodded, as if she'd been complimented. "Seven is an important birthday, the extra money is worth it."

Cael asked, "Which color is your favorite, Junia?"

"Red, like the police, see . . ." Junia pointed the chalk toward the road, and it slipped out of her hand, bounced into the street toward a row of armored cars. Junia dashed after it.

"What is she doing?" Behlain said.

Oh shit. Cael pushed ahead of Aelia, already in the road.

"—unia!" Junia ran into the road, five meters from the first car, oblivious as she crouched to pick up the chalk. Cael was right behind her. The soldiers weren't paying attention, and a trumpet squealed: the cars accelerated. No. No, no, no. Someone shouted from the crowd that there was a child in the road. But the cars sped closer—Junia saw them, froze—and Cael scooped her up with one arm. He wasn't going to, not going to have time. A gust of wind slammed the cars, stalling them—but they didn't stop. Aelia was rushing across the street, a car blocked her view, and she heard a metal-bone snap. Aelia started shaking, still running.

Behind her, Behlain was shouting, "Why did you let her go? You should never have let her into the street!"

Horns blared, police hustled over. The parade shuddered to a halt. Aelia came around the stopped cars: Cael's legs were twisted under the front bumper, and she heard Junia crying.

"Junia!" Aelia's arms shuddered as she yanked her daughter away from the car. There was a bloody streak on the bumper. She checked Junia's head, her shoulders, back, arms, all of her—okay. Junia was okay. No blood. "Are you hurt? Where are you hurt?"

Junia cried, "Daddy!"

Cael sprawled sideways, his torso twisted almost backwards at the waist. Now she saw the gash along his scalp. He was reaching for a square of red chalk. Cael blinked at her, confused. "I don't understand," he said. "Aelia?"

There must be a way to fix this, she thought. Someone can fix this. A doctor. Find a doctor.

Junia buried her head in Aelia's neck and cried.

The parade picked up again, circling around the stopped cars and Cael's limp body. Still blinking, Cael murmured, "Aelia, I can't see . . ."

A Sogjuk soldier in a khaki uniform brought a stretcher, and Behlain hurried to help him.

"We have to move him!" the Sogjuk soldier shouted.

Aelia felt Tes's hand on her shoulder. "Aelia, step back."

"I'm sorry, mommy," Junia said. "I tried to help daddy."

Aelia saw Behlain and the Sogjuk soldier hoist Cael onto the stretcher, then lost sight of them in the crowd. "Where are they taking him?"

"Stay with me," Tes said. "Come on, Aelia—girls—we're going home."

CHAPTER TWO

The whole world felt different after a gut punch. And that's what this was. The spirit holding everything together sucker punched right out of Aelia's chest, so that she was trembly and weepy and angry and always trying to be strong for the kids. Now, Aelia held Subeia's cold fingers and watched Cael sleep. As Cael's first and oldest wife, Tes knelt and stroked his forehead bandages and prayed, "Under Lunda's light, I will shelter you. By the grace of Saturna, I will protect you. And I ask Onne, the white face of Ponu, to watch from the gray river, don't take my husband yet."

Lunda's light. Was this punishment? Had the gods done this, because Aelia had walked away? Because she had left the alley and refused to listen? Don't take Cael, she thought. Please. Was I supposed to blindly trust and agree to anything, because a damn statue started talking to me? That made no sense. I'm sorry, she thought. I can't trust, I don't know what I believe, but that couldn't have been real. Leave him be. Subeia lit incense in a silver bowl on the bedside table and handed Aelia a goblet of holy oil. Outside, from three floors down, Aelia heard people shouting and laughing, as if nothing had changed. As if this weren't the worst day of her life. Cars passed. Gods, he was so pale. No color in his cheeks even. He looked like a corpse already, except for the shallow, raspy breathing. With her right thumb, Julia dabbed oil on his eyelids. And she didn't cry. That was something, that was good. She kept it together. She did what she was supposed to do without collapsing in a heap. Because he wasn't dead, just hurt.

Tes held Cael's limp left hand. "By Volcein's furnace, I will keep you warm. I ask Minet's mercy. It is not his time."

If the gods were listening, now was the time. Subeia took Aelia's hand again and guided her back a few steps. Tes was barely keeping it together. The praying was good for her. And she knew the words better than any of the rest of them. She knew what to say, which gods to ask for what. If the gods were listening, Tes was the one they would listen to.

"Let Perspunte keep the bone lands in peace," Tes said. "I will not hang pine nor cypress, I will not take his wax face, I will not call his name . . . it is not his time."

Aelia heard Behlain and the Greek doctor talking in the hall outside. After the doctor had examined Cael, Behlain had cornered him. Say what you will about Behlain, she was good in a crisis. Strict, no nonsense, ready to jump into the mix. Like with the stretcher at the parade. Now, she was cross-examining the doctor. Probably making sure they got their money's worth. No, Aelia told herself. Don't think like that. Mother is helping. The girls were playing downstairs with Domitus, and Aelia went into the hall to see what was what.

"Operations are messy and expensive," the doctor was saying. "In his condition, you may know tonight."

"When will he wake?" Aelia asked.

The doctor frowned. "I'm sorry, I have to go. I've explained everything to your mother. If he wakes up, it'll probably be soon."

If he wakes up. Behlain thanked the doctor. He tore her a yellow receipt from a binder and left.

Subeia and Tes came out too. "Behlain," Tes said, "we should talk about it now. Away from the children."

Subeia said, "They're downstairs, they can't hear. How bad is he?"

"He may pass soon," Behlain said. "Or he could stay like this for who knows how long."

"Or he could wake," Aelia said. "I heard what he said—the doctor said he could wake tonight."

Behlain waved the doctor's receipt in her face. "How much money do you have saved? All of you?"

"Not much," Tes said. "But the corporation will pay."

"You should call them," Behlain said. "Subeia, you do it. You're the only Batrian here. Find out how much money you can expect to receive. This is a two-thousand dinat doctor's bill."

"*Two-thousand?*" Subeia said. "The doctor barely looked at Cael. How can he charge us that much?"

"Check your savings," Behlain said. "Think about what you can live without."

Aelia said, "Please don't talk about money right now. What are we going to do? We're just going to *wait*? There are other doctors."

Behlain smiled in an ugly, self-satisfied way. "You can't afford to . . ."

"Stop it," Aelia said. She wanted to smack her, almost did.

"We'll tell the children that Cael is resting," Tes said. "We don't have to explain anything now."

"Domitus is too smart for that," Subeia said. "He'll start asking questions. What if he asks to see him?"

"Their father is *resting*," Tes said again. "Not to be disturbed." She started downstairs without waiting for an answer from any of them. Tes was a hard woman, and she was in kill-mode now. Aelia had only seen it a few times before. She wasn't negotiating, she wasn't asking. She was going to keep the kids in line, say the prayers, and wait for Cael to wake up. Period. Subeia followed after her.

As they left, Behlain told Aelia, "I want you to know that you're lucky the children weren't here to see you just now. That was very disrespectful."

The screaming adrenaline from the parade had mostly drained away, leaving Aelia weak. She felt like crying, screaming, or just curling into a ball and closing her eyes and waiting for this to pass. But no, can't do that with the kids here. Have to stick to the path, keep it together.

"Stop, mother," Aelia said. "Please."

From downstairs, Aelia heard Domitus's voice in the atrium, "Is father dead?"

"No," Tes answered. The rest was too quiet for Aelia to follow.

"You embarrassed yourself," Behlain went on. "And you hurt my feelings."

Aelia closed her eyes, tried to focus on her breathing. Make each breath the exact same speed as the one before it. Calm down. "I'm sorry," Aelia said.

"You've had it very easy here," Behlain said. "You've never had to budget or think about anyone but yourself."

"Stop it, mother."

"But hey, you don't have to listen to me," Behlain said, and Aelia could hear the smirk in her voice. "What do *I* know? I'm only your mother. I can't wait until you have to go through this with your own daughter."

"I'm going downstairs."

"You need to budget . . ."

That was it. Aelia opened her eyes and smacked the stair-banister. "*Stop talking about money.*"

"You're being so selfish."

"My husband is *dying*," Aelia said. And there they were: sudden tears. No, she fought them back, blinked them away.

"These things happen for a reason," Behlain said. "I sacrifice to the gods everyday. I wish they had chosen me, but they gave the cancer to Carbo. How will you afford property payments? What if he has debts you don't know about?"

"What do you want me to say?"

"*Why* was he hit by the car? *Why* did he run into the street? *Why*, Aelia?"

Because I left the alley, because I didn't listen. "He saved his daughter's life," she said. Behlain clucked, as if that were absurd, so Aelia asked, "Okay, then tell me what happened. I was there, mother."

Behlain said slowly, "You need money."

"Is that the only thing you can say? Money, money, money? That's all you think matters right now? The doctor was just here. Money didn't change anything with him."

"And you haven't paid him yet." Behlain handed her the doctor's receipt. "If you don't want to make the tough decisions, I will. That's what mothers are for."

"What are you talking about?"

"Pray for your husband." Behlain kissed Aelia's forehead. "I'll take care of it, bluebird." She left without saying goodbye to anyone else.

Bluebird. That was good. Using Aelia's nickname for Junia. That had never been Behlain's name for Aelia. It was just a way of co-opting things, getting her cloying, controlling hands all over everything. Aelia went downstairs, following Domitus's voice through the entry hall, open-air atrium, and into the dining room. Three Roman couches were arranged in an open square with Cael's black marble table in the center. Everybody was here. Subeia and Domitus were on the far left couch (the lectus summus), with Jean, Alvra and Junia flat-forward on their bellies on the center couch (the lectus medius). The lectus imus was empty. Cael's spot. At the back wall, Tes was talking quietly with the Sogjuk soldier who had helped Cael with the stretcher. Maybe we have to pay him too, Aelia thought. Wouldn't that be nice.

When Junia saw Aelia, she said, "Mommy, can I play hop-squares with grandmother Behlain?"

"She's gone now, love," Aelia said.

"*Finally*," Domitus said. "She doesn't do anything but complain."

"Be nice," Subeia told him.

"Why? She isn't nice."

"I want you all to pray for your father," Tes said. "Offer to the gods and to our household Lares. When you're done, Domitus, you watch the girls in the back alley—they can play outside."

"Why do I always have to watch the babies?" Domitus said.

"I'm not a baby!" Jean said and to Tes, "Mommy, I'm three and a half!"

"You act like one," Domitus said.

"What did I just say?" Subeia said. "Try to be nice."

"*Try to be nice*," Domitus said, mimicking his mother. "Why can't I see father? He wouldn't make me supervise the babies all afternoon."

When Jean protested again, Tes snapped her fingers. "No more. You'll honor your father by doing as I ask. Or I will have words with you all. Go on. Domitus, when I look out the kitchen window, you had better be right there and not all the way on the Wyekje sidewalk, understand?"

He grunted and got up. The girls ran through the kitchen doorway and out the backdoor. When they were all gone, Subeia said, "I am sorry, Tes. I don't know why he's like this lately."

"It's not easy for him," Tes said. "Behlain was right, you should call the corporation. Aelia and I will fix something for the children to eat."

Subeia went into the atrium and took a curly ear-pebble from the wall-hook. She popped it into her right ear, said, "Lagma corporation offices, please."

Tes told Aelia, "Subeia is going to be childless very soon, if you don't knock some sense into that boy. If I have to deal with him again, I might strangle him."

Normally, it would have been funny. It wasn't now. There was a frantic, half-hidden edge in Tes's voice.

"It must be difficult for you as well," the Sogjuk soldier said.

"Thank you for staying," Tes said. "But there's no need now, there's nothing we can do."

"If you don't mind, I am happy to help," he said. "Besides, if I go back, they'll have me marching in the damn parade again. There should be a man in this house while your husband is asleep."

And a Sogjuk soldier, Aelia thought. Cael wouldn't have minded, but plenty of their neighbors would just love to murmur and speculate. Oh my, the foreign soldier stayed *all afternoon*. No way to avoid that now. And screw it anyway.

"We're fine," Tes told him. "We appreciate your concern, but you *can* go."

"If you ask me to leave, I will," he said. "Otherwise, consider this a gesture of cross-cultural goodwill."

Tes went into the kitchen to make a salad with lettuce, eggs, and blue-mold cheese. Aelia heard her shout out the kitchen window, "I see that! Domitus, stay with the girls!"

Aelia poured the soldier a glass of tap water. "It's not necessary," he said, but then he drank without pausing for a breath.

"Looks necessary to me," she said.

"I didn't want to offend you. It would have been impolite not to drink."

"Thank you," Aelia said. "For staying. For the stretcher at the parade, I don't know what we would have done."

"He is a good man," the soldier said. "I don't think a man like that will die today. I've prayed that the Divine Emperor will save him."

More prayers, different god.

"What's your name?" she asked.

"Maten. And your name is Aelia. It will be all right, Aelia. Trust me"

But she didn't, she really didn't.

CHAPTER THREE

That night, Aelia, Tes, and the three girls went out on the town, as if nothing was wrong. Everything might be collapsing, but the kids— keep moving for the children. It was still the eve of Junia's seventh birthday. Aelia sat with the girls at an open-air table at the Pleneir Market, while Tes brought over a tray of *sapolin*—corkscrew noodles, chopped tomatoes, and white cheese. Junia's favorite. The Venci chefs spoke almost no Grest, but they'd known Junia since she was a baby and always gave her free sugar noodle cups when Aelia stopped by.

Across the square, black-skinned street musicians played foreign violins, but most of the market stalls were already locked up for the night. And the music wasn't that good. As the girls dug into their noodles, the table wobbled on ancient cobblestones. Where would they go after this? Maybe to the playground further south? You had to know where to look, but a few blocks south of Pleneir Market the Doldair ruins actually hid one of the most elaborate public playgrounds in the city. The ruins themselves were boring gray stone covered in ivy, all fenced off from the main roads. There was no sign, and the metal climbing structures were set back a ways, hidden from view behind ruined walls, and you usually couldn't even hear kids laughing or get any indication there was anything more to it than rocks. Aelia had learned about it from Subeia years ago, who somehow knew a family in the diamond district, which bordered the ruins. They kept the playground hidden on purpose, of course. All the people in their fine togas in those honey-comb apartments saw the playground as *theirs*, a part of *their* neighborhood, even if it did technically belong to everyone in the city. Every time she'd been there, Aelia had to make a point of ignoring whispers and stares. She knew how to dress like she belonged, but Aelia couldn't change her face—she just looked too foreign, too *Eastern*. On second thought, screw the playground tonight. *I should go back to the fountain statue, apologize. Promise to do whatever Lunda wanted. But why? Go to the east, find some barbarian king, why?*

Junia was having a good time, so that was something. Her cheeks were smeared with tomatoes and she was still holding that damn chalk that Behlain had given her. The reason Junia had run out into the road.

"And there were sixteen squares," Junia was telling Alvra. "But not all of them were green. I colored eight of them red."

"It's good that we're here," Tes said to Aelia. Her daughter, Jean, was refusing to eat, and so Tes was involved in a complicated game of strategic bluffing to see who would get to the noodles first. "I couldn't look at anyone else."

There had been a few visitors from the factory and messengered condolence cards, as if Cael were already dead. But really Tes probably meant Domitus. He had responded to the crisis by arguing, almost as if he hoped he could be a big enough prick to cancel out his father's coma. So far, no dice.

"Mommy, I'm full, can we go to the playground?" Junia asked. Her fingers were gooey red.

"I don't know, bluebird. It's late and the playground is far away."

"It's not far," Junia said. "And I'm not tired—*please!*"

There was no fighting it. Aelia gave in, and they left the market, waited for a break in the horse- and ox-cart traffic on Leir—still busy, even at this hour—and entered the open gate of the Doldair grounds. They followed a dark path through a network of high mossy stone that opened abruptly to the playground. It was basically empty, with just two families and four other kids, all of whom already knew each other. Aelia and Tes found a bench.

"Your mother was right, you know," Tes said. "In two weeks, we will run out of money."

Aelia wanted to get up and walk out. Not here, not on Junia's seventh. What the hell? Was it too much to ask to take one moment, just one breath that wasn't about the danger they faced? "My mother is crazy," Aelia said.

"She's still mourning, and she's sick. It's not fair to blame her."

They watched as the girls laughed and played. The first few times Aelia had come to the playground it had just looked like a hodge podge; only later did she realize it was supposed to be an eagle, with a triangular slide as its beak, a bridge leading to ropes for wings, tunnels for a torso and so on. The girls were chasing a boy who had come with another family. Growing up, there were areas of the Hukon where girls couldn't play with boys until the girls turned seven—that was when girls became citizens of Gredan; boys got to be counted at birth. She'd heard rumors of some Batrian families reversing the practice (counting girls first, boys second), but for the government, that was irrelevant. At midnight tonight, a little blinking piece of circuitry somewhere would click or hum or maybe make no noise at all, as a digital file was created recognizing that Junia existed. Amith was the capital, after all, which meant that all Gredan citizens here were first priority when it came to tallying people.

Aelia watched as Junia climbed up the slide, slipped, and caught herself. "Be careful," Aelia called. "Why don't you use the ladder, Junia?"

Junia reached the top, and a sharp wind whipped through the yard. "Mommy, did you see?"

"Yes bluebird, very good. Tes, I have to tell someone."

"What?"

"Before the crash at the parade, I saw something. Lunda spoke to me. I know this doesn't happen, but a statue of the god Lunda spoke to me."

Tes waited, as if she thought it were a joke and the punchline were coming. "The goddess of the moon spoke to you? What did she say?"

"She told me to go east, to find the king of the Tartars or something, past the Sogjuk Empire."

"What—why?"

"I don't know."

"Why would a god speak to you like that? Aelia . . ."

"I'm not making this up."

"I'm not saying you are, but I don't understand."

"Neither do I."

"What are you going to do?"

"I don't know. The statue stopped talking, and we just left it there. It asked me to leave Gredan, to just go east for no reason. Why would the gods want me to do something like that? It's crazy."

"It is," Tes said.

Tes didn't believe it. Of course she didn't. Aelia wasn't even sure that she still believed it. But no, it had happened. Somehow that had happened. She should go back. Apologize to the goddess, offer to her, find out why she was supposed to leave. The gods *were* real. "I don't know what to do," Aelia said.

Tes asked, "Did you get her something?"

Changing the subject, back to Junia's birthday. "It's a surprise."

"Oh come on, what?"

"I'm not telling. On the walk home, we'll pick it up. You'll see."

Two men with the other kids in the playground left their wives on another bench and wandered over toward the exit. Their voices were loud, as if they owned the world and didn't care who heard what they had to say—every one of their thoughts was *so* important.

"Dehlfa in a week?" the first man was saying, as they passed Aelia and Tes. "How could they move that quickly?"

The second man: "They're not visiting for a feast day like you do— they're *conquering*."

Batrians. I'm getting riled up, Aelia realized. Truth was, she didn't know many Batrians, never had. There weren't that many around. In Gredan, there were two forms of Batrian divinization: Earth and Fire. Men did Earth; women did Fire. Male priests outnumbered the women three to one, but the Batrian women were pretty solidly in charge, because divinization passed down through the maternal line. This meant that back home Domitus was a Batrian, just like his mother, but *his* kids would all be ordinary Docians unless he married another Batrian. The Batrians claimed to have direct power from the gods, but Aelia had never seen any sign of it. Subeia had never so much as shaken a candle flame, and those passing Batrian men had ducked under low-hanging vines to leave the playground, rather than moving them with their powers or whatever. None of it was real. She had to go back to the fountain.

"We should probably have a plan," Tes said.

"After we pick up her present, we can go back to the parade route," Aelia said. "The fountain is . . ."

"Not *that*," Tes said. "Aelia I'm serious. A plan for staying alive, for paying for food."

Back to this. "Cael is alive," Aelia said. She watched an orange haze in the sky. The light wasn't from the sun or the stars. She was facing west, which meant that was probably the glow from the fires on top of Vumin's Temple. Maybe more prayers and sacrifices would help. But sacrifices cost money, and apparently that wasn't going to last.

"When Behlain left, it sounded like she had an idea to do something," Tes said. "Like she knew about some kind of reserve or other account we haven't heard of. Do you know where she was going?"

"Home probably." Maybe she would give them enough to make it through, probably not. And before Tes said anything else, Aelia got up. It was time to go. They called the girls and started home.

Rather than follow Wyekje north, Aelia led them to the twisting streets where the crumbling Nmu't Wall met the larger remains of the broken Boldii Wall. Both walls were heaps of old stones, but the Boldii had been reinforced all along the way with concrete and held up by nets to keep it from collapsing entirely and squishing passersby.

Junia asked, "Why are we going this way, Mommy?"

"Because it's a nice night for a walk," Aelia said. It kind of was. But of course that wasn't the whole story. The girls skipped past late-night pedestrians and workers hurrying home, until they were following a track of brick apartment buildings across the street from the paths of Uin Park. Aelia took Junia to a bookshop on the corner. Someone had graffitied red circles near the door.

"It's your seventh birthday," Aelia said. "It's important, bluebird."

Junia was trying to look excited, but she was obviously disappointed.

Inside, the owner looked up from a jumbled pile of scrolls. "Ah, there's the seven-year-old."

"Not yet!" Junia said.

"Almost," Aelia said. "I got something for you here."

The owner went behind a counter, and Junia struggled to appear enthusiastic. "Thank you, mommy. What is it? A book?"

The owner gave Aelia a big brown bag, and she handed it to Junia. "Happy birthday, bluebird."

"Let me see!" Alvra said.

Jean pushed closer alongside the counter. "Me too!"

Junia took out a square writing mirror. Her eyes lit up. "I can draw on this!" She showed it off. "Mommy, I can draw and erase, and it'll glow in the dark!"

"You can even *draw* in the dark," Aelia said.

"I want one!" Jean said.

Tes said, "Wait until you're seven. It's Junia's birthday."

"On the walk home, you have to be careful," Aelia said. "Don't swing it around, okay?"

"Thank you, mommy!"

Tes vetoed going back to the fountain, and Junia hugged her bag all the way home.

When they got back, all kinds of new, horrible-nice offerings were waiting for them. The entryway hallway was overflowing with flowers, cards, and a vase of goat's blood. Maten, the Sogjuk soldier, was still there too.

"Mommy, can I show daddy my mirror?" Junia asked.

"No, bluebird. Daddy's still resting. Why don't you show Subeia in the dining room?"

The girls ran for the atrium, and Tes asked Maten, "Any change?"

"No," he said. "I was just up there an hour ago. I have to apologize, but I do need to go." He smiled at Aelia. "I wanted to wait until you got back. Your daughter's birthday is important."

Yep, and just like that we are big into the crisis, Aelia thought. She didn't want him to leave. Somehow having this stranger standing watch in their house made it less real, as if keeping an outsider around would prevent Cael from dying.

"Of course, we understand," Tes said. "No one expected you to stay this long."

"I'll return in the morning."

When he left, they joined everyone else in the dining room. Junia was showing off her writing mirror, and even Domitus seemed impressed.

"Did my mother call?" Aelia asked.

"No," Subeia said. "Why?"

"I don't know, nothing."

Tes was right. Before she left, Behlain had seemed to have some kind of plan. And now Aelia had a faint nagging feeling. She was missing something. What did Behlain say—I can't even remember, Aelia thought. But she had made a decision, something she wanted me to do. What?

It was bedtime, and Aelia and Tes walked the girls upstairs. Junia asked again to show her mirror to Cael.

"Maybe tomorrow."

The clock at the top of the stairs read 13,15: the thirteenth hour after sunrise and fifteen minutes. It was late; tomorrow was less than three hours away. The girls all slept together in a room on the left. Jean was kicking and fussing, as Junia and Alvra got ready, still admiring the drawing mirror.

"I want to sleep in your room, mommy," Junia said.

"Not down here with the other girls?" And before Junia could even respond, Aelia said, "Okay." She realized that she didn't want to let Junia out of her sight. Maybe it was the birthday, it certainly had to do with Cael. Whatever, it didn't matter. She needed her daughter with her now. They went up to Aelia's room on the third floor. Junia changed into a tunic nightdress, and Aelia tucked her in. Outside, the lights of the eastern city glowed yellow and orange.

"Junia, you can't sleep with your present."

"Please."

"No bluebird, put it on the floor. Against the wall, so you won't step on it if you get up."

Junia did as she was told, then Aelia kissed her, flipped off the light, and said, "I'll be right back."

Tes was still with Alvra and Jean; Subeia with Dominitus on the first floor. We are all the same family, but we're separate, Aelia thought. Those are sort of my children, too, but they really aren't. Junia is. Only Junia. Aelia went to check on Cael. His bedroom smelled worse, all sweat and sinus-stinging incense. He was trembling, sweaty and hot to the touch.

He shouldn't be this warm. Downstairs, Subeia had said she'd given him more antibiotics. But it didn't seem to be working. This was bad.

That damn chalk. It wasn't my fault, blaming the fountain goddess was crazy. If Behlain hadn't given the chalk to Junia, she would never have dropped it and run into the street. Stop it. Blaming her won't fix this either. But the world isn't random. Someone help me, Aelia thought. Lunda, protect this man. Whatever I've done, I'm sorry. I'll try to understand. Please. I love him, please.

Cael wheezed.

A wet rasp, horrible sound. She shivered and took his hand. "Cael? Can you hear me?"

A long silence. A long nothing. Please don't die, she thought. What will we do? What will I tell Junia? That Sogjuk soldier, Maten, said you're too good to die. I can't think that the gods would punish us like this. Please.

She waited for what felt like a long time, then finally got up and went to bed. Junia was already sleeping. Aelia curled behind her, arms around her bluebird, and she slept. Good, there was peace in sleep. Rest.

Until the door opened.

CHAPTER FOUR

Aelia blinked awake. Except for the window-square of light on the floorboards, the room was completely dark. She didn't know what had woken her. Junia was still fast asleep in her arms. The door creaked, stopped. Aelia stared at the gray outline of the door. Maybe Alvra had come to sneak a look at the mirror. The door widened, and Aelia saw a figure in the black hall. Someone whispered.

This wasn't a child. It was a man probably. Someone big. Aelia's grip hardened on Junia. A break in? Tes or Subeia—anyone she knew would never stay silent like this. A man stepped in, murmured something to someone else in the hall. He crept toward the bed. This wasn't real. Couldn't be, except stop it, it was. Slowly, the man extended his arm toward Junia.

Aelia sat up, pulled her daughter back, and shouted, "Cael!"

Junia started awake. "Mommy, what?"

The man shoved Aelia into the wall in a shock-flash of pain. He was dragging Junia out of the bed. Junia kicked, screaming. Aelia lunged, but he was ready, and his knee hit her hard in the stomach. She went down, no air. Help. Someone help me! She started to get back up, but Junia was already across the room, and now a second man picked her up from behind.

"Mommy!"

The hall light came on. Both men were bronze-skinned, foreign, with short-cropped hair. The one near Aelia had web tattoos along the left side of his face. Junia's arms flailed, still shouting, as the second man carried her out.

"*Stop*," Aelia said, and the tattooed man knocked her down. She hit her shoulder and the back of her head again, tasted blood. Somewhere, Junia was crying. Aelia grabbed, found the window, and pulled herself up. The bedroom door slammed and locked from the outside. They were gone. She couldn't hear Junia anymore.

No, don't just sit here. Move, think. Her heart wouldn't slow down. Tears streaked her cheeks, and Aelia's palms were shaking, bleeding too: glass. But the window hadn't broken. Junia's paper bag. It was ripped wide open, and the mirror had smashed everywhere. Even the chalk case was cracked. Someone shouted outside, and Aelia saw a waiting van, with the side door wide open. A man was struggling with a kicking child, trying to get her in.

Aelia pounded the window, felt the glass shards bite into her fingers. "*Junia!*" The man shoved Junia in the van, closed the door, and walked around to the front door, nursing his wrist. Aelia hit the window. The glass cracked.

The man got in the van and slammed the door.

"*Junia!*"

The van pulled away.

"Gods, no! Someone help me! Someone—please, Lunda, please! Not her!"

A breeze rustled her hair. The van disappeared around the corner. Aelia's shouts became an animal scream, and she slammed the window again. The air was suddenly alive, as if an electric current had spiked through it. The bed and furniture shook, and then the entire wall with the window exploded, as if a bomb had gone off. A cloud of brick, plaster, and glass showered down three stories to the street below. Cold air sucked into the room. Aelia jumped out, caught the gutter, and scrambled down to the pavement. This was impossible. What just happened? All of this was crazy. But she didn't listen, didn't care. She ran.

AELIA IS FORTHCOMING
FROM FOX POINT BOOKS

www.ingramcontent.com/pod-product-compliance
Lightning Source LLC
Chambersburg PA
CBHW011424010726
47494CB00011B/2496